I0630883

THE JAR
AND OTHER STORIES
A COLLECTION OF EXTREME HORROR

EDWARD LEE

Alex peered downward and saw, at the bottom of the bucket, some rust, some tiny flecks of things that could've been skull splinters, and some splotches of a dark desiccated material that was otherwise difficult to describe with any clarity.

"So that little bit of stuff at the bottom is a tiny bit of JFK's brain," he said more than asked.

Lena nodded, almost as if embarrassed. "Brain is brain, if you ask me. I don't care if that brain belonged to the country's most beloved president, or just another guy who schlonged Marilyn Monroe. It's just *brain*. But to Clifford?" She shook her head.

For whatever reason, Alex wasn't terribly impressed, and was not inclined to ask or even wonder how much Sombrack had paid for the bucket, nor how he'd managed to procure it.

He looked at the second curtain.

Now Lena was grinning rather sardonically. "Okay. This one's a doozy. Who's the greatest singer in American history?"

Alex thought for a moment, was about to answer, but then was hit by a jolt of alarm. "No. No. Please say you don't have Elvis Presley's head behind that curtain."

"Not Elvis's head," she said and opened the curtain. "Try Elvis's *shit*."

Alex gave a thousand-yard stare at this next Lexan box.

No, was all he could think. How such a thing as this could be preserved, he couldn't fathom. Sealed in a vacuum? Suspended in epoxy? Alex didn't know and didn't want to know.

Contents

GPS

"You have arrived at your destination, Number Three, Mirror Lake Road," informed the GPS navigator in a drab female voice.

Deb was relieved to hear the sound of gravel crunching under the red Fiesta's tires. *Finally*, she thought. The four-hour drive seemed like eight, what with Kipper in the passenger seat the whole way, jabbering about himself, fiddling with the Sirius, and constantly bitching about being hungry and horny.

She parked just as Uncle Nort's cabin loomed into view within the copse of trees. It was bigger than she'd remembered it, a genuine log cabin with a metal roof.

"Ooo." Kipper made the hackneyed remark. "A cabin in the woods. Creepy."

It kind of…was. It had just the right amount of wear and tear and surrounding overgrowth to actually look sinister. In truth, Deb had always been a bit skittish about such stuff: the idea of ghosts or knife-wielding madmen or the things that went bump in the night. But she simply couldn't pass up the money.

"So this is your Uncle Don's place?" Kipper said. He had a bad habit of squeezing his crotch anytime he wanted, which he did at this precise moment.

Deb frowned. "My Uncle *Nort*. He rented it for two weeks each summer since I was a little kid—I used to love coming here. Then he flat out bought the place when he retired, kissed the city goodbye, and never looked back. Wish I could do that."

"What, leave the city? Leave me?" Kipper joked.

Damn right, leave you, you walking sperm-machine. She'd gotten sick of Kipper's sexual prowess long ago, a prowess which included a nine-inch dong as fat as one of those big dill pickles floating in the barrels at the deli. *So what?* she thought. *A lot of good that got me...*

Just before Deb got out of the car, she caught an inadvertent glance at her thirty-year-old face in the rearview. *Fuck,* she thought. *I look forty.* Vague dark circles under the eyes, crow's feet, and some preliminary wrinkles. *Where's my life gone? Partying with pretty-boy ex-cons like Kipper. Too old to strip, too beat to do porn anymore. Fuck...*

Now, this was likely too severe a condemnation; her face still retained some vestiges of its former cheerleader prettiness, and her body, though starting to sag in places, could still walk the walk in the right light. But Deb was at that grim moment of revelation all women encountered just when they least expected it. She wasn't a young hottie anymore.

So I better make the best of it...

She popped the trunk, grabbed her suitcase with one hand and her equipment box with the other. Kipper slung his own duffle over his right shoulder but ignored the remaining grocery bags. "Come on, Kip!" she barked. She trudged toward the cabin's front door. "You can carry more than that!"

"Naw, babe. See, I need my left hand free so's I can feel up your beautiful ass," and then his left hand slipped around and...felt up her ass. Next he slid down her tacky sweatpants to expose her bare rump. "Yessir, that's angel food cake, the cutest, tightest ass I ever seen." He rubbed around and squeezed. "Like a eighteen-year old's."

Deb half-smiled. She knew he was bullshitting, but at least it made her feel better.

"Nice digs," Kipper said as they entered, immediately greeted by a nice piney, woody scent. As large as the house seemed on the outside, it felt much closer inside, much more cozy. The long half-log walls lent a perfect in-the-wilds ambiance, peppered with framed photos and paintings of such stuff as one would expect: wildlife, endless stretches of landscapes and forest tops, one even with a single ranger-tower poking up out of the infinite sea of pines.

Kipper dropped his duffle bag on an oak-framed couch, then rubbed his crotch. "So *how* long do we have the place?"

"Ten whole days. Uncle Nort's vacationing in Switzerland."

"And *how* much is he paying us to house-sit?"

"Kiss my ass, buster. He's paying *me* a grand. It's *my* gig, and so are my webcam and OnlyFans gigs. A setting like this is unique."

"Yeah. Unique."

Just as Deb was essentially unemployed (since she'd been shown the door of the last strip joint in town), Kipper was unemployed as well, unless one considered selling his grandmother's painkillers employment, exploiting his power-of-attorney over her bank accounts (just a nip here and a nip there. No big deal, right?) and "slinging" whatever petty drugs he could downtown. Together, the two of them were on a slow boat going down, but at least they hadn't sunk yet. And the grand she'd be getting for this house-sitting venture would help out a lot.

Several throw rugs topped the main room's shiny hard-planked floor, mostly rife with rustic scenes embroidered on them, and even one faux bearskin rug complete with a dummy head. The rusticness fell a notch when it came to the entertainment center facing the couch: surround-sound stereo, multiple video-game platforms, and an 86-inch 4k flat panel.

Kip was astonished. "Wow! Can't wait to see some porn clips on *that* screen!"

Deb groaned to herself.

In the west wall was a huge, screened fieldstone fireplace, not that they'd be needing it in the summer. Even if it were winter, Deb knew that cutting firewood was *not* something Kipper might avail himself to. *Cutting farts? Yes. Cutting lines of coke? Yes. But not cutting firewood, nope, no way. All those muscles for nothing...*

More rustic decor was found in the kitchen, the only items being out of place were an extra-wide double-doored refrigerator, a separate freezer, and a wine fridge. Kipper didn't even ask; he was popping open a pricey-looking bottle of wine before Deb had finished looking around.

"Give Uncle Nort a break, huh? A least drink the cheap stuff," she said.

No glasses were necessary, evidently; Kipper just started chugging from the bottle neck. A moment later, he'd found a big jar of peanut butter and was gouging out divots with his fingers.

"For fuck's sake, Kip! You're a Neanderthal."

"A meander-*what?*" he asked, sucking blobs of Jif off his big fingers.

Next, the bedroom, she thought. There were actually several, but she couldn't remember what the master bedroom was like.

Wow... A high four-poster bed took up half the room, and the posts were fashioned by varnished larch logs. This would make for some great shots for her OnlyFans page and her Patreon. It would give her typical stuff a brand-new look. *This'll work just fine!* She brought in her case full of her sexy lingerie and all her "toys," then she set up her laptop on the bed, because she knew she'd get no work done in the living room, where Kipper would no doubt have his eyes glued to every T&A flick on cable.

She went back outside to bring in the groceries, realizing then that she'd forgotten to buy a lot of what she'd intended. She half noticed the GPS navigator screen fizzing in and out, and a message that read CALIBRATING ALTERNATE LOCATIONS, whatever that meant. *That fuckin' thing cost a fortune; it better not be crapping out!*

Outside was gorgeous, perfectly still and silent, save for a few chirping birds; the blaze of the day was slipping away. She grinned at the new, cool, tranquil environment, which seemed enchanting; it made her feel as though she were falling under a spell that she could never experience in the city. Between the distant trees, a westering sun dragged molten orange light down between the trunks, and wisps of mist seemed to exude from the plush carpet of detritus that reached beyond as far as she could see. At once her oblique mood dissipated, and she could actually say she felt happy for the first time in a while.

Kipper was asleep on the couch already, snoring. Was it possible he was actually rubbing his crotch in his sleep? Deb didn't want to know. She returned to the bedroom and set up the camera and tripod right at the foot of the bed. Some of her clients paid extra for "private" shots and vid clips more explicit than most. *All in day's work*, she realized. *A girl's gotta do anything she can to make money. In THIS day and age? You ain't kidding...*

She smiled when she got down to the bottom of the suitcase; she'd almost forgotten. What she pulled out was a Ouija board, the glow-in-the-dark kind. One client was paying righteous money for Deb to do a naked Ouija board session and attempt to call up any spirits that might be lingering. The prospect daunted her a little, but what harm could there be? Even if there were such things as ghosts, she'd read someplace that there was no record of a ghost ever hurting anyone.

She showered languidly, relishing the water carrying away the grime of the long ride. Next, she plopped herself belly-side down on the bed and began to half-doze at once. Her brain felt cluttered with all the goings-on of the day, but just as her mind approached the dusk of consciousness, all these cares were usurped by feelings of comfortable contentment. She smiled as the promise of sleep titillated her, and she seemed to be imagining herself roaming silently through the woods, through the fragrant scents of nature and beneath dappled starlight—just as she had when coming here as a child. Chasing fuzz-balls and whirlybirds, swimming in the lake, watching the squirrels frolic in the towering trees...

She fell into the most pleasant sleep she'd had in a long time, until—

A sudden phantom weight pressed the wind out of her; she gasped as her entire body tensed up. Something huge penetrated her with no warning—a *cock*, a *hard* cock, lubricated with God knew what. The throbbing thing seemed to barge right up her sphincter, like a rat plowing into its lair. Then it banged briskly in and out of the tight confine. Each stroke flattened her more on her belly, pressing more air out of her.

But at least it only lasted a minute.

"Damn you, Kip, you inconsiderate *fuck!*"

"What?" He was already finished, already getting up from the deed. "I thought you liked it up the heinie."

"Well, I *don't!*" she snapped back. She felt the warm spurtle of semen lolling around in her bowel like a hot tadpole. "You don't just fuck a woman in the ass when she's asleep!"

"Huh?" He refastened his belt. "Oh, sorry. I'm gonna cook some hot dogs. You want any?"

"NO!" she bellowed.

Kip moseyed off to the kitchen. Her senses couldn't have been more disarranged: her rage at him, her rage at herself, and then the avalanche of despair that always stalked her when she realized what a mess she'd made of her life.

Feeling icky, she took another shower, and didn't even want to think about the semen that was still loitering up her butt. *I'll get rid of it later...* She had things to do tonight, and she was surprised when she looked at the clock: 10 p.m. It was time to get online and address some of her webcam fans. She put on a pink teddy with a split crotch and logged on.

Here was HARD4EVR, putting $35 into her Venmo to insert the vibrating egg in herself and have an orgasm (in reality, *pretend* to have an orgasm.) No problem. The next guy, FarKingHell, tagged her with fifty, to see her max out her nipples with the nipple pump. No big deal, and it actually felt sort of electrifying. Here was another fifty, from DickStanding, to strip nude and rub baby oil all over herself. SORRY, she typed to him, THAT'S MESSY. 75 OR NOTHING. A moment later, her Venmo dinged, and she was in business. It went like this for over an hour, but then a few regulars started slapping down a hundred at a time. Usually she'd get an oddball, and sure enough, here he was: BrownEyeSly.

His text read, I'LL PAY 500 FOR YOU TO LUBE UP A BAGUETTE AND STICK IT IN AS FAR AS IT'LL GO. Deb winced. YOU MEAN LIKE A FRENCH BREAD? she typed back, irked. YES, he replied. IT DOESN'T HAVE TO BE TOO FAT, JUST LONG.

What is with these guys?

Then she typed back I DON'T HAVE A FUCKIN FRENCH BREAD! and to this he responded quite reasonably, WELL, DO YOU THINK YOU COULD GET ONE FOR 500 BUCKS? TOMORROW NIGHT, SAME TIME?

An image locked in her mind's eye: herself, spread-eagled on the bed...

With a French bread stuck in my cooch.

But it was five hundred dollars...

YEAH, SURE, she typed back. WHY NOT?

At the end of the session, she saw she'd made out pretty well. She could go to one of the other cam sites and do live-mic, but... *Fuck it. I don't feel like talking dirty tonight.* That gig was more tiring than one might think.

Remaining online wouldn't be necessary for what came next; she was merely to videograph herself, naked, using the Ouija board. *No time like the present*, she reasoned. She rearranged the camera, diverted the angle a bit, then placed the board on the bed. The client, whose screen name was MILES LONG, was paying a lot for this private job, and he'd amplified his credibility by transferring half of the money up front, always much appreciated.

MILES had communicated some modest instructions too: only candles burning, no electric lights, have a partner watch the board closely and write down any letters that the planchette might indicate. Was there anyone specifically Miles wanted to reach on the "other side"? A dead relative, etc.? No. Were there any specific questions she should ask, any special way he wanted her to conduct herself? "No," Miles had texted her. "Just be naked and ask whatever you want. Just ask stuff like the ghost people on TV ask."

"Piece of cake," she muttered to herself.

She got rid of the teddy and walked out of the bedroom, but stopped as if hit in the face with a two-by-four. There was Kipper, lying nude on the couch with his legs spread like a wishbone, masturbating a mile a minute.

"*Really?*" she yelled. She could feel veins beating in her forehead. "You're jerking off? You *just* butt-fucked me a few hours ago!"

Kip shrugged, looking over his shoulder. "Well, studly fellas like me, shit, we gotta cum, three, four times a day or we have a fit."

Deb's countenance of outrage doubled when she saw exactly *what* Kip was jerking off to on the huge TV.

"*Really?* You're jerking off to *Granny* on the *Beverly Hillbillies?*"

"No, no, hon. Ellie May and…sometimes Miss Jane. That's one pipe cleaner bitch I'd *love* to lay me some dick on." And then he continued with his mission.

If Deb had had a gun in her hand—yes, she would've shot him. Rage reddened her face; her big bare breasts swung as she bolted forward. Why didn't she just *dump* Kipper and end the humiliating nightmare? He was a loser and he was making her more of a loser too. Why didn't she rectify this slow strangulation that was her shitty life?

She supposed she knew the answer: she was terrified of being alone…

"*EEE*-doggie!" someone said on the TV. Ellie May was just now getting out of the *cee-ment* pond. They had brick shit-houses even back in 1962.

Deb snapped off the TV.

"Shit, baby!" Kip complained. "Ya ninja'd my nut!"

Fuck your nut and fuck YOU. What the hell was WRONG with men? They were all just a bunch of potato-head goat-horny schmucks who didn't care about anything but their next orgasm. She cranked her anger down like a water shut-off valve, or at least tried to. "Come on, Kip! Put that away! You gotta come in here and help me!"

He made a face. "Help? With what?"

"The Ouija board thing, like what we talked about. Come on!"

"Oh, yeah—" His long muscled body swiveled off the couch, his splayed butt-crack in full view. *Just what I needed to see,* Deb thought. She thunked barefoot back into the bedroom, while he lackadaisically followed her.

Kip continued to play with his half-hard penis. Perhaps it was subconscious. "So I'm supposed to—what? Write down—"

Deb ground her teeth. "We went *over* this. You stand out of the way of the camera, and while I'm doing the Ouija session you watch the planchette—"

"What's a blanchette?"

"The planchette!" she growled, and testily held it up. "This! Got it?"

"Oh, yeah."

"While I'm doing the session, you watch the planchette, and if it points to any letters on the board, you write those letters down. I can't work the board and remember the letters at the same time."

Kipper nodded, lower lip depending. "Uh, ok. I write down the letters…"

"Then we'll see what it spells."

Kips eyes popped wide, and he touched his temple. "Deb! A spirit just *told* me what the letters'll spell!"

Deb shook her head.

Kip grinned. "The letters'll spell…B…U…L…L…S—"

"Kiss my ass, Kip!"

"And then, after that—H…O…G…W…A—"

"Just write down the fuckin' letters if the planchette goes to any!" she practically screamed.

She lit the candles, whose flickering orange light made the room's dimensions shift in and out. Suddenly the room felt genuinely spooky.

"Here!" she snapped. She handed him a pad and a pen.

She turned the camera on, rechecked the frame, then got back on the bed and sat lotus-style behind the board. "Okay, here we go. Don't say anything during the session. I need to concentrate."

Kip nodded, grinned, and squeezed his raw genitals.

Deb closed her eyes, trying to pinpoint her concentration on the task. She recalled what the client had said: "Just ask stuff like the ghost people on TV ask."

Here goes... With one fingertip on each side of the planchette, she made a couple of circles then put the pointer on HELLO.

"Hello," she said.

"And hello to you too," Kip said and chuckled.

"Shut the fuck up, you fuck brain!" *Damn him, I'll have to erase that...*

Through her grimace she recollected her thoughts, recalling Ouija sessions from ghost-hunter shows. "Is there anyone out there who wants to talk to us?"

A long pause but the planchette didn't move.

"Are there any ghosts or spirits here? Make your presence known."

Another pause but still nothing.

Suddenly the flickering orange light felt hot on her face and bare breasts. "Are there any demons here?"

Something like sparks seemed to jump into her fingertips, and then the planchette shot quickly to YES.

Holy shit!

Kip chuckled. "Come on, Deb. Everyone's gonna know you pushed the planchette thingie."

Her eyes bulged up at him. "I swear to God I didn't! I was barely touching it!"

"Sure, sure…"

"Shut up! Let me do this!" She took a deep breath and focused on the board. Then she said, "I'd like to talk to you if you don't mind. What's your name?"

Deb's belly flopped as if she were on a roller coaster when the planchette moved quickly over the ranks of letters. "Write the letters down!" she wailed at Kip.

He scribbled something in the pad, then chuckled. "Looks like your friend's name is Jerry."

Deb's brow furrowed. *Not a name I would expect from a demon,* but she shrugged and went on, "Hi, Jerry. I'm Deb and this is Kip."

The planchette scratched back and forth.

Kipper chuckled again. "He said, 'It's a pleasure to meet you both.'"

Her mind spun for another question. "Where are you?"

The planchette burst into action, skidding from one letter to another. It was scary yet thrilling at the same time. This *had* to be real. She knew she was *not* moving the planchette on her own; the planchette moved so fast she couldn't even see what letters it was indicating.

After a few more moments the planchette abruptly stopped.

"Damn, that was somethin'," Kip said.

She looked up fretfully at him. "*Please* tell me you wrote down everything."

"Shore did, I ain't the dummy you might think I am. When you asked Jerry where he was, this is what he said back," and he handed Deb the pad.

Deb's breasts bobbed when she jumped up and turned on the lights. She looked at the pad.

In answer to her question of where he was, Kip's chicken-scrawl writing was thus:

341 Amelia Dyer Road, Namaqua Prefecture, 544916

"What the hell?" she uttered, perplexed. "Looks like the road Jerry lives on is called Amelia Dyer. But what's Namaqua Prefecture?" She scratched her head. "I think a *prefecture* is what they call counties or states in Japan..."

Kip squeezed his bare genitals. "Jerry lives in Japan? Cool! Ask him for some egg rolls!"

Deb smirked as if at a mouthful of lemon juice. *Fuckin' idiot...* But he might be right about Japan. Then the number: 544916. *That must be the zip code but it's definitely not a U.S. zip code...*

"Ask Jerry some more stuff," Kip suggested. "This is startin' to get fun."

Deb turned the lights back off, then knelt back behind the board. But when she looked down...

"Holy shit..."

The planchette was pointed at GOODBYE.

"I *KNOW* I didn't put it there!" she yelled.

"Huh?"

She put her fingers back on the plastic device. Now the orange light flickering on her face felt almost like hands caressing her. She took a deep breath, closed her eyes again, and began, "Jerry. Do you live in Japan?"

A long pause, but no response.

"Where *exactly* do you live?"

Nothing.

"Were you once a human being and then turned into a demon?"

Nothing.

"Are you alive in the same way I am?"

Nothing.

"Give it up, hon," Kip said, yawning. "Your new boyfriend Jerry's done talkin', it looks like."

She guessed he was right. "Damn it! That was all for real, Kip."

Kip shrugged. "So maybe it was. Maybe there *is* a demon somewhere named Jerry and you were just talkin' to him. What's the big deal?"

Deb winced. *What's the big deal? Fuck you! I just proved there are demons!* But how could she ever really convince anyone? *I know it wasn't faked, but no one else will.*

Kip yawned again. "I'm tired as a ant haulin' a bail of cotton. Let's go to bed."

Deb was disappointed, though she had no reason to be. *I contacted a DEMON on a Ouija board!* And she was anxious to talk to Jerry some more, but—

I guess that's it for now.

At least she got what she came for. MILES LONG would be intrigued by this little private clip, and she'd also get the rest of her money for the job.

"Beddy-bye time," Kip insisted. He gave the pad back to Deb, then unfolded his long body on the right side of the bed. He chuckled. "And I promise, I won't even jerk off on ya whiles yer asleep!"

Deb sighed. "Thanks, Kip. You're a real gentleman..."

The night granted Deb an atypically solid and restful sleep, and she awakened energized and enthused rather than hungover and glum. Beside her, Kip lay sprawled, snoring and nude, of course, his cock and balls exposed. *God, I'm so sick of looking at his junk...*

But her excitement re-found her only seconds after getting up: the Ouija board, the obvious preternatural contact she'd made, and her brief conversation with "Jerry." She *knew* the board hadn't somehow been rigged; Jerry's responses had been far too particularized for Kip to have faked himself, and it would be absurd to think that she was moving the planchette subconsciously. *That was REAL last night,* she thought. *It HAD to be real!*

She bounced naked out of bed, unabashedly pulled open the curtains, and grinned out at the beautiful morning. Various birds cavorted in the plush tree branches, a family of possums waddled across the side yard, and the forest stretched forever. *What to do today?* she asked herself, teeming with excitement. Of course, later tonight they would pursue more contact with Jerry, and she suspected they'd be doing the same every night for the remainder of their stay. *I'll film every session, put 'em on YouTube, and—who knows?—maybe they'll go viral!* She'd do her regular webcam and OnlyFans stuff early, and make herself more prepared for the next Ouija sessions, have more articulate questions prepared, and maybe do a little online research as to the proper use of spirit boards.

But the thought of her webcam responsibilities only reminded her there was one thing she needed to do before any of this other stuff: *Get a baguette!*

With a smirk, she jostled Kip awake and said, "Hey! I'm going to the store after my shower. If you want anything write, me a list."

"Store?" he said groggily. "Fuck, I'm horny... What'choo need at the store?"

Deb sighed. "A baguette."

He peered at her through slit eyes. "What the fuck's that?"

"A fuckin' French bread! Don't worry about it. Just make a list if you want anything."

He gulped, closed his eyes, nodded, and squeezed his flaccid genitals.

What a great life I have, she groaned to herself.

When she was showered and dressed, she was surprised to find Kipper up and in the kitchen making coffee. Naked, of course. He pointed behind him to the plaid-topped table. "Right there's a list I made for ya, babe. Some important stuff we need."

She picked up the paper and immediately thought, *Asshole…* The first thing on the shopping list was *Anal-Eeze*.

And the rest?

Beer.

Chips, lots of 'em.

Slim Jims.

Twinkies, lots of 'em.

Bottle of Black Velvet.

Cheese dip.

Beer.

"They're not gonna have Anal-fuckin'-Eeze at a little grocery store out here in the sticks…"

"Crisco, then; it don't matter. Just thinkin' of you, babe."

"Terrific. I'll be back later."

"Toodles!" But before she got out the door, he stopped her. "Wait! Hon?"

She turned. "What?"

"Ya think when ya get back we could maybe play some *Hide the Salami*?" And then, no surprise, he grinned and flapped his cock at her.

"I'd much rather play *Cut the Salami Off*," she said, and stalked out of the house. Kip's honking laughter followed her out.

In the car, she recalled there was a small grocery store a ways back, so she typed CLOSEST GROCERY STORE into the GPS and it immediately popped up a Hull's Grocery & General

Store, about twenty miles away. Then she tagged it and let the GPS guide her.

"Veer left at fork on Turkey Neck Road in point-five miles," instructed the voice, like a fussy, stuck-up woman.

Deb followed the instructions while her attention was sidetracked over her excitement about the Ouija session; she couldn't get it out of her head. Would Jerry communicate with her again tonight? Would some *other* entity? Would Jerry ever ask *her* questions?

Damn, once I'm done with this French bread gig, I'm back on that board!

Before long she found the little convenience store, and she took in the list that Kip had made. Right off, she was delighted to find a bread barrel full of long, thin baguettes. She held one up and smiled at it. *I'm gonna make five hundred bucks because of you!*

The old proprietor behind the counter had a white mustache like that of a walrus. He smiled, nodded, then—

You fuckin' old asshole!

—shot a glance right at the crotch of her jeans. She was infuriated when men did that, or blatantly ogled her breasts, but she never admitted the contradiction: every night on her webcam she eagerly offered up glimpses of her bare body to the same kinds of men—for money—and she was all too happy for their attention.

Beer, Slim Jims...what else did he want? She opened the list that Kip had prepared and now noticed that he'd written it on the back of the sheet he'd used last night, where he'd transcribed Jerry's Ouija responses.

She read over the letters Kip had copied from the board: *341 Amelia Dyer Road, Namaqua Prefecture, 544916.* The response intrigued her in its uninterpretability. *When I get back, I'll look it up online...*

The hayseed proprietor with the walrus mustache rang up and bagged all of her items. Now he was eyeing her breasts fairly overtly, and it didn't help that she was braless and the friction against her blouse caused her nipples to stand up.

God damn, man! Make it obvious, why don't you?

"Reckon you're fixin' to throw yourself a big shindig, huh, dearie?"

"You reckon right," she replied, paying with her card. "Say, have you ever heard of Amelia Dyer Road?"

His bushy eyebrows slanted down. "Naw, ain't no road called that anywhere near here."

"And I don't guess you've ever heard of Namaqua Prefecture?"

The old man paused. He was staring right between her legs again.

You old pervert! she thought.

He blinked out of his stare. "Nama-*what?* Naw, dearie, don't know where you're gettin' these names, but there ain't no place neither called Nama—whatever you just said."

"Okay, thanks anyway…"

But the proprietor's gaze snapped right back to her crotch again.

Fuck. I guess all men are the same when you get right down to it. She put one of her webcam cards on the counter. "If you want to see my pussy that bad, log on to this website sometime, and don't be chintzy."

Back in the car, she noticed ranks of almost-black storm clouds sliding in behind her. *Damn it. Where'd they come from?* There'd been no clouds in the sky when she'd gone in the store. She pressed the RETURN TO LAST LOCATION button, and the GPS voice said, "Proceed fourteen-point-six miles down Pig Neck Road, then veer right onto Turkey Neck Road." *What is it with the 'necks' out here?*

Then the GPS beeped, and the voice warned, "A storm may be coming your way. Please execute caution..."

Fuckin' great! she thought. At the same time, the sky above her darkened further. She jumped in her seat at a loud boom of thunder, and seconds later, rain was being dumped on the car.

Deb *hated* driving in the rain.

She flicked on the lights and wipers, her hands tightening on the wheel. The rain was now falling in sheets so relentless she could see almost nothing ahead of her. *Too dangerous to drive in*, she realized. Since she was able to make out the shoulder of the road, which seemed substantial, she pulled over, stopped, and put on her flashers. Then the rain fell harder; it sounded like multiple tons of bb's being dumped on the car. *Fuck this*, she thought. She'd just have to wait it out.

Twenty minutes later, the rain had still not let up. *All I can do is sit here with my fuckin' baguette and wait...*

Deb was the kind of woman who got bored easily. Just sitting there was driving her nuts. She looked at her phone, thinking there'd certainly be no reception in this storm but—

Eureka!

—she had four bars. She considered watching a movie on Tubi but then a better idea occurred to her. *Jerry's address!* She could Google it!

She turned the shopping list over and typed in the address "Jerry" had given them on the Ouija last night.

More disappointment. The reward for her efforts was this (0.55 seconds) NO RESULTS FOUND FOR "341 *Amelia Dyer Road, Namaqua Prefecture, 544916.*"

Then she advised herself, Try removing the quotes, which she did and immediately got pages and pages of results, starting with:

Amelia Dyer, (1836-1896) popularly dubbed
as the "Ogress of Reading" and the "Baby

Farmer of Berkshire," was a trained nurse-turned-serial-killer, credited with murdering at least 400 infants via the process of "baby farming" — i.e. the enterprise of adopting unwanted babies for money. But instead of raising the infants as promised, she would strangle them and dispose of the bodies, usually in the Thames River. She was found guilty of infanticide and hanged at Newgate Prison on June 10, 1896.

"You gotta be SHITTING me," Deb muttered to herself. "Who names a road after a serial killer, especially one who kills *babies?*" Next she tried the arcane zip code, and hundreds of pages popped up, but the first one was this: "544916, notably the Nazi Party membership number for Obergruppenfuhrer Rinehard Heydrich (1904-1942), who, with Adolf Eichmann, set into motion the plans for the Holocaust which killed at least six million Jews."

"What the FUCK?" she said aloud. Her eyes opened fast on the screen. *This is some wacky shit!*

Next, she typed in *Namaqua.* The result was instantaneous and it left her mouth hanging open in disbelief. It read:

Namaqua Massacre (1904-1908): an 'ethnic cleansing' campaign conducted in South Africa by the German Empire, against the native Nama people. The German Colonial Army drove the Nama into the desert, where at least 10,000 died from dehydration, and thousands more were starved to death in concentration camps. This was the first genocide of the twentieth century.

Deb was dumbstruck by the inexplicability of these revelations. She'd never heard of any Namaqua Massacre, nor of anyone named Rinehard Heydrich or Adolf Eichmann. Again, she considered that perhaps Kipper had faked all this for his own amusement but—

No way. He's way too dumb. He doesn't even know who George Washington is, much less any of these people...

The rain kept pouring and more belts of thunder jostled the car. *Damn it, when's this shit gonna stop?* Just as the thought came into her head, she nearly shrieked when a fat bolt of lightning lit up the teeming sky and seemed to strike not far from her.

Distracted, she looked back at the sheet where Kip had written the Ouija responses. It seemed so bizarre. She tried to sort it all out objectively, but how could that be possible? "Jerry" claimed to be a demon. If this somehow were true, where was he? Was he here on Earth, or was he in hell? And what was the explanation of this crazy address he left for himself?

Zip codes referring to Nazis? A street named after a serial killer? Some other place—a county or town, she guessed—named for a horrific genocide?

Without much conscious focus, she pressed the CHANGE DESTINATION tab on the GPS and quickly input: *341 Amelia Dyer Road, Namaqua Prefecture, 544916*

It can't hurt, she figured.

Then her face went blank when the GPS voice said, "Destination found."

What the FUCK?

She squinted at the little screen and saw the red line which indicated the route. It appeared to be southeast of her location. The distance was revealed to be thirteen miles.

Now she was frenzied. As impossible as this event seemed, she sat on pins and needles to proceed, but the rain was still pouring and lightning still flashing. *I can't drive in this shit...*

Over the next thirty seconds, the rain stopped completely, and the thunder and lightning were no more.

Unbelievable... She started the car back up, put it in gear, and pulled back onto the road. "Proceed south on Pig Neck Road," instructed the GPS voice. "Then turn left at unmarked service road in exactly six-point-six miles."

Deb zeroed the odometer and drove on. She was barely thinking now; she was simply excited to see where this inconceivable trek would lead. The storm had ceased with the abruptness of flicking a light switch, but the sky overhead remained dark above black clouds that seemed to be lowering. The downpour on top of the sweltering humidity caused steam-like mist to rise between the stout trees on either side of her. Was it her imagination or did the trees appear fatter, taller, and more twisted now? Here was one that *had* to be four feet thick and over a hundred high. The boughs of other trees rocked up and down with the inordinate amount of rainwater they still held; the impression was almost primaeval. When she squinted ahead, she could've sworn the road was more narrow than before, and spiderwebbed with cracks and potholes.

Freaky, she thought. But then, she *did* smoke a little pot last night before bed, and Kipper always managed to buy some heavy-hitting stuff.

"Reduce speed and turn left at unmarked road," said the GPS woman.

Deb had to squint again, but just as the odometer clicked to 6.6, she saw the unmarked road entrance, a barely discernible gap between more fat, black-barked trees. The road appeared to be unpaved, and as she proceeded she was almost certain she saw...

Is there a cemetery in there?

Farther back between the trees were several uneven rows of what looked a lot like old gravestones. *Who would put a fuckin' cemetery way back there?*

The GPS woman said next, "Continue another six-point-six miles and turn left on Amelia Dyer Road."

"I can't believe it! It really *does* exist!"

Her excitement was unprecedented; her heart thunked in her chest. *What if I find Jerry's house? What if I knock on the door? Will a DEMON really answer?*

Her car rocked over the next six miles; her eyes widened as she approached. The distance to her destination was closing on zero, yet the trees on either side remained thicker than ever. *Jerry lives in the middle of the WOODS?* she wondered.

Nailed to one leaning tree was a sign: WELCOME TO NAMAQUA PREFECTURE. *Fuck! This is it!* But what she was seeing suggested less than a town or little woodland village... *This is the boonies, all right.* At periodic increments, narrow entrances to the right and left suggested driveways, and next to nearly every opening a crooked, leaning mailbox was either nailed to a tree or mounted to a rickety pole.

A few names caught Deb's eye: DeSalvo, Grese, Chessman. Before she could refocus on the thread of her thoughts, the GPS voice announced, "Turn left onto Amelia Dyer Road," and just to her left a muddy, unpaved road appeared.

Deb's stomach filled with butterflies as she turned. The road was a tunnel through more dense, heavily boughed trees, and between the trees grew odd batches of ill-colored mushrooms, fungous, weird ivy, and twisted kudzu-like vines.

"You have arrived at your destination," the GPS voice announced.

And there was the opening which proceeded into something like a narrow driveway. A beaten mailbox read 341 - JERONYMOUS ANDRAS.

Jerry, Deb could only assume. *Short for Jeronymous...*

She turned up the drive and slowly moved forward.

What a place to have a home, she thought. This deep in the trees made everything even darker. She had to rub her eyes several times, because whenever she looked right or left, she thought she detected movement. Branches, she guessed, but no. It almost seemed as if the spread of twisted vines between the trees was *moving,* slithering even.

She noticed something like pine cones hanging from more malformed tree limbs, but *these* pine cones—

That-that can't be...

The pine cones seemed to be oscillating, quickly enlarging and shrinking like small brown beating hearts.

But of course that was impossible. It had to be her imagination, generated by her excitement. And the poor light combined with her lousy vision.

Next, a breath lodged in her chest.

A small stone house came into view, with a slate roof and lancet-type windows.

This is it, she thought numbly. *It really is here...*

She parked, opened the car door, and almost fell back into the vehicle at an upheaving stench that could only be called ghastly, like slaughterhouses in high summer.

God Almighty! she exclaimed to herself. *That's fuckin' AWFUL!*

When she got out of the car, the charnel stench even seemed to burn her eyes and seep into her mouth such that she could taste it. *Get on with this!* she yelled at herself. *This is what you came for, so don't let some bad smells turn you into a pussy!*

Her footsteps squished as she walked slowly toward the brooding house. It must have been the bad light, but the mud beneath her feet seemed to carry a red hue. An ornately carved front door seemed to move toward her more than she moved toward it.

There was a tan doormat just below her, on which had been stitched the word TODESANGST and then a little smiley face.

Deb's breath grew short. She blinked, heard her teeth chattering, then raised her knuckles—*I'm really going to do this...*—to knock. But, like a horror movie cliché, before she could do so, the door swung open on its own.

It even creaked.

What should I do now?

Only vague slants of light could be seen within the house, from windows, she supposed. She knocked on the doorframe, was about to call out for "Jerry", but didn't have time because a bright, lively male voice with an indeterminate accent said, "Ah, Deb! That must be you. I've been expecting you."

"Is that...you, Jerry?" she peeped.

"Yes, yes! Please come in!"

How did he know I was coming? she asked herself.

She could no longer detect the stench from outside. Instead, there was a strong acrid smell like burning plastic. "Jerry, I think I smell something burning here..."

"Oh, no worries, that's just the Acclimation Incense, on the center table."

Acclimation—WHAT? She looked at the table covered with black linen and now saw the obvious incense bowl, with threads of smoking spiraling off of glowing embers within. But it didn't smell like any incense she'd ever encountered.

Jerry's voice drifted back to her. He must have been in a room deeper in the house, likely a bedroom. "I lit the incense because it masks that appalling stench from the city."

Deb's eyes flicked up at the words. "What city? You mean Jacksonville?"

"No, no. Just make yourself at home; I'll be out presently and all your questions will be answered…"

Squinting, she glanced around the dark, clutter-filled room. Framed pictures hung on the wall but little could be made of them, as if smoke, dampness, and grime had deposited such an opaque black sheen that nothing remained of the painter's original artwork. Against the next wall stood an elaborate half-table where several sputtering candles burned. Between the candles lay a large book that read PHOTO ALBUM.

He DID say make yourself at home…

Unable to resist, she picked up the album and opened to its first leaf.

And stared.

The pictures were old, yellowed black-and-whites. Instead of square- or rectangular- shaped, they'd been fixed onto hexagonal photographic paper. *What IS this?* she wondered, feeling woozy. One picture detailed a down-sloping cemetery that extended for as far as the limits of the photo paper would allow, and above, in the dim night sky, there was a thin sickle moon that was black instead of lambent white. And next—

What in God's name?

—was a long gibbet atop a hill. From the gibbet exactly thirteen newborn babies were hanging by their necks.

Before Deb could close and drop the book, her eyes detected another photo: soldiers in unrecognizable uniforms marching in formation, all bearing rifles with severed women's heads mounted on bayonets; the last split second of the glimpse detailed the faces of some of the soldiers: faces more like those of cadavers than those of living men.

Deb backed up in shock, a hand to her chest. Some sort of mental vertigo was skewing the rational aspects of her thought processes. *This is IMPOSSIBLE! I can't really BE HERE! Kipper must've put drugs in the pot!*

"Forgive me for taking so long," Jerry's voice floated back out, and he chuckled. "An oldster such as myself needs a little extra time to get presentable."

But she had to admit this: "Jerry, if you want to know the truth, I'm beginning to doubt my sanity right now —"

"Oh trust me, my dear. You're not insane by any stretch of the imagination."

She gulped. "Okay, fine. But...did you really give me directions to your house through a *Ouija board*?"

"Indeed I did. My board is on the kitchen table, if you'd like to see it."

Deb's brain only half-registered the words, and she stumbled around till she found a room fitted with the appurtenances one would expect in a kitchen, only these were very old-fashioned: a barrel-shaped woodstove, black pots and pans hanging from hooks, and, instead of a refrigerator, one of those ancient "iceboxes" people used a hundred years ago. On a table below a curtained window she saw the Ouija board, but this one seemed to be made of gray slate. There was no sign of a planchette.

By now her shock and disbelief was prolapsing into mental numbness. The tiles on the floor were a hideous checkerboard of dull carmine squares, with threads of blue in them, almost like veins. Were there drugs of some kind in that weird incense? Now everything she looked at took on a warped aspect, like a vague fisheye effect, and with it came the impression that much of what she attempted to look at shifted in and out of focus.

I'm either high as fuck or...

Or what?

Deb flinched at the notion of a shadow crossing the room.

"We meet at last," Jerry's voice seemed to flutter. "I'm sorry if my appearance is upsetting; I was quite handsome back in my day. I was the Masterbuilder of Arīhā, which you might know as Jericho, the oldest city on earth. That was—what? Twelve thousand years ago?" Jerry chuckled. "As you say, time flies. I built the cenote in which thousands were sacrificed to Yareakh; *rivers* of blood poured in Yareakh's name, and every drop was credited to me. Yareakh was thought of as the moon god, but that was simply camouflage for another *greater* deity—"

Deb felt the urge to scream but was too stifled to do so. It was as though a fist had been rammed down her throat, bulging her eyes in their sockets.

The shifting image of what she now looked at could only be called inscrutable. The figure stood slightly taller than her and had either an oblong head or was wearing an oblong hat of some sort. It seemed also to be wearing a cloak, a sickly black mixed with green, but in the intermittent shifts in and out of focus, a more ghastly observation was made clear to her: it wasn't a cloak, it was a caul of skin the color of decomposing swamp scum. Arms and legs seemed to throb but thus far she was not able to see a face, a fact she would be grateful for had she any ability to think coherently.

But she was coherent enough to croak this conjecture: "This is hell, isn't it? I'm in *hell* right now, right?"

"Of course." Jerry's voice, like his image, shifted back and forth in nature, from sharp, bright, emphatic speech to something like gargling, like someone drowning in sludge. "You arrived at that conclusion much more quickly than most, so I commend you for your keen perceptivities. Some scream themselves to death, others desperately try to make away with themselves." Jerry's measured pause seemed like someone in bemused contemplation. "But not you. Such an adventurer you turned out to be. I'm thrilled."

He seemed to pick up a broom from behind the icebox, and held it out for her examination.

Now Deb *did* scream, but quite ineffectually; it was more like a scratching sound issuing from her throat.

The head of the mop was a human scalp with very long hair.

"And how do you like my parquet flooring?" Jerry said next, extending a tumorous but blurred hand.

Deb squinted down at the glistening carmine squares. The blue etchings she'd noticed earlier were indeed veins which throbbed now in three-dimensionality, beating as if to the rhythm of some evil, unseen heart.

Deb began to shiver in place. She wanted to throw up, but still she managed to ask, "How did I get here? When I left, I wasn't in hell, but now I am…"

Jerry's dark, barely identifiable form began to pace back and forth. "First I'll tell you how *I* got here. It's a matter of reward, you see. So successful was I in spilling so much innocent blood for my dark lord that, when I died and came to this unholy firmament, I was transmogrified into the subcorporeal being you're now privileged enough to look upon. Believe me, very few of your kind ever see such a sight while still part of the Living World. And how did you get from there to here? I'm afraid it's just a particularized manner of happenstance. On the infrequent occasions when the stars are propitious and aligned to maximize my god's accessibility, a veil is raised, so to speak. The barriers between your world and this one are reduced to a barely extant membrane through which persons such as yourself are able to pass. It's that simple, Deb. A door was opened, I provided you with the directions to get to that door, and here you are, my guest in the flesh." Another gargling chuckle. "But you can't really blame me, my dear. You're the one who asked for the directions."

It was true; she couldn't deny it. *And it looks like I'm getting what I asked for...*

"And now, my pretty inquisitive friend, before I depart on my little jaunt, I'm afraid I must intrude on your good nature and do something I haven't been able to do for quite a long time..."

This time Deb screamed louder than she'd ever screamed in her life, when this thing, Jeronymous a.k.a Jerry, hauled her to the floor, pulled her earth-made clothes off, and lifted its caul-like cloak of skin to display fully erect genitals: something akin to a baby's leg but the color of phlegm and with an abundant uncircumcised foreskin...

Deb was drooled on, crudely squashed against the throbbing floor, and her breasts were kneaded by long-fingered hands that writhed like enslimed, hot octopuses. She'd not yet been able to see the exact nature of Jerry's mouth, but she did feel the demon's appalling lips open against hers and begin to suck. Jerry chuckled into her mouth as he began to inhale all the breath out of her lungs.

For long alternating moments, each as much as several minutes, she was unable to breathe, and she frenetically convulsed under her captor's incomprehensible body mass. Each time her consciousness slipped away, she knew she was about to die on the living floor of this maniacal kitchen in hell. By the dozenth time, she knew she would've welcomed death. Anything had to be better than this nauseating, otherworldly molestation.

She partially revived as something unspeakable penetrated between her legs and began to derrick in and out. It was at this point that some notion of mercy was bestowed upon her, inasmuch as her sentience divided and she could no longer feel what was being done to her. Whatever cerebral provision allowed the brain to block out severe trauma had engaged, and next thing Deb knew, her rapist was getting off of her.

"Thank God," she muttered.

Jerry chuckled phlegmatically. "Really?" Then he picked up her jeans and retrieved her car keys. "There have been a few visitors in the past who've been generous enough—with a little instigation, mind you—to instruct me as to the proper operation of these clever machines of yours known as automobiles, and the even more clever—what are they called? GPS navigation systems?"

At last Jerry looked down, and Deb was able to see the details of his face: it was like a great pile of cow excrement, with two red-irised eyes and a mucky hole for a mouth.

"I shall return at some future time but, until then, treat my home as though it were your own." With that, Jerry turned and moved out of the house through the front door.

Demonic motherfucker! Deb thought.

Against crushing fatigue, she rose nude to her feet. She was more infuriated than mortified. On the kitchen counter lay a meat cleaver, which she picked up at once. *I will fuck him up! I will cut off his demon dick and chew on it like jerky! I'll butt-fuck him with it!* Due to the rigors of her rape, she was unable to run after him; she could only limp. Her belly constricted when she felt Jerry's semen ooze down the inside of her leg; it was nothing like typical semen but more like dark, wriggling cottage cheese.

Once she got outside, Jerry had already started her car and rolled the window down. "Until we meet again, my friend. But I'll be sure to give Kip your regards."

Deb was too exhausted to pursue further. She heard several beeps coming from the car, and she knew this meant that Jerry was pressing the GPS system's function tabs. She could hear that drab female voice saying, "New direction search," then, "New destination found: Number Three, Mirror Lake Road."

The car pulled away and proceeded down the driveway until it disappeared amongst twisted, noxious trees and stinking mist.

Holy fuck, she thought. She dropped the cleaver and limped back inside.

Back in the kitchen, she picked her jeans up off the floor and got her cellphone out of the back pocket. She posited, *The GPS worked from my world to this one. I wonder if my cellphone will work from this one back to mine...*

She dialed Kip's number.

Kipper, as was his usual habit when Deb wasn't home, watched porn and vigorously masturbated several times. He got off the first one to his all-time favorite smut flick, *Backside to the Future,* then he got off another one to some homegrown video of himself banging Deb like a two-dollar whore on the garage floor at home. A little while later, he popped a third one eyeballing the brick shit-house chick on the Tubi commercial for eHarmony.

If one thing could be said of Kip, he was a very *virile* young man.

Then, he lay back nude on the couch, frowning and bored and rather irritated. *Where the hell is she? How long does it take to get French bread?*

He grabbed his phone and just as he was about to call her, she called him.

"Well, hey, babe," he grumbled. "I'm gettin' a bit lonely sitting here all by myself. Did you get your dang French bread?"

Her voice on the other end sounded winded and frenzied. "Kipper! Listen! You're not gonna believe this, but just for the hell of it, I typed Jerry's address into the GPS, and it worked!"

"Huh?"

"The address! That you wrote down from the Ouija board last night. It took me to where Jerry lives, and I'm there now!"

"You're-you're in *Japan*?"

"No, you numbskull! I'm in Jerry's *house*! The directions were spot-on!"

Kip frowned and rubbed his raw crotch. "Awright, fine. So where's he live?"

"In-in," Deb blabbered but then said, "Never mind!"

"Well, what about the French bread?"

"*FUCK* the French bread! Listen! Jerry, he-he, well never mind. But he stole my car!"

Kip chuckled. "Is he really a demon?"

"Yes!"

Kipper's thoughts stalled. One thing about Deb—two things, actually. One, she had a genuine snappin' pussy. Two, she had absolutely *no* sense of humor.

"Babe, I don't know what this jive is you're talkin', but how 'bout you come home right now so I can lay some proper dick on ya, give ya the kind of lovin' ya deserve? And I won't even cum fast this time. I just jerked off three times!"

Deb's voice blasted like a truck horn. "Damn it, Kip! Would you fuckin' LISTEN? Jerry stole my car. He typed in the address back to Uncle Nort's cabin and he's on his way there *right now*! Get out of the cabin!"

By now, Kip was getting ticked. He didn't mind a little leg-pullin' on occasion (he'd done plenty of that himself) but this was getting annoying. He didn't much like bein' yelled at or called names like fuck-brain and numbskull. And just as he was about to make his protests known to Deb—

Well, ain't that a pain in the neck...

—his cellphone stopped working. The battery died.

However, only moments later, he hopped off the couch because he heard a car pull up in the driveway outside, and then—

thunk...

—a car door closed.

Finally, the smart-ass bitch is home. Well, I'll give her a greetin' she won't forget for some time...

With that thought, he rubbed his crotch.

What he heard next was the front door opening.

THE BABY SHOWER

PROLOGUE

One would think that the placement of a live jellyfish into a woman's rectal vault would present considerable difficulties—but this is not at all the case. And, to be sure, L.E.G. Unit 133 was seasoned by *much* practice.

First, the subject, via the use of a common Paralysis Spell, would be "rigored" while bent over some convenient object (for instance, a couch), and then one administrator would manually part the woman's buttocks, and another would apply a rectal speculum. There are a number of different styles and types of specula and dioptra: devices made especially for the forced opening of bodily orifices. Many such devices have, sort of, "pistol grips." A pair of hinged, stainless-steel spoonlike protrudments extend, like a duck beak, which is then inserted into the desired orifice, and when the pistol grip is squeezed, the "beak" spreads apart. Other leaf-style specula exist as well, fashioned quite like a leaf shutter on a camera. Circular in shape, when closed there sprouts from its center several, say, two-inch-long studs with rounded ends all bunched together. These ends are sufficiently lubricated and then pushed all at once into the target orifice—in this case, an anal sphincter. Then a mast-mounted screw is turned, and with each turn, the studs come apart, and the screw continues to be turned until the sphincter has been stretched open to its physical limit.

This is when the jellyfish is pushed into the agape orifice and then the speculum is closed shut and removed.

And from there? The desired spectacle ensues in grand style.

First, the Paralysis Spell is extinguished, and the naked victim thunks to the floor while being wracked in throes of agony very few humans have the experience to describe, and even less describable are the vociferations of protest. The jellyfish is too big to shit out, so there it would remain, in the recipient's nerve-jammed bowel, and not even the jellyfish's death would end the stinging agony. Why? Because with each contact of a tentacle (and most jellyfish have dozens or even hundreds of tentacles), thousands of these tiny things called nematocysts detach and embed themselves (via stingers, of course) into any available flesh. Then the venom is injected, causing mind-boggling pain, and those little nematocysts continue to inject venom even after the host jellyfish dies.

Hence, the spectacle, which might be likened to a screaming gymnastic repertoire of twitching, writhing, shrieking convulsions and seizures. Eventually, the recipient would either go unconscious or die, depending on the genus of jellyfish.

It may be worth mentioning that this process can almost as easily be used with a victim's *vaginal* barrel, where the nerves are much more abundant and sensitive, but in the absence of a sphincter muscle, a surgical stapler would be necessary to keep the jellyfish from falling out.

For it would be a shame, wouldn't it? To waste a perfectly good jellyfish?

For a more expeditious process requiring less intricacy and less fuss, the speculum can be dispensed with. Instead, the administrator (wearing thick rubber gloves, mind you!) merely takes hold of the jellyfish by its head (or mantle, as it's properly called) and then uses it to swab the tentacle-cluster briskly up and down and around the subject's vaginal area, much in the fashion of a dish mop. The process is repeated in the woman's ass-crack and then all around her neck, with special attention paid to the face—foremost, the lips and eyelids. Though less interesting than the speculum-route, the end result is still the same: absolutely excruciating agony apportioned to the victim's most sensitive parts.

But all this is neither here nor there, as they say. Let the above words serve as a preamble to the curious sequence of events that took place in Suite No. 415 at the famed Collinswood Hotel, on April 30, 20—.

(1)

Alison wouldn't have guessed in a million—no, a billion...er, well, no, a *trillion* years—that her friend's baby shower would officially commence via the act of her being forced to swallow diarrhea. No. Not even in a *septillion* years.

Yet it would be so.

But even before this rather atypical beginning to such a traditional celebration, Alison, and Kirsty as well, may have had an inkling that the evening was manifesting itself into something a little off-kilter. For instance, it was now 8 p.m., yet the shower had been scheduled to begin at 7:30. True, friends of young prissy society types such as Kirsty, Alison, and Teresa were steadfast in adopting the practice of "fashionable lateness," but this was a bit much. Only the three of them were present, plus Kenneth or, as Teresa called him, The Kenster, and, come to think of it, he had disappeared to the kitchenette twenty minutes ago with orders to bring out the first bottle of champagne (Perrier-Jouët, *not* Dom), yet he seemed to be—to use his wife Teresa's words—"taking his sweet motherfuckin' time about it."

"What's the prob, hon?" Alison asked from the plush couch. "You can't drink anyway. Not while you're pregnant."

"Oh, I can have a fuckin' *sip!*" insisted Teresa, plopping down in the opposite couch. The busty brunette cradled an eight-and-three-quarter-month pregnant belly, which threatened to erupt from her $500 Rachel Pally maternity dress like a Jiffy Pop too long on the stove.

"My mother drank when she was pregnant with me," Kirsty added, distracted. She fingered a blonde tousle off her brow and looked forebodingly in the direction of the large suite's door. *This is too weird. NO ONE has knocked on the door yet, and NOT ONE shower gift has been brought except for mine and Alison's...*

"That's probably why your daddy had to pay off the professors at that pissant college you went to, just so you'd pass," Alison remarked with a chuckle. "Fetal Alcohol Syndrome it's called. That's why you fucked up in school."

"That's mean! And it's not true," Kirsty shot back, even though it was.

"Relax, sweetie, I'm only kidding. You know, when you're mad, your black roots show big time."

"I DON'T dye my hair. YOU dye your hair! Nobody has hair THAT red!"

"She's a natural redhead," Teresa interjected. "Don't you remember junior high phys. ed.? The showers? That big red bush sticking out? Looked like somebody took a piece of sod and spray-painted it the color of a fire truck."

Alison toked demurely on her lime-sherbert-flavored electronic cigarette. "Yeah, well, I shave it now."

"Figures," Kirsty spat. "You gingers are all hillbillies. Classy ladies don't shave, they go to laser hair-removal parlors."

Alison leaned up in her seat. "Oh, so then I guess you DON'T go to those parlors 'cos you're about as classy as a rubber machine in a gas station bathroom…"

Though it may seem so, this is not digression, but instead a sample of discourse to alert the reader as to the overall intellectual capacity of the trio. They were mid-twenties, Daddy-Rich high-society princesses, all reasonably attractive, enhanced by saline, rhinoplasty, etc. Hefty components of deductive surmise are NOT required to put the reader in possession of their nature, just as FURTHER development of their character would be a useless expenditure of the reader's attention.

That said, however, a small dose of passive narrative in the way of a situational synopsis might prove appropriate to the onlooker's interest. Kirsty, Alison, and Teresa were the snooty offspring of wealthy families in an up, upscale neighborhood (this, you've already gleaned.) Teresa's baby shower was underway; her youthful, well-to-do husband, the Kenster, was nearby purveying some refreshment but, oddly, he'd deputed himself to this task roughly twenty minutes ago; whereas, it was no more than a two-minute job. This oddity imbued in Kirsty quite a disconnected feeling of foreboding; in fact, her thumbs itched.

Though she'd not given voice to it yet, Teresa was downright uncomfortable, not just because she had the equivalent of a fifty-pound fuckin' basketball in her stomach but more because of the twentyish guests who'd RSVP'd back a positive reply, yet not one had yet shown up, which meant that *all* the guests were now running late by just shy of the better part of three quarters of an hour. Hence, Teresa's biggest worry: that none of her so-called friends gave enough of a shit about her even to attend her baby shower and drink free high-end champagne and wolf down several thousand dollars' of hors d'oeuvres, including lobster pot pies from Hancock Gourmet, foie gras, caviar, truffle terrines from D'Artagnan, and dim sum from Peking Gourmet. Oh, and an impressive fondue platter, encircled by squares of artisan bread, Argentine shrimp, and roasted lamb cubes. Teresa would never live it down if her baby shower was a dud.

And though Alison, the redhead (the eyebrows told all), tended to exist in an unremitting state of pre-occupation, she, too, felt something untoward about the evening's overall complexion thus far. The Kenster had spent a fortune for this affair; the Presidential Suite at the world-famous Collinswood Hotel alone must've cost a king's ransom. It stood fairly to reason that even the snobbiest blue bloods in the social nexus to which the trio belonged would *never* blow off a party at such an establishment.

There was a wet bar on the room's other side, and several linen-covered tables *loaded* with the fanciest appetizers money could buy. In fact, at just that moment, Alison was marauding those appetizers, wolfing down raw Hokkaido scallops and Pacific Hamachi at the sushi section. "Oh, this is so good," she said with her mouth stuffed. Then her eyes bugged at the next section: "My favorite! Pigs in Blankets!" she squealed and started scarfing.

"They're not Pigs in Blankets, you moron. This isn't a tailgate party," said Teresa. "They're Kobe Beef sausages in phyllo dough. Expensive as fuck, so take it easy."

Alison wasn't hearing it; she stuffed three more into her mouth at once, and then grabbed a fondue fork and continued to dig in.

"What a rip-off," complained Teresa, rubbing her distended belly. "She can stuff her face like that Japanese guy who ate a hundred hot dogs, but she never gains an ounce. Fuck, if I just *look* at that stuff, I'll gain weight."

"High metabolism," came Alison's next cheek-stuffed comment. "Besides, I burn off lots of calories every night when I fuck the Kenster."

Teresa's mouth locked open. "Whuh-*what?*"

"Oh, for fuck's sake, girl. I'm *kidding!*" She eyeballed more delectable food on the table. "And there's no point letting all this great food go to waste." Next she stuffed in several toast points loaded up with Iranian caviar, and after that, tea-smoked partridge tenders.

Go to waste, Teresa thought. *Is that what's going to happen? Nobody's coming to my baby shower?* The question made her stare off into space.

Alison crudely stuck her fingers down her top to adjust her ludicrously expensive La Perla's bra. "Shit, Teresa. Not one single guest has bothered to show yet. What did you do to piss everyone off?"

Teresa's lower lip quivered. "I...can't imagine..."

"You *are* kind of obnoxious sometimes," Kirsty said. "I mean, no offense."

"Oh, none taken, cunt!"

"Easy there, hon," Alison said. "But what gives? Where *is* everyone?"

Teresa was beginning to percolate, then her face collapsed into her hands and she began to blubber.

Alison and Kirsty, both frowning, sat down beside Teresa to comfort her. "Don't cry, honey," Kirsty said, arm around the mother-to-be. "They're all just running late."

"No they're *not!* They all hate me! I'm a shitty person, and nobody wants to come to my baby shower!"

Kirsty and Alison both exchanged raised brows. "Calm down, Ter. You need a drink." Alison looked over and bellowed, "HEY, KENSTER! WHERE THE FUCK IS THAT CHAMPAGNE, YOU BUTT-NUGGET?!"

At last, the kitchenette door swooshed open, and the champagne was brought in, but—

"Who the fuck are you?" Alison and Kirsty barked at the same time.

—*not* by the Kenster.

It was a perfect stranger who'd just alighted from the kitchenette, holding a bottle of the aforementioned Perrier-Jouët. He was balding, with a gray straggly beard and wearing a rust-colored tweed jacket with elbow patches and not-very-well-matched khaki slacks. He might've been in his fifties. The clothes looked a bit frayed and, well, dirty, and so did the gentleman's face; dirty, that is, not frayed.

One other thing:

He didn't smell good.

"You weren't invited to my baby shower!" Teresa blared.

"Yeah," the big-titted Alison joined in. "Who are you and—" She sniffed. "Holy shit, buddy! You stink!"

"Yes," the man replied, and stroked his bearded chin. "My body odor is just one element of my plight, the gist of which you are all about to become all too grimly apprised. My name is Professor Artimus Peasley, and until my relocation into my current situation, I taught physics and calculus at none other than Harvard University." He set the champagne on one of the buffet tables. "Would one of you be so kind as to open this? And in the meantime—" He withdrew a small LCD-type timer, like a fancified egg timer.

"What's the timer for?" Alison inquired.

The strange man set the timer then, and its front read 66 MINUTES REMAINING. "It's to let me know how much time I have," said this man, this Peasley.

Kirsty glowered at him. Who the fuck *was* this guy? "Time for what, old man?"

"How much time I have to royally *fuck* with you," he said with a bit of scorn. "And that 'old man' remark will be remembered."

"This guy's off his rocker," Alison deduced. "One of those people from the Tent City."

Teresa coughed at the man's alarming body odor. "And why do you *stink* so bad? Don't you ever wash?"

The man—Professor Peasley—smiled. "Well, no, actually. I'm not allowed to. In fact, I haven't washed since the day of my induction into the Unit, and that was in 1958. Each volunteer gets a sixty-six-year stint. I'm happy to say that I'm on my sixty-fifth year—only one more to go!"

"Oh, fuck this!" Alison snapped. "I don't know what this asshole's talking about but I'm calling security. How could a crazy homeless bum like this sneak into the *Collinswood*?"

"Go ahead and call security," Peasley authorized. "Just know that when you're *done* calling security, you'll be taking your clothes off. To be frank, I'm rather anxious to see your bare breasts and—you know—the goods between the legs."

Alison stared open-mouthed at him. "The only thing you're gonna see anytime soon is the backseat of a cop car, you stinky whack job." She picked up the phone. "That's funny, the hotel line's dead." She whipped out her cell phone, dialed 911, and then stared at the screen. "There's no signal! It was working perfectly earlier."

"Ah, yes," Peasley said, "but that was then and this is now."

All three women stiffened up in shock when, next, Peasley reached into his pocket. The natural assumption was that he was about to pull a gun but…not so. However, what he *did* pull out were two irregular oval objects about the size of plums; they were whitish in hue with a rough finish.

"These," he announced, "are talismanic totems. They're actually the petrified balls of a famous warlock and serial killer named Gilles de Rais. When utilized by an experienced practitioner—such as myself—they are—and believe me when I say this—magic."

"Magic?" Alison laughed. "Magic balls? You mean like *balls* out of a guy's *sack?*"

Peasley nodded, smiling. "And when I rub them together, they will facilitate what's known as a Subservience Spell, and you will do anything I command." With that, Professor Peasley began to abrade the two hardened objects in his hand, as one might rub together a pair of dice. "Now. Alison, is it? Take off your clothes."

Alison shuddered in place…and took off her clothes.

"My, oh my," remarked Peasley, "that's quite a mammarian endowment." He squeezed his crotch. Then he looked at Teresa and Kirsty, continuing to rub the balls together. "Get out of those clothes, girls. I need to see the merchandise."

"This is crazy!" Kirsty complained. "I'm trying with all my might not to do it but—"

"Me too!" cried Teresa.

They were both out of their clothes as fast as they could take them off.

Teresa stood, crossing her legs and trying but failing to conceal her milk-laden breasts, which were really *very* large now. The near-full-term stomach stuck out pin-prick tight; in fact, it was so tight and so distended that Kirsty could see a semblance of her own nude reflection in the shiny belly skin.

"Wow," said Peasley. "That's what I call pregnant. Fuck. You got a belly sticking out like the fuckin' Octomom." He turned back to Alison and Kirsty. "Now, Alison, Kirsty, take these next few moments to decide amongst yourselves which one of you will first go down on Teresa."

Both girls' eyes popped open. "Go...*what?*" Kirsty said.

"Go *down.* You know what I mean. Which one of you will perform cunnilingus on Teresa."

"*Huh?*" Kirsty replied.

"He wants one of us to eat Teresa's pussy!" Alison said. "And I guess he can make us because of that dude's balls in his hand. What the fuck's going on?"

"It will all be explained in due time," Peasley said.

"Something's *really* fucked up here," Teresa whispered.

"Indeed, there is." Peasley was appreciating the red stubble between Alison's legs. It was, like, a scarlet five o'clock pubic shadow. "And here's more proof as to just *how* fucked up things are." He pointed to the suite's fancy nine-paneled entry door. "Alison. You're free to leave if you'd like. Go on. Go open that door."

Alison stood duped. She looked at the door, then at Teresa, then at Peasley. Then she said, "Fuck it," and stalked nude to the door, tits bouncing, grabbed the knob, and yanked open the door.

She expected to see the plushly carpeted hallway but instead she saw—

"What the fuck is that?" Kirsty asked.

Alison stared at whatever impossible material it was that filled the doorway. It was like a flat face of pale yellow rock, roughly cut.

"What's this stuff?" yelled Alison.

Peasley perused one of the hors d'oeuvre tables, sampling foie gras cubes and delectable little rumakis made with steamed anglerfish liver. "It's raw sulphur, also known—biblically—as brimstone."

"You-you mean like 'fire and brimstone?'" Teresa's voice quavered. "*That* kind of brimstone?"

"Yes, Teresa," Peasley affirmed. "*That* kind of brimstone. The most abundant raw material in Hell. So now you'll be wondering, 'Why is there brimstone just outside our hotel room door,' right?"

All three naked women nodded dumbly.

"It's because of an occult science known as 'spatial transposition.' A special process is enacted—in Hell, mind you—that, by the utilization of life-force energies, ancient evocations, and a variety of refined black magic, causes an area of space in the Living World—this hotel room, for example—to *transpose*, or trade places, with an identical area of space in Hell. In this case, that identical area is a rectangle of brimstone the exact same size as this room. Understand?"

"Fuck no!" yelled Alison.

"You're fucked up in the head!" blurted Kirsty.

Teresa started blubbering again. "This crazy bum is ruining my baby shower!"

Peasley chuckled. "Okay, the whys and wherefores aren't particularly pertinent to the three of you. Just take my word for it. It's by pure happenstance that I'm here with you now and, trust me, it's nothing personal. I'm part of a—" He glanced at the champagne bottle on the table. "Wait a minute. What's the guy's name in the other room? Kent?"

"Kenster," Alison said. And then pointed to Teresa. "Her husband."

"My! It looks like he emptied his beans in *you* more than a few times." Peasley yelled toward the kitchenette door. "Hey, Kenster! Get your ass out here and bring that old suitcase!"

The kitchenette door was heard swinging open, then came a dragging sound. Eventually, the "Kenster" appeared around the corner, totally naked and pretty haggard looking. He was walking as if with significant back pain, and his hair, one of those fussy razor-fade haircuts with a poof on top, was severely mussed up. His decidedly *un*excited penis dangled perhaps as limp as it had ever been and, well, it had a smear of some mysterious brown stuff on it.

"Kenneth!" wailed Teresa. "Why are you naked?"

Kenster sighed and released the suitcase he'd been dragging. "Same reason you are, I'd imagine. This guy *made me* take off my clothes—"

But now Teresa was grimacing at Ken's genitals. "And is that...is that...is that...*shit* on your dick?"

Kenster, stooped shouldered and exhausted, nodded. "He made me fuck him in the ass."

Teresa's expression crumbled to one of grave suspicion. "Do you mean to tell me that...you're homosexual?"

Kenster winced. "No! I knocked *you* up, didn't I?"

"Then how could you get it up for a man's *ass*?"

"It was some magic jabber he talked," Kenster answered. "One minute my dick was dead meat, the next it's hard as a rock. It's some satanic magic shit this guy knows."

"I'll concur," Peasley said. Now he was trying Peking duck buns. "I'm afraid the Kenster's claim is true. I forced him to comply with my wishes by using these," and he held up the two petrified warlock testicles. "And then I uttered a simple Excitation Spell so to erect his penis sufficiently to perform sodomy on me."

Teresa stared at him, befuddled and wincing. "But...*why?* Why would you do that?"

"Well, Teresa, because there are some men who enjoy the feel of another man's cock up their ass, and I happen to be one of them. Cock, pussy—it's all enthralling to me. I suppose that makes me *bi*, yes? Isn't that what they call it in this day and age?

And I'm happy to say—though Kenster's not quite as *large* as I prefer—his performance was satisfactory."

Alison's big tits wobbled when she barked back, "I think what she means is, why would you want to make *anybody* do something against their will?"

"The same reason I'd want to make you eat my spit off the floor." Peasley coughed up some phlegm and spat it on the floor. He rubbed the two testicles together and said, "Alison? Eat my spit off the floor."

Alison's expression was one of sheer infuriation; nevertheless, there she went, down on all fours, to lap up all of the lumpy expectoration.

"Kenster?" he said. "Please open that bottle of champagne, set out five glasses, but only fill *one* glass. And while you're doing that, I'll start getting set up."

The three girls continued to stand naked and dumbfounded. Kenster popped the champagne cork, set out five flutes and filled one, as instructed. Meanwhile, Peasley—there were actually flies buzzing around him, he stunk so bad—opened the carob-brown and rather battered suitcase and removed what appeared to be an egg-shaped piece of glass about the size of a Nerf football. Four little legs stuck out of one end, so the egg-shaped object could stand on end, sort of like a football on a tee.

"What the fuck's *that?*" Kirsty asked, hugging her bare boobs together.

"It's called an Oculere," Peasley answered. "I'll explain momentarily, along with much else. It needs a little time to warm up." Then the man approached the table on which one glass of champagne sat, along with four empty glasses. He smiled and addressed Teresa and her prodigious stomach. "First, we must *officially* begin Teresa's baby shower." Then Peasley opened his pants and pulled out his unwashed-for-

48

sixty-five-years penis. Even ten feet away, the girls all gagged and stepped back.

"That's-that's the worst smell I've *ever* smelled!" Teresa gagged.

Peasley smiled. "If you think this is bad, just wait till you're sucking it."

Most of the color drained out of Teresa's face.

"Ug, fuck," croaked Kirsty. "I think I'm gonna throw up…"

"If you do, *Teresa* will have to eat it all up off the floor."

"DON'T throw up, Kirsty! I'll kick your ass if you do!"

It was at this point, then, that Peasley pissed into each empty champagne flute, one at a time. Then he passed a flute to each of the girls and Kenster.

"And now?" Peasley raised his own glass, the only one with champagne in it. "Allow me to propose a toast. To Teresa, her baby, and this wonderful baby shower!" He sipped some of his champagne, smiled with his eyes closed, and remarked, "Mmm, yes. Remarkable feather-light body with an edgy burst of citrus buoyed by an intricate nuttiness—almonds, perhaps. All married with a fascinating mousse-like texture and exorbitant bubbles. Girls, Kenster? Do you agree?"

Kenster knew better than to resist. He slugged his glass down, grimaced, and gasped. "Fuck! Do you have kidney disease or something? Piss can't taste *that* bad!"

"That's my boy," Peasley replied lightheartedly. "Girls? Don't be party poopers. Down the hatch."

Alison, Kirsty, and Teresa all stood still, eyes and mouths shocked open, each, with a shaking hand, holding their glass. Kirsty at least ventured boldly enough to *sniff* her glass, after which her expression collapsed into a rictus of horror. Alison, less than wisely, snapped and said, "You're a horrible misogynist! I'm not doing it!" And then Teresa piped up, perhaps emboldened by her friend's declaration. "I-I can't!" she exclaimed. "It'll be bad for the baby!"

"Bad for the baby?" Peasley questioned. "How about a spontaneous, projectile miscarriage? Would *that* be bad for the baby, Teresa? I can make that happen right now. I can make the Kenster jump up and down on your big stomach until that baby shoots across the room. I can make him put the baby in the bathtub and walk all over it like a Frenchman squashing grapes." Then he shot a grave glance to Alison and Kirsty. "And you two, hear me well. Either drink my piss or…I will fuck you up."

Alison's big tits stuck out like monuments of defiance. "Damn it, girls! Are we gonna take this? Are we gonna let this asshole humiliate us just so he can get his jollies? Women have been letting men exploit them for thousands of years, and why? Because we *let* them. Because we're afraid of the power they exert over us. We're not *sheep*. We're not dummies or slaves. We're *women*, damn it! We're just as smart and we're just as strong as them, and we're *not* gonna take this anymore! Girls? Are you with me?"

Teresa remained standing in place with her mouth still hanging open, looking at her champagne flute full of piss. Kenster was just slowly shaking his head.

But Kirsty stomped her bare foot, raised her fist (in a manner which exemplified the physiology of her already awesome breasts) and declared, "You're right, Alison! We're not gonna live our lives in fear of this sick, perverted bum!" She glared at Peasley. "Did you hear that, asshole? We're *not* gonna drink your piss! Drink your *own* damn piss, fucker!"

Peasley's shoulders slumped. "Wow. It looks like I have absolutely failed in securing your attention with any degree of credibility. That's too bad…for *you*."

"Go ahead and kill us!" Kirsty blurted. "I'd rather die than degrade myself for you!"

Kenster just kept shaking his head.

"Alison," Peasley said. "Lay down on the floor and open your mouth as wide as you can."

"Fuck you!" Alison yelled back. "My will is stronger than your...whatever it is!"

Peasley rubbed the two testicles together, and Alison lurched forward as if on marionette strings, and then, in short choppy movements, and with bugged eyes, she lay down on the floor and cranked open her mouth.

"I'm afraid this is a bit Old Hat," Peasley commented, "but—" He rubbed the testicles together again. "Kirsty, sit on Alison's face, position your anus directly over her mouth, and shit in her mouth."

Kirsty's fists clenched. "You can't make me do it! I am woman! Hear me r—" Kirsty jerked out of her stance, sat on Alison's face and—

"Oh nooooo," Teresa said.

—released a very loose bowel movement into Alison's mouth. It was quite noisy as well.

"I told you not to order the Kung Pao last night!" Teresa said.

Alison gurgled beneath her friend's squat, clenching at each diarrheic gust.

Peasley continued to abrade the sorcerer testicles. "Now be a good girl, Alison, swallow it all right down into your tum-tum..."

Making retching sounds, Alison swallowed everything that Kirsty's bowels offered up. At the conclusion of the process, poor Alison wrapped her arms around her stomach, rolled over, and groaned.

Peasley smiled thinly. "Okay. It's not fair to let Alison have all the fun. Kirsty? Lay on the floor and open your mouth. And Alison…you know what to do."

The order was followed and, in comparison, Alison's stools were stout and firm—she'd clearly eaten more roughage last night at the Chinese place. Kirsty made a noble effort to scream but such screams were stifled as each big turd was pushed into her mouth.

"Damn, Alison!" Teresa commented. "Those are some *logs!*"

"Chew it up before you swallow," Peasley advised. "I suppose the texture is a bit like pâté—the *texture*, mind you, not the *taste*."

When a third "log" was pushed into Kirsty's mouth, she began to squeal in her throat, and wagged her fists around and stomped her feet.

"Please, Kirsty," Peasley implored. "Don't make a fuss. There are people starving in the world."

After Kirsty choked down the last of it, she began to shudder.

Peasley turned back to Teresa with the full intention of unleashing some cabalistic wrath but stopped short.

Teresa was chugging her glass of piss, and then Alison's and Kirsty's glasses. "There! See? I drank it all!"

"That you did, my fine bulbous friend," Peasley complimented. "Good girls do as they're told, and I hope this will be a lesson to the others…"

The "others," incidentally—that is, Kirsty and Alison—both remained half-paralyzed on the floor their arms wrapped around their bellies. They were both groaning like a pair of sick donkeys.

"But I can't let you off *too* easily, can I?" Then Peasley ordered, "Get down on your knees, Teresa. And Kenster? I do believe your lovely wife has not quite yet quenched her thirst. Give her some straight from the tap."

Teresa thunked down on her knees, while the Kenster contemplated his instructions for a moment, sighed, and then inclined his pelvis toward Teresa's face. She looked up beseechingly. "Ken, my God. Why is he doing this to us?"

"I don't know, babe."

"And *how*? Is it really magic?"

"Yeah, I think so. It's some kind of satanic juju. He's, like, a warlock, I think, and he has to do this stuff for sixty-six years before he's released. He sold his soul to the devil, so, I guess, the devil gave him special powers."

"Chop, chop, folks." Peasley looked at his watch. "Time's a-wasting."

"I gotta piss in your mouth, sugar plum," Kenster said, "and you gotta drink it. Otherwise, he'll fuck us up, or worse, he'll fuck up the baby."

Teresa, now wearing a mask of sheer dread, nodded acknowledgment, then closed her eyes and opened her mouth.

Kenster leaned back, hands on hips, and began to piss—like a proverbial racehorse—right into his wife's mouth. Teresa did a fair job timing her swallows against each mouthful but by the time the Kenster's bladder was voided, Teresa's big tits and belly *shined* in piss.

"God *damn*, Ken," she muttered, dripping. "That was a *lot* of piss."

Kenster shrugged. "Yeah, well I had a couple Kirins earlier."

But when Teresa looked up, she noticed that Peasley was holding that oblong glass thing with the little feet on the bottom. It looked different now, though. Before it had been completely clear, but now, behind its surface, there seemed to be something like moving fog inside.

"What *is* that thing?" Teresa asked as if aggravated. "It looks like it's filled with fog now, and…is there something *moving* in it?"

Peasley's free dirty hand bid one of the couches, while he sat down on the couch opposite. "Ladies? If you'd all be so kind as to sit across from me, and with your legs parted, I'd be much obliged."

"Why do our legs have to be parted?" Teresa challenged.

"So I can look at your pussies while we talk. Any more questions, Miss Priss?"

Teresa's belly sloshed when she sat down, while the other two girls staggered to the couch and plopped down, still holding their midsections.

"Damn, Alison," Kirsty complained. "I'm *full up* with your shit!"

"Yeah? Well, fuck you!" Alison blared back. "I'm full up with your fuckin' *diarrhea*, and it's *spicy!*"

"I told you not to order the Kung Pao," Teresa repeated.

Peasley set the oblong glass-thing on the table in front of them. Yes, there was fog inside it, and something else lurking around. "The explanation for which you've all been waiting is now at hand. The Kenster is fairly correct in his observations. I'm sort of like a warlock, in that I've been granted occult powers for the entirety of the sixty-six years that I've agreed to serve in the Unit. What is the Unit, you may ask? It's a detachment, shall we say, that exists to serve the interests of…" Peasley grinned. "Can you guess?"

"Satan," the Kenster said.

"Yes! Satan is, for lack of a better term, my boss. And the Unit of which I am a part is fully called L.E.G. Unit 133. I am the one hundred and thirty-third member to volunteer my services to the Group. L.E.G., by the way, stands for Luciferic Entertainment Group."

Teresa, Alison, and Kirsty all stared back in silence.

"Back in 1958," Peasley continued, "when I was teaching at Harvard, I...ran into a little...trouble—let's just say, trouble of a sexual nature. I was about to be incarcerated for fifty years when, in the wee hours, in my cell, I prayed to Satan to help me. I promised I'd forfeit my soul if he got me out of that mess. And, would you believe it? He did! He transported me from that dreary cell into a training class where I learned all the ins and outs of degradation, misogyny, torture—you name it. Along with that, I was granted certain occult powers. The term of my enlistment, if you will, is sixty-six years, and during that time period it's my job to maraud random persons—such as yourselves—and provide entertainment for my lord and savior, Lucifer."

"Entertainment?" Alison finally broke the awkward silence. "For the *devil?*"

"Why, yes. You can't expect him to be content sitting on a throne in the midst of demons, damned souls, and fiery rocks. And do what? He wants to be entertained just like anybody. Now, he can't walk the Earth, but he *can* see the Earth and what goes on in it with certain devices and machinations. That's where I come in...and this." He pointed to that weird oblong glass sitting on the coffee table. "Like I said, it's called an Oculere. It's like...a video camera. With my awesome infernal powers, I perpetrate atrocities and human outrage—quite often of a *sexual* nature—in front of the Oculere, and via the vast occult science instigated by Satan's hellbound sorcerers and technicians, the images are transmitted into Hell, where Satan can see them." Peasley smiled. "Not unlike cable TV, really. Or what is it they call it now? Streaming. The Oculere is Lucifer's favorite mode of entertainment. I travel the world, royally fucking people—mostly women, I'm sorry to say; Satan *hates* women—up. You might say that those fortunate few who serve in the Luciferic Entertainment Group, are the Prince of Darkness's cable provider."

"Oh my God, he's right!" Alison said, leaning forward and pointing at the Oculere. "Look at that thing! There's an eyeball in it!"

Kirsty stared, astonished. "And it's looking at my pussy!"

Indeed, the Oculere was now sufficiently "warmed up." Within its milky fog, an eyeball floated, looking back and forth at each girl.

And it was a *large* eyeball too, much bigger than human, more the size of a billiard ball.

"It's actually the eyeball of a flying species of demon called *Buteogallus Occularus*—a demonic version of an eagle, with exemplary eyesight."

Teresa's big tits sat on the top of her gargantuan belly. "You mean, everything that eyeball sees…Satan sees too?"

"Exactly!" Peasley sipped more champagne. "Think of it as a camera, and I am the cameraman. All of us inducted into the L.E.G. Unit are responsible for Satan's entertainment—as I've said previous—for sixty-six years. And there are many fringe benefits."

"Like what?" Alison said, smirking.

"Well, for one, for those sixty-six years of duty, we don't age. Believe it or not, I was born in 1903, but I sold my soul at the age of fifty-five, which is how old I am now. This duty allows us to see much more of the world's history, and, well, we can experience more things."

Alison was still smirking. "What happens at the end of the sixty-six years?"

"I'll live out the rest of my natural life, starting at age fifty-five. Then I'll die, go to Hell, and live like a king for all of eternity. Sixty-six years of fucking with women is a small price to pay for infinite riches, wouldn't you say?"

Teresa could feel the gaze of that monster eyeball roving up and down her belly and breasts, and staring between her legs. "So that's your job, huh? You provide entertainment for Satan. You travel all over the place by some kind of supernatural magic, and you make girls drink piss and shit in each other's mouths? Because Satan likes to see stuff like that?"

"Oh, all that and much, much more," Peasley said. "We've only broken the ice so far." He glanced at the timer, which read, 52 MINUTES REMAINING.

Several moments of grim silence followed that statement. Then Kirsty asked, "So what's with the business about you not washing? Did you say you haven't washed for sixty-five years?"

"That's a fact," Peasley said, then, to Kenster: "Ken, I'll have a lobster pot pie now, and how about a plate of those dim sums?"

Kenster proceeded as ordered, then Peasley returned his attentions to Kirsty's interrogative. "That's quite correct, Kirsty. Sixty-five years without washing. I stink so bad that sometimes I all but pass out—"

"I'm about to pass out *now*," Alison remarked.

"Well, you can believe me when I say that there's nothing I'd like more than to take a bath but, you see, the terms of my induction forbid it. I'm simply not allowed to."

"But that doesn't make sense!" said a very aggravated Teresa.

"Oh, but it does, Teresa. It makes *lots* of sense, if you're Satan. See, he doesn't merely want you humiliated and exploited, he wants you *appalled*. And you'll see what I mean right now. Teresa, come over here and suck my dick."

Teresa's eyes watered, and her lower lip quivered. "Oh, please, please, sir. Please don't make me do that."

"Your choice," Peasley offered. In the meantime, Kenster brought the plate of food; Peasley sampled several dim sums with his dirty fingers. "You can suck my dick or you can suck my ass. I'd highly recommend the former." He opened his pants and extricated his genitals from underpants that had never been washed.

"His dick must be bad enough," Kirsty said, flapping her hand in front of her face "but can you imagine having to suck an *ass* that hasn't been washed in sixty-five years?"

Teresa looked like she was about to have a fit. "No! I *can't* imagine it! And I shouldn't have to! I don't deserve any of this!"

"Ah, now you're starting to get it," Peasley informed. "It's true. You *don't* deserve any of this. You're completely innocent. And *that*, my dear, is why Lucifer insists that you be degraded."

"That's fucked up!" Teresa yelled.

"Teresa, just hold your nose and suck his dick," the Kenster suggested. "There's no getting around it, so just get it over with."

"Are you going to make me use these, Teresa?" Peasley held up the two petrified testicles.

White as a sheet now, Teresa cumbersomely slid off the couch, crept on all fours to where Peasley sat, pinched her nose shut, and then started performing fellatio on Professor Peasley's atrocious erection. The cock was slimy, malodorous beyond conception, and covered in some mysterious grit. Teresa's plump physique seemed to be actually *vibrating* in disgust, and though she was holding her nose, the smell of that utter horror found its way to her olfactory senses through her mouth to her sinuses.

Peasley's hips bucked. "Here comes dinner. Please be good enough to swallow it all. Don't make me be mean."

Teresa mewled as one salvo of semen after another rocketed to the back of her throat. Then came repetitious gagging. She was pounding her fists on the floor holding it all in her mouth, her eyes crossed, then—

gulp

"Good girl!"

—she swallowed the entirety of the intrusion, then fell over and thunked like a sack of bricks.

Peasley beamed. "There! The job is done. It wasn't all that bad, was it?"

Teresa looked up, drooling. "It was the worst experience of my entire fuckin' life. If I'd known it was that bad, I would've killed myself."

Peasley's brow rose. "Wow, that's not exactly a confidence builder." He buckled up his pants, then told her, "Lie back on the floor and spread your legs." Then, to Kirsty, "Kirsty, hunker right down there and start licking Teresa's pussy." Then, to Kenster, "Kenster, get right up behind Kirsty while she's going down on your wife...and fuck her in the ass."

"No, please, sir!" Teresa begged. "Don't make my husband fuck another girl right in front of me!"

"In the *ass*, remember," Peasley said. "The *unnaturalness* of it all is so much more degrading."

Kenster went right to work, sliding his erection deftly in and out of Kirsty's puckered star. "Wow, this is primo action. Tight."

"Shut up, Ken!" Teresa bellowed, looking up over her enormous belly. "I'll hang you upside down by your balls till your nutsack snaps!"

But Kirsty was having a bit of trouble getting with it in the cunnilingus department. Peasley clapped three times as if to root her on. "Come on, Kirsty. Use that tongue for something more than yakking."

Kirsty had her face an inch away from Teresa's bald and slightly protruding snatch. She sighed aggravatedly. "But-but...I've never done this before—"

"Oh, bullshit, Kirsty!" Teresa objected. "You've eaten tons of pussy—you told us all about it!"

"Yeah, Kirsty," Alison piped in. "Remember? Your Girl Scouts stories?"

"Oh, yeah. Fuck." So Kirsty just shrugged, lowered her face, and began the wet, noisy process. "Gimme a break, Teresa. There's enough yeast in here to start a brewery."

"Fuck you! There is not!"

Kirsty chuckled. "I'm just kidding...sort of."

Peasley picked up the Oculere and moved it around the action, like an energetic camera man: long holds on Ken's, Kirsty's, and Teresa's faces, then close-ups of Ken's brown-smeared cock sliding in and out of Kirsty's butt and macro shots of Kirsty's pink tongue roving fastidiously over Teresa's glistening vulva.

Evidently Kirsty's style was formidable because Teresa's big ass began to squirm and she pressed the back of Kirsty's head to increase the mouth-to-pussy contact. "Damn, girl," Teresa murmured. "You do that better than Ken."

"Thanks a lot!" Ken exclaimed and started reaming Kirsty with more deliberation. "Bitch!"

"That's the spirit!" Peasley approved. "Dissension! Just what Satan wants!"

Ken grabbed Kirsty's hips hard, driving it home. "Professor? I'm about to cum. Where do you want me to put it? Back, ass-cheeks, head, where?"

Peasley held the Oculere closer. "Pump it all right up her ass where it belongs."

"Roger, that." The Kenster quivered where he knelt, and went, "Ah-ah-ah-ahhhhhhhh..."

Kirsty smirked. "Fuck, Ken. It feels like I'm getting an enema with a pint of egg drop soup."

"Be happy it's not hot and sour," Peasley added.

Meanwhile, Teresa cringed off several orgasms right in Kirsty's face.

"Like that, did ya?" Kirsty said wiping her lips with her wrist. "Now you can do me. Fair is fair."

"Fuck *that* shit!" Teresa cracked.

Peasley chuckled at the vocal antics; the situation was almost amiable. "Okay, girls, the warm-up's over. Now it's time to get down to business." He looked at the timer. "We still have forty-five minutes left."

"What happens at the end of the sixty-six minutes?" Kenster asked, wiping his dick off with the white linen tablecloth.

"Then I must go," Peasley said simply.

"Go where?" Teresa asked, looking up over her huge stomach.

"I'll go back to Hell for a while, for a little R&R, then sit in on some atrocity training classes, and then…" He upturned his hands. "It's off to the next mission I go, my next block of duty for the Luciferic Entertainment Group."

"You mean find more innocent girls to fuck with," griped Kirsty. "Just to entertain the devil."

Peasley sampled a few scallop-mousse pastry puffs. "That's correct,"

Teresa, infuriated, lumbered up on her elbows. "For fuck's sake! You've made us eat shit, drink piss, suck dirty cock and swallow cum, and take it up the ass! Isn't that enough?"

Peasley's smudged face bloomed in wonder. "Oh, believe me. There's *never* enough…" He turned to Ken. "Kenster, while I'm retrieving some things from my bag, please go to the bathroom and bring back a toilet plunger."

Kenster's mouth hung open a moment but he knew the mistake of asking questions. "Yes, sir."

From the battered suitcase, Peasley withdrew a small leatherbound book whose binding consisted of metal hinges. "Here we have the infamous *Ars Goetia*, part of the coveted tome *Lemegeton* of which only one genuine copy remains." He held the little book up higher. "This copy. King Solomon was known to whisper in his sleep, and he always had night-sitters posted to write down everything they heard. The *Ars Goetia* contain those decipherings, many of which are transitive spells and other mechanisms of diabolic magic."

Very quickly, then, Peasley swiveled his stance toward the far corner of the room where Alison stood sheepishly, as if in hiding.

"There she is! You're missing out on all the fun. What are you doing way over there?"

Alison stepped nude out of her little sconce. "I-um...I..."

Peasley grinned. "Thought I'd forgotten about you, huh, sweetie?"

Alison quivered in place. "Yuh-yes, sir, or I thought that, um, maybe you like me more than the other girls so maybe you were gonna give me a break."

"I must say, that's some honest answer, isn't it?" Peasley remarked. "And it's true in one respect—I *do* like you more than the other girls. Teresa's a stuck-up condescending fuss-pot, and Kirsty's an oblivious dunce. There's really nothing likeable about her, is there?"

"Oh, I can't tell you how much I appreciate that!" Kirsty stood up, holding her butt, then winced as she sat down on the couch. "Fuck, I can still feel Ken's nut moving around in me. Feels like hot worms."

"How lovely!" Peasley replied. "It's something unique you can tell your grandkids someday, hmm?" Then he addressed

Alison. "Get ready, dear. I'm about to read a Levitation Spell. I think you'll find it thrilling."

Alison frowned, uncomprehending. "What?"

And then Peasley read aloud from the little book. "Ixedox iktob, iaglrub, ayptob…"

A moment after the strange utterance, Alison rose off her feet to float on her back in mid-air. "You're right!" she squealed. "It *is* thrilling!"

"Mmm, yes. But it probably won't be for long." When the Kenster returned with a toilet plunger, Peasley ordered, "Ken, what I'd like you to do now is defecate into the cup of that toilet plunger."

Kenster looked at Peasley, then at the plunger. Then he shrugged. He flexed his knees a bit, positioned the plunger cup directly under his butt-crack, and—amid some grunting—displaced a liberal bowel movement into the plunger's cup. It looked like a big brown ice-cream cone.

Peasley, with more than a modest look of satisfaction on his face, took hold of the plunger. Kirsty and Teresa stared, unblinking.

But Alison, floating almost shoulder-level in the air, was staring with a bit more severity. "What…the…fuck…ARE YOU GONNA DO?"

"It should be elementary, my dear Alison," Peasley answered. "I'm going to pump shit into your pussy with this toilet plunger," and with that simple, forthright response, the professor did just that: he pressed the poop-filled plunger cup against Alison's vulva and—

Alison screamed at the top of her lungs.

—and pumped shit into Alison's pussy.

On the table that big eyeball inside the Oculere watched intently.

"Wow," Kenster muttered.

Kirsty gulped.

But Teresa was outraged. It took some effort, but she stood up and then began to rail, "That's ridiculous! That's the dumbest-ass thing I've ever seen! Only the most childish little perverts would get their kicks watching something disgusting like that!" She pointed to the Oculere. "And yeah, I'm talking to *you*, Satan! You're an asshole, and I'm *glad* you got kicked out of Heaven! Dickbrain! Fuckface! Someday Jesus is gonna whoop your ass!"

The room fell silent. Peasley was looking down, pinching the bridge of his nose. "Teresa, there are some things one should *never* say to the Prince of Darkness, and I'm afraid everything that just came out of your mouth is a prime example."

"Honey," Ken suggested. "You probably shouldn't have said that…"

Peasley picked up the pair of magic petrified testicles and began rubbing them together. "Teresa. Bend over the couch so your ass is sticking up."

Teresa grimaced, resisting, like someone pulling against a tether. "Nnnnno! Nnnnnn—" but her resistance was short-lived and a moment later she was bent over the couch till her ass was sticking up.

Next, Peasley retrieved several items from the old suitcase, and instructed, "Kenster. Spread your lovely wife's butt-cheeks, will you please?"

Like an automaton, the Kenster obeyed, displaying with great clarity every detail of Teresa's asshole. If an asshole could even remotely be called "pretty", Teresa's was just that. Dainty, inconspicuous, petite.

Next, Peasley held up one of the items he'd retrieved from the suitcase…

"This," he began, "is a leaf-style rectal speculum. The way it works is, you insert this cluster of rounded metal posts into the recipient's sphincter and then, by way of this screw, open said recipient's rectal vault." Peasley spat on the posts and did exactly as he'd just explained.

Each twist of the screw made the metal posts move farther apart...until they could part no more and, hence, the sphincter muscle was stretched open as far as it would go, and poor Teresa's rectal vault was wholly exposed.

Teresa was yowling while Ken and Kirsty stared with a fair amount of curiosity. "I didn't know a butthole *looked* like that when it was opened all the way," Kirsty observed.

Peasley grinned. "Well, now you do!"

Indeed, the forced-open pink-rimmed aperture looked like a bottomless black hole in the middle of Teresa's splayed butt.

Teresa maintained her frown from her bent-over position on the couch. "And what now? Let me guess. You spit in my butt-hole, or pee in it? Or make Ken fist me—"

"No, no, no, my dear Teresa. Nothing nearly so pedestrian," assured Peasley, and then he grasped the second object he'd procured from the suitcase: a largish Mason jar. Something milky and gelatinous seemed to be floating in the jar.

"What," Ken began.

"The *fuck* is that?" Kirsty finished.

"I'm glad you asked." Peasley looked proudly at the jar. "This is a young *Chrysaora chesapeakei*—also known as the Maryland sea nettle. It's about the size of a dinner roll, with clusters of short tentacles, and is quite malleable, since jellyfish have no skeletons. Each tentacle contains over a thousand tiny stingers called nemotacysts—"

"No!" Teresa blared. "You're not gonna put that thing in my—"

"In your rectal vault?" Peasley questioned. "Why, yes, I'm afraid I am. All for the pleasure of my master, not to mention the technique's proof of the efficacy of the human nervous system." Peasley arranged the Oculere into a position on the table that provided a "bird's-eye view" of Teresa's cranked-opened backside. "Pain is the name of the game, Teresa, and I regret to inform you that you're about to find that out firsthand." He twisted the top off the Mason jar, poured the jellyfish into Teresa's rectal cavity, and then quickly reversed the speculum's screw until the opening was fully closed.

As the nemotacysts began firing their microscopic barbs into Teresa's most tender flesh, time and time again injecting venom, poor Teresa rolled off the couch onto the floor in what appeared to be a non-stop grand mal seizure. She flopped around hard, thunking loudly with each flop, such that one might think of a giant Mexican jumping bean, but one with monumental tits and a belly the size of a beach ball. But even more profound than the thunking were the noises she made in reaction to this absolutely incalculable agony: not just screams, shrieks, yells, and bellows, but squeaks, chirps, yelps, and barks, and everything conceivable in between—indeed, an amalgamation of vociferations quite possibly never before generated at once from a human throat.

Peasley turned from Teresa's wailing rigors, then reassessed Alison, who still levitated stupefied—with a pussy, mind you, still packed to the brim with Ken's feces. Then he turned back to Kirsty of the bright blonde hair.

Oblivious, Kirsty looked at him. "What? I licked Teresa's pussy, took Kenster's load up my ass, and ate a whole lot of Alison's poop. I'm done, right?"

Peasley bubbled laughter. "Done? Oh, no, you silly girl! I've saved the very worst especially for you."

"Why?" Kirsty yelled.

Peasley grinned. "Because, though Alison and Teresa may have their faults, they also possess traits that are *likeable.* They're animated, congenial, and interesting. But you, my dear?" Peasley tsked, shaking his head. "You're self-centered, morose, boring, and about as interesting as a bag of sand. You *suck,* Kirsty. You're absolutely worthless and, your phenomenal implants aside, you have no redeeming qualities whatsoever. It's women like you that make Satan *bristle,* and that's why I've arranged a very *special* surprise for you tonight." Next, Peasley popped several petit fours with gold flake into his mouth, and then removed another jar from the briefcase.

"Not another jellyfish!" Kirsty pleaded.

"No, no, it's something much more diverse than that." Peasley winked at her. "It's actually magic. I think you'll be impressed."

By now Teresa's screams and annoying thunking had abated, leaving her to quiver unconscious over by the 72-inch TV. Ken stood aside, awaiting more instructions, and Alison continued to float in mid-air, her neck craned in order that she might observe the action. All the while, that big abominable eye watched over all from the Oculere, moving from subject to subject, the single iris jittering as if with fervid excitement.

Peasley held up the jar he'd just withdrawn, then he began to shake it up as if it were a martini. "This will *really* blow your minds. It's a special occult concoction called an osmotic reagent. Simon Magus referred to it as a 'high and mighty veil-lifter.' Rather than bore you with a long-winded technical explanation, just watch…"

Peasley gave the jar one last shake, opened the top, and tossed the jar's blackish contents against the wall. This produced a large oval stain on the fancy hotel wallpaper. But in no time, there was a barely perceptible glitter about the oval's edges, and then that big black stain became a hole: four feet wide, perhaps, and six feet high.

"What *is* that?" Kenster asked, squinting at the marvel. "It melted a hole in the wall?"

Peasley rubbed his crotch for no apparent reason. "Not quite. You might say the ingenious substance, manufactured by Lucifer's most talented Chymists, has effected a temporary *portal* of sorts."

"A portal to where?" Alison asked, crook-necked. Her fabulous implants sagged not a bit in spite of the more extraneous effects of gravity in her levitating position.

Peasley grinned at the question. "Put your thinking caps on."

More than several seconds ticked by, then Ken blurted, "Not a portal to Hell!"

"Yes!" Peasley celebrated. "A portal to that very place. It won't last long, but it'll last long enough to produce the desired situation."

"Which is?" the Kenster ventured.

"You'll see." Peasley faced the great black hole in the wall and began to move his hands slowly backward, over and over, like someone ground-guiding a truck. Eventually, a giant pair of bare human feet emerged from the hole, and then a bare human body, quite muscular and rather hairy. It floated out of the hole, levitating much like Alison, until it had completely emerged, and then slowly lowered itself to rest on the floor.

"Oh my God!" Alison shrieked. "It's a giant corpse from Hell!"

Kenster staggered in place. "And it-it-it…*STINKS!*"

Indeed, the air fouled instantly, like concentrated tear gas only B.O. instead, and much much worse than Peasley's B.O. It smelled like butt-crack, armpit, and bad breath—but the *worst in history*, all distilled down to the most incalculable potency.

"Goddamn, man!" Kirsty bellowed. "That thing smells worse even than you! What the fuck?"

Peasley nodded with a sly grin. "You think I'm bad from not washing in sixty-five years?" He gestured at the giant corpse on the floor. "Our guest here hasn't washed in *three thousand!*"

Ken bent over and spontaneously threw up at the stench, then Kirsty thunked down to her hands and knees and did the same. Even Alison, still levitating, threw up as well, in a gushing loop that landed on her boobs. Alison and Kirsty had previously been forced to eat each other's shit—in sizable amounts—and this only added to the otherworldly stench that filled the room.

Alison looked down aghast at the giant nude corpse. "That fuckin' thing must be nine feet tall!"

"A bit more, actually," Peasley corrected. "He is six cubits and one span—in biblical measurements. And I couldn't tell you how much he weighs. God knows."

"Why did you bring that thing here?" Kirsty yelled.

"You'll find out in due time," Peasley answered. "But let's not get ahead of ourselves. This is a ground-breaking occasion. Take a few moments to really *look* at our colossal guest."

Still all gagging at the abominable stench, Ken, Alison, and Kirsty visually surveyed the outrageous nine-foot corpse lying before them. It was hairy from head to foot—like Ron Jeremy— its contours sculpted in muscles that seemed to be growing over even *more* muscles. Its head alone must've weighed a hundred pounds, sprouting with dark shaggy matted hair full of bugs, and a fat black beard flecked with chunks of food. Its ears were the size of bear's claws in a bakery, only full of detestable wax. But the genitals?

"For fuck's sake," croaked Kirsty. "Look at its cock..."

The figure's cock looked like a three-foot-long cutting of an elephant's trunk (only flesh-colored), situated atop a great crinkled sack containing two veined coconuts.

There was an oddity or two about the figure's head. One: its neck seemed banded by scars. In fact, Alison couldn't help but inquire, "Are those *scars* around his neck?"

"In a manner of speaking," Peasley answered at his elusive best. "They're actually welding marks, from a device called a Flesh-Welder."

"Huh?" Kirsty uttered.

"You see, our big friend here encountered some regrettable business long ago, in a place called the Valley of Elah, and his head was cut off. But we couldn't have him walking around Hell with no head, so our Teratologists welded the head back on. But isn't there something else that strikes you as odd?" The professor was referring to the second oddity: a poker-chip sized hole in the corpse's forehead. "In fact, I'll make a deal with you, Kirsty, if you can guess the identity of our nine-foot guest, I will let you out of here, and you can go home."

Kirsty began to shake. "Huh? Guess—what?"

"Guess this person's name," Peasley reiterated, pointing to the great reeking corpse. "You see, Kirsty, I'm betting that you're *so dumb*, you'll never in a million years be able to guess who this gentleman is. In fact, if you do, not only will I let you go, but I will personally suck this cadaver's dead-for-three-millennia dick."

"Come on, girl!" Alison rooted. "You've got this! Make this snide fucker suck this thing's dirty dick!"

"Think!" Kenster prodded. "Think of Sunday school!"

Kirsty looked up, terrified. "Huh? I never went to Sunday school! This isn't fair!"

The Kenster stood well behind Professor Peasley, and with quite a bit of emphasis, he was silently mouthing the name GOLIATH! with his lips. GOLIATH!

"Come on, Kirsty!" Peasley chided. "He's got a fuckin' *hole* in his forehead and he's giant! You must have some inkling."

Kirsty was now in tears. "Huh? Fuck—I don't know! How can I know who it is?"

Peasley ruefully shook his head. "Kirsty, you should have to pay a tax for the space your brain takes up, rendering it useless. It's Goliath, as in David and Goliath, from the Bible?"

"Huh?" Kirsty sobbed. "David *who?*"

"Fuck, are you shitting me, Kirsty?" Alison griped. "You've never heard of David and Goliath?"

The Kenster just pinched the bridge of his nose, looking down.

"And now let's continue." Peasley set the Oculere on the floor, affording it an ideal view. Then he began to rub the two petrified testicles together. "Kirsty, dear? Suck Goliath's dick."

Kirsty's eyes bugged. "I'm begging you—noooooooooooo!" But the professor's testicular spell left her no choice. She began to trudge forward on her hands and knees, toward Goliath. And Goliath's sheer stink not only permeated the room, but it was so evilly *dense* that she could actually *see it* wafting off the giant's body like heat waves on asphalt.

"Oh, and I might add," Peasley informed, "Goliath was a Philistine and an arch enemy of the Israelites. Remember, the Israelites practiced circumcision but the Philistines did not."

Kirsty looked up, puzzled. "Huh?"

"You can bet that Goliath's foreskin is *jam-packed* with dick-cheese, which you, of course, will orally extract and have to swallow." Peasley kept rubbing the occult testicles.

71

Once arrived at Goliath's groin, Kirsty, going pale in the face, picked up the giant's cock in both hands. She gulped, made a few croaking sounds, hitched out a few more tears, and then stuffed the flaccid organ into her mouth. Anything close to typical oral sex was not really possible since the cock was as wide as the fat end of a baseball bat; nevertheless, Kirsty did her best packing several inches into her mouth and moving her head falteringly up and down. When she came up for air, her opened mouth did indeed reveal a hefty deposit of smegma.

She looked pleadingly to Peasley with eyes that said *Can I please spit this out?* but the professor, true to form, answered, "No. Swallow it. Consider yourself uniquely privileged. That's three-thousand-year-old dick cheese, Kirsty. Yet another exciting experience you can tell your grandkids."

Kirsty went back to trying to suck the mammoth organ, then gagged out, "But this is stupid! Why make me suck a dead guy's dick? Nothing's gonna happen. He can't get hard. He can't cum…"

"That's where you're wrong," Peasley informed, sucking down several mango-and-grilled-shrimp kabobs. "You see, Goliath isn't really *dead* in the way that you think of the word. He's more in a state of *half*-death. When our incarnation technicians deliver a damned human soul back to the Living World—as is the case here—the personage's former physical body is re-assimilated as it would be as if he'd never died. Some small amount of life must be re-instituted into the body so that the damned soul can be possessed of awareness. In fact…aren't you detecting a slight *hardening* of Goliath's penis?"

Kirsty had to intermittently hold her breath, but she re-grasped the monstrous penis with both hands, squeezed, and exclaimed, "You're right! It's getting hard! He's pulling a boner! I can feel it beating!"

"Amazing, isn't it?" Peasley replied. "Now keep sucking, or I'll turn your pussy inside out and you'll have a tail. And it won't hurt you to go the extra mile and play with the balls either."

Shuddering, Kirsty did as commanded. Her entire *face* squeezed shut as she impaled her head on Goliath's now fully hard and very long erection. Aside, her hands fiddled with the reeking, slime-covered balls, which began to draw up in the horrific scrotum.

Everyone—except Peasley, that is—was getting lightheaded from the monstrous stench emanating off Goliath's gargantuan body. Tears came to Alison's eyes as if from riot gas; Ken stood jittering in place, trying to breathe through his mouth. If one harnessed a roomful of all the bad smells *ever produced* by the human body all throughout history, and compounded that a hundredfold, *that* would give some abstract idea of just what Goliath's stench was like. It was so concentrated that the wallpaper was starting to fall, and the sheetrock beneath was warping, and even the corners of the carpets were curling up. All the while (and with a resolve that was really quite impressive) Kirsty kept deep-throating the vanquished dead/not-dead Philistine. Eventually, Goliath's giant hips began to buck, he groaned like a just-gelded walrus, and his orgasm took place. If one took a garden hose with a sprayer on it, and squeezed the lever on and off, on and off, that would give any onlooker an idea of the sheer *force* of Goliath's ejaculation. Kirsty squealed in her throat, pulled her mouth off the throbbing prong of flesh with a mouth *full* of lumpy, discolored semen. More appalled, perhaps, than any woman in the annals of humankind, her eyes crossed, putrid semen fell out of her mouth, and she began to convulse. "My God, it's *rotten!* His cum is *rotten!*"

"What did you expect, you silly ninny?" Peasley said. "That's his first ejaculation in three millennia. The stuff builds up."

"Man, that takes the cake for blue balls," the Kenster commented.

And this was no exaggeration, for Goliath's monumental erection was still pulsing and ejaculating as he lay there, the jets of rotten semen firing all the way across the long room, splattering against the wall.

Stupefied and nearly insane, Kirsty began to thunk away from the scene on her hands and knees, gagging, retching, mumbling, and sobbing at the same time.

"And just where do you think you're going, little miss?" Peasley asked, arms crossed and tapping his foot.

"Huh?" Kirsty uttered. She looked back in horror. "I'm done now, right? For fuck's sake, I just sucked *Goliath's* cock and took the rotten load in the mouth, not to mention the dick-cheese!"

"Done? Is that what you said?" He sarcastically cupped his ear. "Did I hear you right? That you think you're *done* with your remaining responsibilities? Hmm?"

Kirsty started crying outright, like a little kid. "Oh, come on! Why are you being such a dick?" She pointed a shaky finger at the timer, which read 10 MINUTES REMAINING. "There's only ten minutes left! Can't you give it a rest?"

"No," Peasley informed. "That would be a waste of Satan's entertainment time. I've been charged with a duty for my master, and I will never fail that duty. The degradation will go on until the timer runs out, pure and simple. In other words, Kirsty—you're *not* done."

More outright bawling. "What do you want me to do *now*?"

"Well, Satan's a completist. Now that you've sucked Goliath, you need to *fuck* Goliath."

"He just blew his load!" Kirsty wailed. "His dick's a giant wet noodle! It's impossible to fuck that limp thing!"

Peasley shrugged. "Then you'll just have to get him up again."

"How?" Kirsty continued to wail. "He just came! Guys can't get it back up that fast after cumming!"

"Oh, I think they can, sweetie. All it takes is a little of the right kind of stimulation." Peasley turned from Kirsty and smiled down at Goliath. "Goliath? Turn around and get onto your hands and knees. Kirsty here is going to suck your asshole."

Kirsty screamed. Alison began to dry-heave. And Ken covered his face in his hands, muttering "No, no, no…"

Goliath needed no goading to assume the position; now the giant hairy figure positioned himself on hands and knees, protruding his rear end such that his butt stuck out grandly.

"Kenster," Peasley said next, "kneel right down there and spread Goliath's butt-cheeks as far as you can. We can't have Kirsty missing so much as a square millimeter of Goliath's mammoth backside, can we?"

"Don't you dare!" Kirsty spat at Ken. "Don't you do it, you cowardly fuck!"

Kenster rolled his eyes. "Come on, Kirsty. I have to, otherwise he'll use those magic ball-things and force me. Just do what he says. Don't be stupid."

"FUCK YOU, YOU YELLOW-BELLY FUCK-HEAD-LOOKING MOTHERFUCKER!" Kirsty yelled louder than ever in her life. Then she jerked her gaze to Peasley. "This is BULLSHIT! *Ken* should have to do it! He hasn't had to do anything today except bust a nut in my ass and open a fuckin' bottle of champagne! Me, Alison, and Teresa go through the wringer while Ken gets nothing! Why?"

"Because," Peasley began, "Ken is a *man*, and the outrage that Satan so enjoys is much better implemented via the exploitation of *women*. I'm afraid it's those warm, fascinating fissures between your legs that make women much more ripe for exploitation, degradation, sexual abuse, and overall subjugation and servility—those fissures, mind you, along with your tits, your menstrual cycles, your rampant hormones, hot flashes and mood swings, and your *femininity* in general." Peasley shrugged nonchalantly. "Quite simply, degrading men is boring. But degrading women? Nothing puts the lead in Satan's pencil faster than forcing a fussy, stuck-up woman to eat shit, or have her ass filled with urine, or blow donkeys, horses, and German shepherds, or get gang-banged by a hundred dirty, perverted men, or sexually abuse her own children. You see, *that's* the ticket, Kirsty."

Kirsty could only stare, her lower lip depending. Kenster's brow rose, and he said, "Gee, professor. I guess you're not a supporter of the National Organization of Women."

Peasley chuckled at the petty amusement. "I didn't quite realize just how *sizable* Goliath's ass is. Kenster, you'll need some assistance parting those big cheeks, yes?" Then he opened the little book he'd used before, and intoned, "Ayptob, iaglrub, iktob, ixedox."

All at once Alison shrieked; the Levitation Spell was broken and she landed on the floor flat on her back. Upon impact, all that excrement previously packed into her vaginal canal made an expeditious exodus.

"Alison," the professor said, "help Kenster pull Goliath's buttocks apart so Kirsty can get her face right up in there and start licking."

Alison stood up, wincing at the shit rolling down the inside of her thighs. She seemed a bit dizzy (who wouldn't, given her experience thus far?), then she walked over toward Goliath.

"YOU FUCKIN' BACKSTABBING SILVER SPOON CUNT!" Kirsty yelled. "You're supposed to be my friend! You conniving hosebag! You cum-gargling *tramp!* Jeez! *How* many abortions have you had? Six, seven? You're a traitor and a coward, just like Ken!"

Alison just sighed. "Shut up, Kirsty." She got down wearily on her knees and pulled on Goliath's right buttock, while Ken did the same to the left.

That great hair-packed ravine that was Goliath's ass-crack spread such that all that existed within extruded outrageously into view. Untold fecal debris littered the horrific valley with much reeking matted ass-hair stuck to the sides. The Philistine's actual asshole looked like some kind of an organic drain, its puckered knot rimmed with ancient pimples. There were other things in there too: curious little mites and beetles frolicking about, blood-curdling dingleberries, whole kernels of corn, and many less mentionable things. The elephantine cock and balls dangled hugely below.

"Kirsty?" Peasley said. He picked up the petrified balls of the Baron Gilles de Rais and commenced to rubbing them together. His grin couldn't have been more nefarious when he instructed, "Suck Goliath's ass-crack. And do it with precision and assiduity."

Kirsty was mewling, eyes closed, and she moved on hands and knees—clearly against her will—toward Goliath's monstrous back end. Her big tits swayed with each begrudging increment. The waterworks returned and Kirsty was blubbering away. "Please! Please don't make me!" but even as she choked out the plea, her face inched closer and closer to the splayed crack. Then, at last, Kirsty's comely face wedged right in there, like some kind of docking procedure.

Peasley rubbed the warlock testicles more aggressively. "Come on, Kirsty. Lick and suck like you mean it. No half measures. Don't stop until Goliath's butt-crack is clean as a whistle."

Indeed, licking and sucking sounds were heard, and before long Kirsty was screaming out loud as she followed the order. And along with this, the semi-living Goliath began to moan with pleasure and his hellish asshole began to flinch.

Peasley nodded. "You go, girl. Isn't that what they say in this day and age? You're doing a great job, Kirsty. Oh, but no holding your breath in there. Take a couple of good deep breaths through your nose."

The first deep inhalation was heard but then—

"Oh, no!" exclaimed Alison.

"Fuck!" yelled the Kenster.

—Kirsty collapsed, toppling off to her side, her face now smudged brown. She was totally unconscious.

Ken rushed over to her, patting her face. "Looks like she's out cold."

Alison rushed over too, feeling for a pulse. She tried both wrists, both sides of the neck… "Holy shit! She's got no pulse!"

Ken put his ear between Kirsty's spectacular breasts, listened, then paled. "No heartbeat. Fuckin'-A. Goliath's butt-crack stink was so bad it fuckin' *killed* Kirsty!"

Peasley stroked his shitty beard; he did not look pleased. The clock read 4 MINUTES REMAINING. "Then revive her. Do CPR. Come on! Do I have to think of everything?"

Kenster straddled Kirsty and began pressing down on the center of her chest. "I'll do compressions," he said to Alison. "You do mouth-to-mouth."

Alison blinked. "Uhhh. How about…FUCK YOU?"

"Oh, yeah," Ken said. "Well, I'll just keep doing compressions." And, wouldn't you know it? Just at that moment, Kirsty gagged and shuddered, and then began to come to.

"You did it!" Alison rejoiced. "You brought her back to life!"

"Thank God!" Ken exclaimed, hugging Kirsty.

Peasley, nearing infuriation, put the balls down and grabbed Kirsty by the hair, yanked her forward as she yelped with each tug, then jammed her appalled face right back into mammoth cleft of Goliath's buttocks. "In ya go, you little floozy. You'll suck till I tell you to stop." He pushed the back of Kirsty's head harder, maximizing the contact between of her face and Goliath's revolting-beyond-description ass-crack. "That's it," he chuckled. "Good little rich girl. Wear that ass-crack like a mask…"

Kirsty's body began to hitch, and rough gags could be heard deep in her throat. She was beginning to convulse.

"Uh, professor?" the Kenster ventured. "I think she's smothering…"

"You're gonna kill her…*again!*" Alison exclaimed.

Suddenly Professor Peasley's hands released Kirsty and he screamed as loud as a truck horn, and by the time Ken and Alison discerned what had happened, they saw one of the fondue forks sticking out of Peasley's right eye. It was the huge-stomached Teresa who stepped out from behind him. Somehow, she'd managed to open the rectal speculum and remove the jellyfish, then grabbed a fondue fork and attacked Peasley. The unwashed professor continued to howl as blood spurted spectacularly from his eye.

"Alison!" Teresa yelled. "Pull his pants down!"

Alison obliged with a festive grin, yanking the trousers all the way down as Teresa pulled out the fondue fork and then plunged it right up between Peasley's legs, sinking the sharp prongs deep into the professor's perineum, a.k.a. "taint."

Much higher-pitched howling accompanied this action, and of this the Kenster remarked, "He sounds like a little girl!"

Peasley grimaced at Teresa, and through his unexpected agony, he growled, "I will incinerate you from the inside out, starting with your pussy!"

"You ain't doing dick," Teresa retorted, and then she proudly held up the pair of petrified testicles. "Because *I* got the magic warlock balls now, bitch!"

Peasley's eyes crossed, and then his face turned white when he realized his oversight.

Teresa, with a vulpine grin, began to rub the two testicles together. "Suck Goliath's ass-crack, you spinach-chin pervert mother fucker," she ordered. "And I mean suck it *good!*"

Peasley had no choice but to obey the supernatural command, groaning, "No, no, please no!" as he knelt behind Goliath and pushed his face resolutely into the crack.

"Suck! Suck that ass-hair that hasn't been washed in three thousand years! Yeah!"

Alison and Kirsty, giggling like insane witches, each grabbed one of Peasley's ears and jammed his face *harder* into that biblical ass-crack, such that he soon began to gasp for air, while Kenster added some spark to the party by snatching up two more fondue forks, one of which he hooked down into the professor's nutsack, catching a ball. The other fork he rammed right up Peasley's anus.

Whether he actually smothered to death or not could not be verified, but just as he was stroking out, a beeping sound was heard. The four naked young people all jerked their glances at the timer on the table, which read 0 MINUTES REMAINING.

"I wonder what happens now?" Teresa asked, but the question was answered in the next split second when Peasley and Goliath...

"Wow!" the Kenster remarked.

...disappeared in dual wisps of foul smoke. Then, so did the copy of the *Ars Goetia*, the old suitcase, the speculum, and that poor dead jellyfish. The timer disappeared as well, and when Teresa noticed the Oculere on the floor, she rushed to pick it up and she stared into it, stared at that billiard-ball-sized bloodshot eye as it stared back at her.

"Fuck you, Satan," she said, and then the Oculere disappeared too.

When the four of them looked at the wall on which Peasley had opened the portal, they were not terribly surprised to see that the black oval hole was gone, as if it had never existed in the first place.

"Holy shit, it's over!" Ken celebrated.

"And we're still alive!" Alison added. She grabbed a linen napkin from one of the hors d'oeuvre tables and began wiping shit off the inside of her thighs.

Kirsty was washing her face in one of the punch bowls. "Oh my God, I'll *never* get this *butt-stink* off my face!"

"Quit complaining," Teresa said. "That prick stuck a fuckin' *jellyfish* up my ass." But, even with all that trauma, she did manage to enjoy a few fancy deviled eggs and pheasant tenders in mustard sorrel sauce.

Then, everything went black...

The Kenster, fully dressed, walked out of the kitchenette, holding a bottle of champagne. His face was blank.

Kirsty, Alison, and Teresa were also fully dressed in their ritzy overpriced designer apparel, all unmussed, unsullied. They were sitting on one of the couches, and not one of them had the aftertaste of human waste in their mouth.

They stared at each other for a full minute.

Teresa was the first to give voice. "Was...was that real?"

"Was there some stinky man here a little while ago," Kirsty ventured, "making us do horrible things? Some guy with Satanic powers?"

"Yeah," Ken said. "I'm pretty sure there was. I'm pretty sure it all happened. That guy put a jellyfish up Teresa's ass…"

"You're right!" Teresa bellowed. "It was all real!"

Behind them stood several long tables bearing exquisite appetizers as well as a steaming fondue pot surrounded by delectable tidbits.

Kirsty gave a thousand-yard stare. "Did I really…*suck* Goliath's ass-crack?"

Everybody looked at her and nodded.

"So…what happened?" Alison queried.

"The timer ran out," Ken supposed. "Everything that Peasley did became *undone* at that moment. That has to be it. And when there was no more time, everything switched back to normal. Everything is back in its proper place. The whole business was only *temporary!*"

The three girls looked at each other, took deep breaths, then burst into tears, hugging each other.

Just then, there was a knock on the fancy door. Ken turned and froze. "Well, here's the moment of truth. If I open that door and there's brimstone behind it, then we're screwed…"

The girls watched wide-eyed as three owls when Ken walked to the hotel room door. He waited a moment, shivered a bit, then opened it—

"Sorry we're late!" someone announced.

"You know how the traffic gets in Channelside," remarked someone else, and then into the room poured over a dozen well-dressed twentysomethings, many bearing wrapped packages.

"Come on in!" Teresa squealed, tears in her eyes.

Amongst a stuffy mixture of upwardly mobile chat, the crowd moved its way to the hors d'oeuvre tables, and the decimation began. "Oh, this fondue is superb!" one prissy woman raved, sucking a cheese-dipped chunk of quail off the fork. "What kind of cheese is this? Camembert du Bocage?"

The Kenster walked around the crowd to the couch. "Girls, who wants champagne?"

A VERY BAD DAY IN HELL

John had no idea how long he'd been waiting in line—of course not. In the Mephistopolis there *was* no time. Clocks didn't tick, it was always nighttime, and the moon always existed in the same phase and it never moved. *Fuck*, he thought. *In Living World time, I may have been standing in this line for years...*

But stand there, he would, for as long as it took. He wasn't very industrious here, just as he hadn't been when he was alive. If there was an easy way out, John would seek it out. Hence, his presence here, in this atrocious line of "people" waiting to sell some part of themselves to the Pay Clerk at this Sales Annex of the Department of Surgical Transfiguration.

There were many such annexes all over the endless city. This one was between Rotville and the Ghettoblocks, this latter prefect for providing an abundance of "inventory." The poor were always more desperate, and John, well, he was always poor since he'd arrived in this fabled city of the Damned.

He watched numbly as a portable compacter on things like tank treads, rumbled to a stop across the street. *This should be interesting*, he thought. Demon legionnaires from the Ludendorf Punishment Battalion ground-guided several steam-powered dump trucks into position, then gave the go-ahead signal. Gears ratcheted and pistons surged as each truck's rear haulage container rose and then tilted until the container's contents emptied into the compacter's long crush pit. What exactly did the contents consist of? People, mostly, the Human damned, mixed in with a variety of Crossbreeds, Trolls, Broodren, and Imps. After the trucks had fully emptied their wares into the crusher bed, one would think the victims would all clamor over one and another to climb out and escape but...not so. Each and every one of them had had their arms and legs broken so all they could do was lie in their squirming, bellowing, and voiding waste. Now the crusher's operators pulled the CRUSH lever, and slowly but surely the hydraulic plate traversed the bed and all the contents therein were squashed. The action released an interesting cacophony of screams, crunching, and squishing. Passersby all stood on their tiptoes in order to behold the mass of demonic goulash, collapsed skulls, and flattened bodies. Later, the contents would be emptied at a reclamation center where it would all be deboned, flensed of all useful flesh, and then the drain plug would be removed so that all the remaining liquid could be tapped for the higher-scale restaurants downtown.

Better them than me, John thought after he'd seen enough. Finally, the malodorous line he stood in got one notch shorter, after a Human woman had sold her face for one hundred Hellnotes. Once she'd signed her permission form at the cashier window, a horned Conscript came out and—SNAP!—pressed a circular device like a bear trap against her face and pulled the spring release. The serrated jaws of the device snapped shut in an instant, and an instant after that, the woman was staggering away, faceless. "That hurt like a motherfucker!" she yelled. The Conscript paid the remark no mind when he retreated back into the annex, holding the woman's face like a scarlet dishrag. "I wonder what they do with the faces," John muttered, more to himself. "All kinds of things," answered a guy behind him. The "guy" was a half-turned werewolf, evidently here to sell some pelt. "Archdukes and Chevaliers buy them to jerk off in, or for toilet paper. Can you imagine that? Wiping your ass with some chick's *face?*"

"Uh, no," John said. "I don't think I can…"

The werewolf nodded. "But if it's a good-looking chick or handsome dude's face, they sell the faces to the upper-class Transfigurists for, you know, face transplants. Human faces on Demons and Trolls are all the rage now, I hear."

"Hmm," John uttered, thinking. He doubted he would get much for *his* face.

"What are *you* looking to sell?" asked the lycanthrope.

John shrugged. "My cock."

"Yeah? Shit, I sold mine a long time ago," and then the wolfman jutted forward his hips to display the fact. Indeed, there was a big bald spot between his legs, in the form of a crusted scar. "Hated to see it go but, fuck… I needed the money."

"I hear ya, man. If you don't mind my asking, what did they give you for it?"

"Seventy-five. Can you believe it? Said it wasn't worth any more than that 'cos I'm a lycanthrope. What a rip-off. Back in the Living World I could've sued the fuckers for discrimination. But here? Fat chance."

"Bummer, man," John tried to commiserate. But, shit, if they only gave him seventy-five for *his* dick, he'd be screwed. He owed the shylocks on Ruby Street twice that much. But then, John was counting on something the rest of these chumps couldn't.

"Next!" shouted the cashier in a cringing Rhode Island accent.

"Good luck, bro," bid the werewolf.

"Thanks. You too."

John dusted lint or something more nameless off his rotten blue/red paisley dress shirt. *Here goes…* He stepped up to face the woman in the cashier booth—well, correction. The *zombie* woman in the cashier booth. *Damn, for a dead chick she's packing some SERIOUS tits*, he thought. In spite of their green/gray hue, her breasts stuck out grandly on her slat-ribbed chest, with nipples like bruise-purple cabinet knobs. Beneath high cheekbones, gouged and rotten flesh showed imposingly, and her eyes were like two open pustules. But, yeah, there was still something cute about her. *Back in L.A.*, he thought, *I'd be putting some serious blocks to this bitch.*

Ah, but such is the verity of fate, yes?

"What are you looking to sell, hon?" came her accent again.

"Well, my dick," John said.

The corroded woman shook her head with a smile. "I guess it's a trend now—more and more guys are selling their junk. But first, let me fill out your receipt." She produced a bone pen and clipboard with vellum paper on it. "First name?"

"John," John said.

"Middle name?"

"Curtis."

"Last name?"

"Holmes."

The cashier looked up. "Wait a minute. I remember you. My asshole husband used to watch your movies. Johnny the Wadd, right?"

John smiled and rubbed his considerably packed crotch. "That's me. Did you catch *The Jade Pussycat*? Or *How Do I Love Thee, Let Me Count the Lays*? I won awards for those. I was also in a big horror flick, *Sex and the Single Vampire*."

The cashier's runny eyes bloomed. "Say, did you really kill all those people in Laurel Canyon?"

"No, I did *not!*" John responded with the emphasis. "I'm a lover, not a killer! But I was in a movie once called *Laurel's Canyon*. I was balls-deep in some chick's ass, and they had to take her to the hospital. "

Now the rotten woman was leaning out of the window, trying to view his crotch. "Well, come on. How big is it really?"

"Fifteen even," John lied. He lied about pretty much everything in his life. In truth, not that truth mattered much in the domain of the Prince of Lies, his erection was only thirteen and a half, and that was on a good day. Right now, he whipped it out flaccid and flapped it around for her. It made for an impressive display. "How about a roll in the hay?" he said and winked. "Then you can tell all your friends you got schtupped by Johnny the C-Man. And it'll only cost you fifty Hellnotes."

The dead woman sighed. "I wish but I can't. I'm on company time and it's against policy. Last time I broke the rules, they—well, have a look…" She raised one veiny leg and showed John the gray-green groove between her legs. "The Constabs stapled my pussy shut. No nookie for me."

"Well, that sucks," John said. But he could think of plenty of women back in the Living World he'd like to use that stapler on, but not on their vaginas, their mouths. Both of his wives never shut up. Nag, nag, nag, yell, yell, yell. Especially Sharon, whom he'd foolishly married in 1964. She was a nurse and she had income. John had beguiled her with his giant dick and figured he'd be able to live off her and not have to work. Wrong. All she ever did was yell about what a loser he was. Get a job! Clean this place up! Get off your fuckin' lazy ass. Well, fuck that. And she was a piss-poor lay. He'd only taken so much of that demeaning shit before he'd gotten resourceful and put that big dick to work—in the porn industry. One reviewer said of him, "John Holmes is to porn what Elvis was to rock and roll." *Damn straight*, he thought. He was out of Sharon's house like a shot and never had to listen to her yell again. *Loser, huh, Sharon? Lazy ass? I was the biggest dick in porn—in HISTORY, so fuck you!*

But still, he would've loved to staple her mouth shut. What a sweet fantasy!

"Okay, John," the cashier got back to business. "Do you want to sell the whole three-piece set?"

John blinked. "The *what?*"

"You know, the whole kit'n'kaboodle? Or just the dick?"

"Just the dick," John said, and then he chuckled. "Can't sell the family jewels, you know. Gotta keep something swinging down there."

The cashier leaned her chin against her palm. "Seriously, John. What good are your nuts gonna do ya without the dick?"

John pondered the query. She had a point. But then there was whole "manhood" issue. It was the balls that made the man a *man.* "Well, how much will you pay?"

"For just the dick? Fifty Hellnotes."

"Are you shitting me!" John yelled. "This is the most famous dick in history—"

"The *second* most famous," the cashier corrected. "Rasputin's is the first. That fucker was hanging *sixteen inches,* limp!"

John didn't know what she was talking about. "My dick is worth more than fifty Hellnotes! Shit, I've fucked *fourteen THOUSAND* women with it!" This claim, too, was bullshit. It was also bullshit that he was a Vietnam war hero, that he was the brother of Ken Osmond who played Eddie Haskell on *Leave It to Beaver,* and that he had dual degrees from UCLA. John was FULL OF SHIT and always had been. But here, now, what did it matter?

"Sorry, John. All I can give you is fifty."

"But you even gave the werewolf seventy-five!"

"Sure, because he's a werewolf. You're a *Human* and Human's are tits on a bull in Hell. They're like old people in Florida. A penny a dozen. Less, even."

Fuck me! "Okay, then what about the whole works, the...three-piece set?"

"Oh, sure. Throw in the nuts and the sack along with the johnson, I can give you, say, sixty-five—"

Why, you-you-you...cunt! This was not going well. *If I don't get some money to my shylocks, they'll cut off my head and take me to an Electrocity generator!* "Really, miss," he pled. "I need more than that. Come on, these are the family jewels of JOHN C. HOLMES, the king of porn! More people have seen my dick than *anyone else's dick! Ever!* It's famous!"

The zombie clerk let out a long exhale. "Maybe it's famous in the Living World, but in Hell? It's just another dick and it's worth sixty-five Hellnotes."

John gave her his best despondent puppy dog look. "Miss, please. I'm begging you with all my heart. If I don't bag more than sixty-five for my dick, I could get pressure-cooked, or the goombas could fill my ass up with Slime-Snakes and butt-plug me."

The cashier tapped a nail on the counter. "Okay, John. Since I like you, I can up the pot a little—"

"Oh, thank you, thank you!" John blubbered and actually kissed her rotten hand. "You have my eternal thanks!"

"I'll give you seventy for the works, and that's the bottom line."

John's entire posture wilted, the ridiculous tube of uncircumcised meat still hanging out of his ridiculous bellbottom pants. "I-I-I-"

"Take it or leave it. You've got six seconds to decide. Otherwise, you gotta go to the end of the line."

John looked over his shoulder at the line, and nearly lost consciousness. The line was miles long.

"Four, five, s—"

"Okay!" John blurted. "I'll sell for seventy! Fuck!"

"Okay, great," she said, and slid a permission form over, which John signed as if a zombie himself. *I just signed my dick away*, he thought. *What could be more fucked up?*

And that was that. The following procedure could be summed up in very few words. A Golem stepped onto the street and pinned John's elbows behind his back, then two white-garbed Transfiguration Surgeons appeared, pulled John's bellbottoms down and—

SNIP!

—cut his genitals off in a single action, with a pair of roofing shears.

There was no need to describe the vibrant tenor of John's screams, or the way his eyes bugged from his head and crossed. If anything, the pain had damn near straightened his famous curly hair.

Pedestrians stopped in their tracks to watch, most of them chuckling. But John didn't see what was so funny.

He hugged his knees to his chest, shuddering on the brimstone sidewalk. Semi-coherent thoughts at last re-entered his head, through the throbbing agony, and then his eyes bugged more extremely when he realized the man with the most famous penis in the world now had *no* penis. The zombie cashier came out, and her awesome corpse-breasts hung low when she bent over and slipped seventy Hellnotes into the top pocket of his ridiculous paisley disco shirt. "Here's your money, John—oh, and here's your cock." She held the severed thing up like a limp salmon, balls dangling. John moaned walrus-like when the image finally registered its reality in his brain.

"Say bye-bye," said the cashier in a baby voice. "John's dick says bye-bye to John," and she coyly waved her fingers at him. "Bye-bye, John, bye-bye!"

The cashier traipsed away, hefting the dick and scrotum in her hand with quite a bit of satisfaction. But poor John could only quiver on the sidewalk, holding a hand to the great bleeding empty space at his groin. When the pain began to throb down, he managed to unsteadily stand up and fasten his pants. If there was a bright side to getting your dick cut off in Hell, John found it by thinking, *Well, at least I can pay off some of my marker now. That's better than nothing, right?*

But the bad day was about to get worse, if such a thing were possible. A barrel-chested, lump-faced Demon in a police uniform waltzed up, twirling a razor-studded baton. "Hate to tell you this, sir, but bleeding on the sidewalk is illegal," and then the cop pointed his stick at the great oval of blood that John's penectomy had voided. "I'm afraid you're gonna have to come with me and face the judge. You'll probably be incarcerated."

John was now twitching as if cataleptic.

"Or you can pay the fine," the cop added, nodding.

"Whuh-what's the fine?" John hacked out.

"Head."

John peered at the cop. "What do you mean? You mean like…"

"Head, you know. That means you *give me head*. You *blow* me. You *suck* my willy till it spits."

Ug, fuck, was the most articulate thought that John could muster, but he said, "Um, okay," and then he got down on his knees and opened the policeman's blue trousers. What flopped out was not anything that John could regard as a penis; it was more like a sea cucumber, green, but with pulsating red bumps akin to cysts. *Just get it over with,* John reasoned, and an instant later, there he was, Johnny the Wadd, sucking cock like a seasoned little bitch. But...was this the first time John had sucked a dick? Well, that's a big negatory. See, toward the end of his life in the Living World, he'd whored himself out to rich gay guys all the time because he was a hopeless coke addict. His pride and joy wouldn't get hard any more, so that was curtains for the porn career. But there were plenty of rich gay dudes who got a kick out of giving it to the famous John C. Holmes right up the poop chute, or fucking his mouth like it was a two-dollar whore. John didn't mind; he just needed the coke money. He could deep throat with the best of them. He was a terrific party favor.

John's pathetic head bounced back and forth like a ball on a spring while he kept up the mouth-love on the Demon cop's junk. We'll leave out descriptions of what that junk smelled and tasted like. John's tongue rolled around the end of it—what would be the "glans" on a Human but, see, he couldn't help but make this incongruent observation: there really *was* no glans, no mushroom helmet, no nothing. Just a nub. Nor did there seem to be a urethral exit or "pee-hole." Of course, John wondered briefly how this cop pissed, but then more than briefly he wondered, *When this guy gets off, where's the jizz gonna come out? There's no hole...*

Or was there?

What John found out the hard way was this: each one of those cyst-like bumps served as a glans. At least a dozen of them, each tipped with its own egress or, if you will, dick-slit. At any rate, eventually John's expert fellatio got the job done, and when the cop quite noisily had his orgasm, each one of those carbuncle holes released copious whitish-yellowish goo with little lumps in it—indeed, less like semen and more like some corrupt manner of tapioca sauce. This is what filled John's mouth aplenty, and with the officer's clawed hand clenched in the back of John's head, there was no pulling his mouth off and spitting the stuff out. The former cocksman's reflexes told him he could inhale the nefarious crap or he could swallow. So…

Down the hatch it went, one spasmodic pulse after the next. John had to gulp as desperately as he'd ever done anything in his life, because every time he'd transferred a big mouthful to his stomach, another mouthful was waiting. *Fuck, and I thought Peter North came a lot!* He thought. *This fuckin' cop must have a prostate the size of a mail bag!* Yes, the cop just kept coming and John just kept swallowing. So far he must've chugged down a half a gallon of the pestiferous semen — no, more like a *whole* gallon. And in his mouth John could feel those "tapiocas" swimming around like pea-sized tadpoles. Fill-swallow, fill-swallow, it seemed nowhere close to abating. In fantasy, he saw himself chomping down hard and biting the policeman's cock off, but such a thing could never happen now: John had sold his teeth to a Concrete Annex a long time ago.

Anyway, eventually the cop *did* stop ejaculating. John fell back on the sidewalk, his mouth agape, and he was now sporting a considerable pot belly that he didn't have earlier.

"Damn," the cop remarked. "You suck dick like a champ, buddy." He patted John on the top of the head, almost as if he were a dog. "But I hate to tell you this, I gotta write you up and take you in."

Rage turned John's face maroon. "What for! I just paid the fine!"

"Well, that was before you committed another crime —"

"What crime?"

"Performing an obscene act on a police officer in public!"

John went cockeyed. Veins bulged in his forehead bigger than the ones in his penis…back when he'd *had* a penis.

The cop stuffed his monstrous genitals back in his trousers. "But you know what? That blowjob was so good, it put me in a

94

better mood. I won't take you in, but you'll have to pay a fine—
"

John was shaking all over. "What, I gotta suck that thing you call a dick *again?*"

"No, no, just a monetary fine this time."

You gotta be shitting me... "Okay, how much?"

The demon constable narrowed his eyes—"Hmm, now let me think," then—

SNAP!

—he snatched the bills out of the top pocket of John's stupid shirt. He counted the money, nodded, "Seventy Hellnotes. Have a good day, sir," and then he chuckled, turned, and waltzed away, twirling his baton.

John, of course, was mortified, but those were the breaks in Hell. He wanted to yell, scream, cry, throw a tantrum, etc., but all this was useless, he knew. He was in Hell, and nobody cared how illogical and unfair things were here. In fact, they were *supposed* to be that way. *I just waited for years in the Annex line, and look at me now. I've got a bellyful of monster cum, no money, and no dick. What am I gonna do now?*

Beat the street, that's what. But just as he hauled himself up from the bone-flecked sidewalk—

SPLAT!

—a delivery truck roared by, hit a puddle, and sent a spectacular splash of diarrhea right into John's face.

John crawled into the nearest alley and sat there for a good long time, blubbering like a baby.

———

Sometime later (a few hours, a few days, a few months? Who knew?) John was awakened by a series of gentle nudges.

"Sir? Sir?" came a man's inquiring voice. The voice sounded distinctive, like a Brit maybe. John had dozed off in the alley

95

and dreamed of the first time Seka had sucked his dick. "It's like trying to blow a telephone pole!" she'd complained. Ah, the good ole days... But now here he was, awakening in the atrocious alley full of Caco-Ticks and Bapho-Rats. Rats had been trying to eat his cock for God knew how long. At least he didn't have to worry about *that* any more.

"Sir, I hope this isn't an imposition," said the British voice. John squinted up and noted detail of the speaker. He was a Human with a bald head and very dapper poise, and he was dressed in tuxedoish apparel, like a butler.

"Fuck, what do ya want?" John opened his pants. "Can't you see I've just lost my dick."

"Indeed, sir, and I'm very sorry that you've suffered such an unpleasant misfortune. But it is my duty to convey to you a message of considerable import, and one of such a nature as to prove quite beneficial to you at this present moment."

John rubbed sleep and the stinging of piss-vapors out of his eyes. "What is this, another rip-off, another scam?"

"I can assure you, sir, that this situation represents nothing of the kind." The butler tapped his heels and bowed. "I am Hollingshead, sir, the personal valet of a very lofty dignitary indeed: the Lady Vesticle, Duchess of Cadaverton. You can espy her thither," and the butler pointed behind him into the street where there sat a motorized carriage car whose sulphur-burner, like the front of a steam train, belched black-yellow smoke from a stovepipe chimney. "The Duchess is quite the humanitarian; her heart goes out to unfortunates such as yourself, and she requests the pleasure of your company."

John peered into the passenger compartment and saw a stately high-collared woman fanning herself with a fan fashioned from the severed, mummified hand of a Deep One. (The webbed fingers provided a very effective "fan" function.)

And even from this low angle John could tell that her bodice was of the topless variety, and—

Damn, that chick is packing a pair of tits like Lisa Deleeuw—er, at least before Lisa Deleeuw croaked from AIDS... John cast an inquisitive glance back up to the butler. "And she wants to see me, huh?"

"Of that I can answer most affirmatively, sir," said Hollingshead the Brit butler. "And it is highly likely to behoove you, sir, to consent to meeting her. She is well known to give large sums of cash to the poor."

John was up and at 'em in a split-second. "Sounds good to me. I don't think I have anything on my schedule today."

"Very good. Follow me, sir."

The butler pulled down a fussy hinged step, then John loped up into the carriage where he got to eyeball the "duchess" with a bit more clarity. The awesome breasts, he could see now, had been surgically attached—such was the case for a majority of titled females—and the rest of her was a cosmetically augmented brick-shit house as well. Her face was particularly captivating; it was covered with metal studs, each inlaid with a variety of semi-precious gemstones—citrines, tanzanites, and agate—all valueless in the Living World but in Hell each stone had more value than the ten Hope Diamonds. The highly polished stones, in other words, made the Duchess' face sparkle fabulously, almost like a disco ball.

"You poor, dear man," said the Duchess. "When I saw you there in your destitution, I knew I just *had* to stop. No one should have to exist in such an impoverished state. Have you eaten?"

"Well, no, ma'am, not in a long time," John said, now sitting opposite her in the cushioned seat. The woman's legs were as perfect and pristine as a top-shelf model's, barely covered by a luminous, incarnadine skirt that looked diaphanous. John relished the memories of a time when legs like this would be wrapped around him every day as the camera rolled and his world-famous cock banged away.

The ornate woman offered a tray of chocolates, each embossed with the sigils of Baphomet, Belial, and the Ardat-Lil. John stuffed a few in his mouth and nearly swooned from the luxuriant taste and texture. "Oh, these are great! It tastes like real chocolate from the Living World!"

"Indeed, they do, dear man. My Occult Chocolatiers work hard preparing them for me. Help yourself to as many as you like, and do tell me a bit about yourself as we make our way back to my chateau. There I will procure for you a million Hellnotes to assist you in your plight."

"Wow! Thanks, ma'am! That's very generous of you!" But what could he tell her about himself? He figured the truth couldn't hurt, right? "Well, let's see. My name's John, I was born in Ashville, Ohio, and, uh—" John paused for further thought and decided it best to skip the part of his porn fame. "I was also a Vietnam war hero."

"Oh, how interesting!" exclaimed the Duchess. "I was born in a nice little place called Renton, in Washington State. Not too far from Seattle."

John nodded, still stuffing chocolates into his mouth. But suddenly he stalled. "Renton? I've heard of it—"

"Yes, there's a big Boeing factory there," the Duchess added; however, something was odd. Was she actually smiling ever-so-slightly?

"Oh, now I remember! My first wife, Sharon, was born there, but I'll tell ya, she was a class-A bitch and duller than dishwater. Fucking her was like fucking a bag of sand and she had *no idea* how to give head."

"Ah, Sharon, you say? As in Sharon Gebanini?"

"As a matter of fact, yes," John replied. "Did you know her?" but by then John's motor functions were slowing down and he was suddenly *very* tired. *Wait a minute... What the fuck?*

The Duchess was now removing the jeweled studs from her face. "You should be feeling it now, John. Those chocolate-covered nether-berries have been Hexed by a paresis spell..."

John gulped, and then sidled over on the seat. And she wasn't kidding; John was fully conscious, but now he couldn't move a muscle.

"I didn't just know her, John," said the Duchess. "I *am* her," and this fact was at last revealed when she's removed the last of the studs to show her true face.

John's eyes bugged. It was her all right—looking just as cute as she'd been in 1964 when he'd met her during his short-lived job as an ambulance driver. "Sharon! Honey! I can't believe it! It *is* you! I've missed you so much! You know, you were the only girl I ever really loved—"

"Save it, John," she said quite calmly. "A Class-A bitch, huh? Duller than dishwater? I was your meal ticket for years because you couldn't keep a job and wouldn't even try! I fed you, clothed you, and drove you all over town to buy drugs, and all you ever did for me was stick that giant dick in my ass *every night* until you threw me over to do porn! That's all you ever were, John. A great big dick!"

John was dumbfounded. "But, honey! I don't even *have* a dick anymore. They-they-they *stole* it from me. Some demons mugged me and stole it!"

"Once a pathological liar, *always* a pathological liar," the Duchess chided. "Nobody stole it from you, you *sold* it. And when my confidantes at the Annex called me, I bought it immediately, for *ten thousand* Hellnotes!"

"Shit, all I got was seventy!" John babbled, now limp where he lay. "And then a cop stole *that!* Seriously, sweetheart! I'm a *victim!*"

"Oh, poor baby. Poor John lost his dicky-dick, his only real identity. I knew it was the right move to sell my soul to Lucifer, 'cos he made me a Grand Duchess the instant I died. Then I devoted my eternity to exacting my revenge against you, you two-bit lying junkie cock-hound motherfucker."

John tried to act dismayed but wasn't pulling it off. "Honey? Revenge? But I *love you*, I always have!"

"And after I bought your world-famous cock, I hired the best surgeon in the Boniface District to sew it on me, and...wouldn't you know it?"

It was with a dramatic slowness that the Duchess raised the hem of her elaborate skirt to display her bare groin, which was now occupied by the preposterously large genitals that had once proudly belonged to John Curtis Holmes.

"Look familiar?" asked the Duchess. It was hard, of course, and its devilish new owner flexed it a few times for effect. It bobbed like a springboard.

The Duchess didn't tarry while pulling down John's bellbottoms and arranging him appropriately, belly-side down, on the carriage floor.

"Sweetheart, please!" John sobbed. "Let's talk about this!"

The Duchess slapped that huge hard tube of meat repeatedly on John's scrawny buttocks. "For all the times you fucked me in the ass and all those other poor girls...*now* I'm going to fuck *you* in the ass...with your own cock...FOREVER..."

John's mewls of objection only stoked the Duchess' desires higher. But when that big glans was jammed right up against John's sphincter, she began to have a little trouble effecting the necessary insertion. "Oh, Hollingshead! Be a dear and fetch me the shoehorn…"

6-THIRTEEN

"So how do you know all this stuff?" Westmore asked when he went through the traffic light where the old Henry's Liquor used to be.

She'd contacted him because she'd seen his piece on the paranormal investigation at what had been dubbed the Central Avenue Murder House. No ghosts had been revealed but Westmore did have to admit seeing an odd shadow in the room where the guy had decapitated his wife (he later put her head on the aerial on her lover's car). Westmore had needed to write something feisty so he'd picked that location in which had occurred not just the sensational head-chopping but a hanging and a baby microwaved. He'd so been hoping that the paranormal team would fake some findings but...no dice. There was only the "shadow," which he'd played up as the possible "revenant" teleplasm.

He was pretty sure he didn't believe in the supernatural, though. Plenty of people did, however, so it gave him something to write about and keep his editor happy. Now he was driving his Prius around the middle of Dannelton, where there was still wreckage from that mini-quake they'd had last month. The upscale psychiatric center had been demolished, and there it sat in a pile just off Clay Street, not even half cleared. Some rowhouses had collapsed as well, and several residents had been killed; several cops and firemen had died too. Backhoes, bulldozers, and cranes were *still* clearing debris, even at this hour—after 11 p.m.—the sound of their engines and ubiquitous beeps filled the air. The only illumination came from the work crews' generator-powered lights, since the quake had leveled all the street lights.

"Huh?" she said, staring intently through the passenger window. Her name was Nia. She was probably thirty but looked late-forties, a former meth addict and not-so-former prostitute.

"Come on," Westmore said. "You promised to prove to me that Hell really exists if I agreed to write an article about it. You've mentioned grimoires and old church theses that I've read about, plus codices and ancient manuscripts that I know exist, so all the time I'm asking myself 'What's the deal?' How does a girl like you know about things like that?"

She grinned from a once-pretty face. "A girl like me? A street hooker, a hype…"

Shit. "That's not what I meant. I—"

"I told you, I'll take a piss test. They sell 'em in Walgreens now, but *you* pay for it. The fuckin' things cost eighty bucks. What a racket, huh?"

"Everything's a racket," Westmore murmured, turning onto another dark street.

"Anyway, I've been clean for five years."

"No offense, but that's hard to believe. If you're off drugs, why do you still work the streets?"

Nia laughed. "Same reason you write for a shitty paper. To make money. What, if a girl turns tricks she's automatically a junkie? Man, you're ignorant. I work the street so I can continue with my studies."

"Your *studies?*"

103

"Yeah. A minute ago, what did you ask me?"

Westmore had to admit, now, that there was something about her that aroused him. What was it? The soap she used? The way the harsh generator light shone through her auburn hair? She wore very high cutoff jeans which demonstrated what any cameltoe afficionado would call a jackpot. "Oh, I asked how you happen to know about this stuff, all this occult stuff."

"Because I'm an occultist," she said very calmly. "I've studied this *stuff* for a long time. I've read the *Book of Eibon*, the *Pnakotic Manuscripts*, the *Eltdown Shards*, *Fuga Satanae*—"

"So you said in your email," Westmore said and smiled. "I looked all that shit up. It's all *fictitious*. It's a bunch of bullhockey that horror writers from the Twenties made up."

Nia laughed, shaking her head. "Man, you've really fallen for it. Translations of all that *bullhockey* are on the Dark Web."

"That doesn't mean it's real!" Westmore almost yelled.

"Then how did I get off meth without rehab? Even a quality rehab is statistically less than ten percent effective for meth. What, willpower? Just Say No? I found an Abstinence Spell in the uncut version of Remingius' *Daemonolatreiae Libri Quattuor*. And here I am"—she smiled at him, showing perfect white teeth—"drug free and raring to go."

Her eyes sparkled with an enthusiasm Westmore used to see in his own eyes.

But not any more.

"And I'm supposed to believe an…*Abstinence Spell* got you off drugs?"

When she shrugged, her pair of cupcake-sized breasts pushed together in the V of a black diaphanous top. "You can believe or disbelieve what you want. But I could use the same spell to make you quit smoking and drinking."

"How do you know I smoke and drink?" he asked, chuckling. "Wait, let me guess. You're psychic too."

"No, but your car smells like one of those Smoker's Station things, and there's a fucking six-pack behind your seat."

She got me there... "And speaking of that..." Westmore parked in a lightless lot with cracks in the asphalt from the quake. In parts, whole chunks of asphalt were shoved up, in great ragged wedges, revealing the soil and clay underneath.

"I knew it!" Nia laughed. "Here it comes! How much for a blowjob..."

Westmore sighed. "That's *not* why I parked here—"

"Twenty-five's the going street price," she said. "But for you? Fifty."

"Terrific," Westmore sputtered. *There must be something about me.* "I pulled in here because I can't drive while trying to pay attention to what you're saying. Plus"—he reached behind him—"I want a beer." He produced a bottle of Peroni. "Could you please get my opener out of the glove box?"

She opened it and froze upon seeing his Webley .455 sitting there. "You know what they say about guys who buy big guns?"

Westmore rolled his eyes.

"And do you have a permit for that thing?"

"Of course, this is Florida. You can get 'em from vending machines."

She handed him the opener and he opened the bottle. He reveled in that fresh European-lager aroma, which put him immediately in a better frame of mind.

"Really? Open beer in the car?" she said. "What if a cop sees you?"

"I know most of them," Westmore sluffed; in fact, he waved to a cruiser that slowly passed them and disappeared into the darkness.

"Okay," he began. "You say it wasn't an earthquake that hit this place last month—"

She was gazing out at the broken walls, downed trees, and collapsed houses. Backhoes, with their incessant *beeping* emptied chunks of rubble into waiting dump trucks. "It wasn't an earthquake; that's what they *want* you to think. Truth is, they—the authorities—don't really know *what* happened here."

"But you do?" Westmore said.

Her hand went out the window to gesture at their immediate surroundings: a perimeter of wreckage. It reminded Westmore of pictures from history books of Berlin in 1945. *Damn. This place really got hit hard.* For some reason, in the urban darkness, the place looked many more times worse than in the day.

"Last month, this *ruin* that we're sitting in experienced the most important satanic event, maybe, in history," she informed him. "I didn't say *seismic* event, I said *satanic.* That event was the result of a process called a Trans-Dimensional Spatial Merge—"

"Ah," Westmore mocked. "One of those…"

"You asked, so don't be a dick. It's the pinnacle of Hellbound occult technology that's taken thousands of years to develop. It's still not perfected but they're getting close, and they're coming up with new tricks pretty regularly. With the help of Warlocks, Bio-Wizards, and a whole lot of sacrificial energy, Lucifer's engineers are able to cause this Spatial Merge. For a very short period of time, and encompassing a very small tract of land, they're able to *transpose* a given perimeter of Hell with a given perimeter of the Living World. These two perimeters share the same space for exactly six seconds, and then *switch.* They trade places. Get it? What's there comes here, and what's here goes there. It gives Satan the chance to directly *fuck with* Earth, a place God created to be separate from the Prince of Darkness' domain. It's Lucifer's chance to give God the finger."

Westmore made snoring noises, pretending to be asleep.

"Oh, fuck you," Nia said, rankled. "If you're not gonna take this seriously, then it's a waste of my time. Just take me back."

Westmore chuckled. "Sorry, I was just kidding. But in all honesty, I don't believe *any* of this. Who would? So it's a waste of my time too."

"Yeah?" Her sparkly eyes leveled on him. "And what would you be doing instead?"

Westmore stalled. "Well, I don't know. I could be out with friends…"

She seemed bemused. "You're hardly the life of the party. I'll bet you don't really even *have* friends."

Westmore's mouth opened to object, but then closed again.

"So you've got nothing to lose," she went on, "and everything to gain. You'll get to witness a Spatial Merge. The article you write will be read all over the world. It'll be your greatest achievement as a writer. You'll be famous."

Westmore couldn't see himself as famous; he doubted that he would handle it well. "All right, I'll pretend that I believe you. So a Spatial Merge is like—what?—a bait and switch between Hell and here?"

"Exactly," she said. "Say you take a shovel full of dirt from your yard and your neighbor takes a shovel full of dirt from *his* yard, then you walk across the street, put your dirt in *his* shovel hole, and he puts his in yours."

Westmore's brow raised. *At least she's got an imagination…* "And this happens tonight…*when?*"

She looked at her tiny watch. "About a half hour. The Merge will begin at exactly *six* minutes after midnight."

"And it will affect this same area, the area of the quake?"

She held up a finger. "Not a quake, a Spatial Merge. And, yes, it'll happen here, the same place as the last Merge. Why

107

here? Because at least three trance-channelers online have said so."

"Trance-channelers, huh?"

"Yeah, dick. Same people who predicted the last one, right down to the minute."

Westmore nodded sarcastically, panning a glance through the windshield across the entirety of the block or so that the quake devastated. "So Satan wants to switch Hell stuff with downtown Dannelton? It's not even that much space—"

"Each Merge encompasses fifteen point two acres," she said and grinned at him. "That's six hundred and sixty-six thousand square feet. Get your yardstick and go measure. That's how big this disaster area is."

"Hmm, six hundred and sixty-six thousand square feet, and the Merge starts at *six* minutes after midnight, and why exactly tonight?"

She huffed. "Like I said in my email, because Saturn and Pluto are in Trine, and Venus is in the *Sixth* House."

"Of course. Another six. The number of the devil."

"It's the number of *error*, one down from seven, the *perfect* number, *God's* number. That's why Satan chose six for his own."

"And let me guess," Westmore went on. "The Merge will last for *six* minutes, right?"

"No, eleven point one minutes—"

Westmore did a double take. "What? Not six?"

She smirked at him. "That equals six hundred and sixty-six seconds. Exactly."

"Of course," he said and sipped more beer.

"That's all the time we'll have to take pictures and video. I've got my cell phone. Did you bring your camera like I told you?"

He reached behind him and hefted it out, a big Canon 5D. He'd inherited it from his dead brother who'd also been a writer but a much better one than Westmore. "Sure did. Oh, and speaking of pictures, didn't you promise to show me some?"

"Yeah, from the last Merge. I found 'em online," and then she opened the gallery on her cellphone.

Online, Westmore thought. *So it's GOT to be true...*

She leaned over and displayed her cellphone screen. Her closer proximity to him rekindled that annoying semi-sexual awareness, urging quick glances at her cleavage and crotch. *Just a dirty old man...* The first digital photo showed broken piles of rubble, and a half-knocked-over sign that read: DANNELTON PSYCHIATRIC CENTER. It was a place where rich people sent their loved ones who were mentally ill. At first, Westmore saw nothing but the piles of rubble and the windowless frames of what was left of the facility, but—

"Look right behind the sign," Nia instructed him.

Westmore squinted and, yes, saw a shadow-shape of some kind, plus two tiny red slits that must be eyes. "It's red eye; it's caused by camera flash. That's all that is."

"Wait..." She tapped open a tool bar at the bottom of the screen, then slid her fingertip up a line that read EXPOSURE. The photo immediately brightened, revealing more details of the shadow's contours. It was some wide-shouldered thing with horns in its head, a human-shaped body, but a head more like a—

"I don't know," Westmore said, not impressed. "Sure, it looks like a guy wearing a bull's-head mask..."

"It ain't no guy in a mask, and it ain't even a guy. Look."

He squinted more and was able to make out that this figure had the contours of a woman, and had bare breasts that any man would find formidable.

Nia said, "It's a Minotauress."

Westmore rolled his eyes again. "Okay. Next picture…"

The next one caught him off guard. It was a Dannelton Police cruiser, one door hanging open, and one officer lying face-down on the street, his arms out, and a pistol in one hand. Right on the back of his neck there appeared to be something like a small black ball, the size of a ping-pong ball, with legs sprouting out. "That's one of the town cops, dead. The thing on his neck is a species of infernal vermin called a Caco-Tick. Its mouth is a cannula that it rams between two of your neck vertebrae and sucks out all your spinal fluid. And here it is after it's sucked him dry—" She swiped to the next; the creature had swollen to the size of a football. "And look at this one"— another swipe. "Here's a wall that thrust itself up between the rear of the Sunoco station and the windshield repair place." She expanded the photo with her fingers, and it was indeed a wall, a concrete wall, but an odd greenish hue. Nothing like bricks could be distinguished, just the single vertical slab of concrete, and inserted along the top of the slab were rusted metal rods, or spikes…

Atop each spike some manner of *head* was mounted, but not all of them *human* heads. One ghastly bald head with a jacked-open mouth showed one fang on the top and two on the bottom, and it had a single centered eye the size of a softball; the next head looked exactly like a gargoyle as one would find atop a European cathedral, only this one looked plainly organic and half rotten. Next was a head with a highly angled face and a sharp chin, with pointed ears, apparently some kind of elf or imp, and next was a head that was only human*ish*: its features looked human but disarranged, the mouth on the forehead, the nose on the chin, and an eye on each cheek.

"I'll admit, that's top-notch Photoshop," Westmore said, shrugging, "but it's gonna take more than that to convince me that a bunch of stuff from Hell traded places with stuff from here."

"Look closer at the wall," and she expanded it further.

Yes, it looked like concrete, but instead of rocks and gravel mixed in with it, he could see—

That's fucked up, he thought.

Teeth, bone chips, skeletal fingertips, and skull fragments were bound into the cement. A jawbone here, a spine there, pelvic nodes and sternums and a coccyx or two. Westmore took particular notice of the front of a skull with eye sockets and slit-like holes where a nose had once been—locked into the cement mixture; next to it another such skull chunk wasn't even close to human.

"Again," he nodded, "that's impressive but I'm sure it's easily achieved by an expert photographic technician."

She ignored his assessment. "And here's the video clip that one of the firemen took that night. It's got, like, several million hits on YouTube already." Her manicured nail tapped the play arrow, and Westmore watched:

A fire blazed in the middle of Church Circle, but there was no Church there anymore; several squat figures were congregated around a woman lying on her back. No details of the woman or the squat figures could be made out, only their outlines, like moving black silhouette-shapes scrabbling in some concerted effort. The silhouette of the woman convulsed, heaved, and screamed as the figures around her seemed to be greedily and chucklingly...pulling things out of her: rope-like squiggly shapes and misshapen blobs that could only be internal organs. Now Westmore noted that the marauding figures each had huge flap-like pointed ears and small horns growing out of their heads. Some ran away with their wet, shining prizes, while another lowered its fanged mouth to the ground, to slurp up blood. Yet another silhouette excitedly seemed to pull its pants down, displaying a curved, throbbing erection which it then sunk into the dying woman's loins.

"Those things are called Broodren," said Nia. "They're like the juvenile delinquents of Hell. They attack humans and eviscerate them, to sell the organs to Alomancers and Extipitrists."

"What the *hell* is an Extipitrist? Did you just make that up?"

"They've been around since the times of ancient Sumeria. They're diviners—they tell the future...with the innards of people who were murdered very violently."

She's got a fast answer for everything... Westmore looked more intently at the cellphone screen: the last thing was video footage of an old man in a wheelchair desperately trying to wheel himself away from the bedlam. He'd almost made it out of the perimeter when some Cessna-sized creature with great black wings swooped down, plucked him out of his chair, and disappeared into foggy darkness.

"Now I suppose you're gonna say that's fake too," Nia said.

Westmore finished his beer. "Well, yeah. Ever heard of CGI? I mean, sure—it's Hollywood quality, but I don't believe that a bunch of *Broodren* ripped out a woman's insides to sell to fortune tellers, and I don't believe that a bat with a fifty-foot wingspan snatched an old guy out of his wheelchair."

Nia pointed out the window at the rubble that was once Church Circle, complete with the collapsed church itself. Not far off, they could see a tipped-over wheelchair.

"Sorry," Westmore said. "Not good enough."

"Actually, I'm glad you think it's all bullshit." Her eyes kept sparkling in the tinged darkness, in something like a demented anticipation. "I can't wait to see the look on your snob face when the Merge goes down. And I guess we better get out of the perimeter—"

"Get *out* of the perimeter?" he asked, still toying with her sentiments. "Why not smack-dab in the *middle* of the perimeter? Won't the Merge be stronger there?"

"Yes, and that's why we *don't* want to be there. We could have our guts pulled out like that lady or get carried off by all kinds of flying Hellspawn. Bapho-Rats could eat us; they have anesthetic in their fangs so you don't feel anything when they're eating all the meat off your legs. We could get sucked down—"

"Sucked down into *Hell*, you mean?"

"Fuck, yeah!" she snapped. "What are you? Stupid? There are gonna be Demons walking around here in a little while, and Constabs, Ushers, and Crossbreeds. Read my lips. They'll fuckin' *kill* us."

Westmore at least had to give her credit for the authenticity of her convictions. "Okay, you're the expert. Where does the Merge perimeter end?"

She pointed. "Just right over there on the other side of West Street where the 7-Eleven is. Go park there. We'll be able to see everything."

Westmore humored her and drove over and parked in the familiar, brightly lit parking lot. SLURPEES - HALF PRICE! a sign promised. He pushed some cash her way. "Here, go in and get us a couple of Slurpees. I want the cola-flavored."

She looked into the store through the big plate-glass window and winced. "No, that nasty Russian girl with the big tits is working. I can't stand that fuckin' bitch. She's about as friendly as a mad dog." Nia grinned at him. "But I will take a Slurpee. Thanks."

See Spot run... But he needed cigarettes anyway. "What flavor?"

"Cherry, please."

"How much time before the *Merge?*" he asked. "I wouldn't want to miss it."

"You've got plenty of time. Over fifteen minutes."

Westmore got out and went into the store.

No customers were present; on a radio, someone was talking emphatically in Russian. Westmore moseyed in and nodded to a bosomy, remarkably-figured woman in her mid-twenties with jet-black hair. She didn't nod back but instead frowned, watching him hawk-like, as if he might shoplift. He paused at the magazine rack, appraising several sets of spectacular breasts on the covers of *Vogue*, *Shape*, and *Women's Health*. His eyes widened abruptly when he spotted a magazine actually called *Bust* and the cover model was soundly demonstrating the magazine's moniker. *Damn. Women's mags are pretty stellar these days!* His eyes flicked up once to the cashier. *And I wouldn't mind seeing THAT rack on Bust...* Westmore even considered that he might pay a pretty penny just to see those boobs bare.

"Hey, meester," said the cashier with a disgusted look. "Theese is no farkin' libry, you know. You like those magazines, you can buy them."

Westmore, not one for confrontations, looked at her astonished. "Are you serious? I just walked in. I've spent less than a minute perusing the magazines."

She had a handwritten nametag that read KASHA that had a frowning smiley face drawn on it. "You *peruse* somewhere else. Theese is *store*. A place to buy things, not a place for *perusing*. You buy somethink or get out. Eeze illegal to loiter in store."

And just as he was not one for confrontations, he wasn't one for ill-will either; however, he could not curtail his thoughts. *I should give her a good hard kick right in the panty hamster. I'll bet a bell would ring and her tongue would pop out.* He shuffled to the machine and dispensed the Slurpees. *Nia was right. That chick IS a fuckin' bitch.* Her narrowed eyes followed him to the counter.

114

"I'll also take a pack of Buffalo Light 100s," he said and got out his wallet.

"Vee don't have those," she said.

"Yes, you do!" Westmore objected. He pointed right at them behind her.

"Oh, yes, you are right, I see. Is cheapest brand, cheap-scape-type people buy them, and bums. Lots of bums in your country—many many bums."

Westmore let his sexism rave when she turned and bent over to reach for the cigarettes. *That ass should hang in the Louvre...the BITCH...*

When she was ringing him up, she glanced out the front window at his car; Nia was plainly visible in the windshield, finnicking with her phone.

"Oh, oh!" said the cashier, "I see you are with that *hoo-er*. Now I see what kind of parson you are, to hang out with such undesirable people. In Russia, it is not condoned. Such *hoo-ers* are all on the drugs and are put in work prisons. Russia makes much more sense than bull-sheet America."

That was it for Westmore. "Well, if America is *bull-sheet*, then why are you here? Why don't you just go back to fuckin' Stalingrad or whatever drab borscht-eating shithole city you came from? Go jump in *Lake Balkash*...but leave your *tits* here!" Then he grabbed his Slurpees and left the store.

"Fark you!" the woman bellowed. "Farkin' sheet-head Americans! Russia eese so much batter than stupid Facebook America! All you iceholes care about is the Starbucks and the Netfleex! Go *fark* yourself! You and your farkin *hoo-er!*"

Nia was laughing when Westmore got back to the car. "See what I mean?"

Westmore passed over her Slurpee. "I'm over it. I'm just not a people person." The encounter winded him. He lit a cigarette and coughed. "So, what now? Just sit here and—"

A hitch caught in Nia's throat as if she were suddenly scared of something. Then—

A rumbling, soft at first, followed by the faintest tremble, and then—

There was a flash of scarlet light accompanied by the loudest thunderclap Westmore had ever heard. Nia screamed; Westmore yelled "Holy fuck!" and he could even hear the Russian girl in the store screaming. Several cracks crawled down the store's plate-glass window; then Westmore opened his car door and saw cracks forming in the asphalt. Both Slurpees jolted out of their hands and upended on the floor.

"Get out of the car!" Nia yelled, and she thought to grab the pistol from the glove box.

"It's another earthquake!"

She ran over and pulled him away from the car. "Does *that* look like an earthquake, you moron?" and she pointed straight up into the sky.

Just as cracks were forming in the asphalt, cracks were forming in the night sky; with each thunderclap a new zigzag appeared, and within those cracks, light that was dark-red could be seen, like the red of de-oxygenated blood but somehow luminous. The thunderclaps were nerve racking; they clacked Westmore's teeth together like the 155 howitzers he'd heard in the Army.

"Is this—Is this—" he stammered.

"It's the Merge!"

"But you said it wouldn't start till six after midnight!"

"Well, I guess there was a miscalculation!" she yelled back. Wild-eyed, she looked at her watch. "It started at six *before* midnight!"

The parking lot was now tipping back and forth under his feet. He was pissed. "And you said we were safely out of the Merge perimeter!"

Now Nia wobbled in place like she was trying to balance herself on a stationary skateboard. "Then I guess I was wrong! It's not *that* precise, you know! A hundred feet here, a few hundred there—"

"Are you shitting me! I thought you were the expert on this!"

"Oh, suck my dick!" she blared back. "You didn't even believe it!"

Next came a grinding rumble, and the 7-Eleven jolted and abruptly sunk a few inches. Inside, the Russia girl wailed, her preeminent breasts bobbing in her work shirt. She was trying to open the front doors but they were jammed.

"Should we help her?" Westmore yelled the query.

"Fuck no! You think that cuntsicle would help us?"

Westmore figured she had a point, but a second later, the question would be moot: the entire 7-Eleven jolted again, tilted once, and *disappeared,* dropping out of sight into the ground. The store's departure left a crater, and from that crater shards of throbbing dark-green light shot up, along with hissing jets of gas that looked like steam from a broken pipe but—

It wasn't steam. Westmore immediately doubled over— throwing up—at the *worst odor* he'd ever encountered.

"Aw, *fuck!*" Nia wretched. "It's a cracked corpse-gasifier!"

"A *what?*"

"Like a propane tank outside someone's house, only they gasify dead bodies to produce Agonicity instead of electricity."

Westmore stared at her, uncomprehending.

"Get your camera!" she ordered. "I'm pretty sure that—"

A new round of rumbling was heard.

Westmore almost fell over a few times, from the tipping ground. He grabbed his camera from the car, then noticed that Nia was pointing her cellphone straight up, snapping pictures. Westmore looked up himself and almost passed out.

All the cracks had cleared from the sky like a screen being pulled back. The sky had changed; there was no more normal midnight-blue sky, no more white stars, and no white moon. Instead, hauled across this section of downtown like a tarp, the sky had completely turned to that previously noticed dark luminous-red color. The moon was now a black sickle-shape, and across it streamed streaks of clouds so black they could've been comprised of coal smoke.

"What the fuck? Where's our sky?" Westmore gibbered.

"It's in Hell, and right now, Hell's sky is here. They traded places."

Now his eyes scanned a landscape that was wholly alien to him. On Church Circle, the rubble from the old St. Stephen's Church was gone—sucked down, no doubt—but what replaced it was a very *different* church, one made castle-like of large cut stones and with a tower of six pinnacles and turrets. Atop each turret sprouted a spike upon which some manner of female— Demon, Human, or Hybrid—had been impaled upside down from throat to groin. Screams issued from the church's gunslit windows, and occasionally buckets of blood and other less mentionable materials were emptied, along with wet flapping sheets that might have been skin pulled off bodies whole, like jumpsuits. From other windows, and from high wall-blocks like ramparts, horned heads peeked over.

Westmore was merely staring, his sentience unable to restart, but Nia kept snapping photos like a madwoman, and she yelled, "Take pictures, damn it! You wanted proof, well, here it is!"

A transom sign above this *other* church's front entrance read: THE CHURCH OF THE UNHOLY TRINITY.

In the distance, other structures were sinking, only to be replaced a moment later by something horrific or inexplicable. Near the main road which led to the interstate, the familiar

Busch Gardens billboard disappeared; what rose up in its place was another billboard that read BELIEL'S VOMITORIUM: FUN FOR THE WHOLE FAMILY! *Guess where we're NOT going,* Westmore thought, snapping his own pix now. Through smoking holes in the ground, street signs popped up: VASCULITIS BLVD, TERATOMA COURT, VULVECTOMY STREET. By now the rumbling had tapered off, leaving only an eerie distant silence. Indescribable stenches issued from cracks in the ground; Westmore had to steel himself not to throw up on his $5000 camera. Where the town water tower once stood, there was now a giant orbicular tank standing on hundred-foot-high iron girders; the tank read CADAVER SLURRY. Westmore groaned when he roved his camera along the quaint downtown shopping promenade; where the old Vito & Pepe's pizzeria should've been there was now a HACKENHOLT'S GAS OVEN PIZZA next to a fashion store (CATHERINE THE GREAT'S SECRET) behind whose dazzling display windows stood mummified corpse-mannequins dressed in all manner of infernal women's wear, including evening gowns comprised of the severed faces of babies, tongue-panties and hand bras, and some very elegant penis garters. A rack of Louis Baton Scrotum Purses was evident as well, some with hair, some shaved. In the next window, a live blue-skinned and six-horned succubus modeled a plush winter fur coat. Westmore had to squint but eventually discerned that the "fur" was made up of dozens and dozens of stitched-together Human pubic patches, like the hefty pubic hair women sported during the '70s and earlier. *For fuck's sake, that's a lot of bush!* he thought. The succubus grinned and showed her forked tongue as Westmore snapped another pic.

"The flux this time is weird," Nia said, as if perplexed. "It's a lot stronger than it was last time," and when Westmore turned toward her comment—

"Holy shit!" he exclaimed. "Your hair!"

— Nia's shiny auburn hair was standing on end.

"Yours too," she notified him. He looked in front window of the Louis Baton and saw that his hair, indeed, was standing ludicrously on end, and so was his beard.

Nia howled laughter and took a picture of him.

"Great, I'll use it for my masthead pic," Westmore grumbled. "And what were you saying a minute ago? Something about the *flux*? What's that?"

"The Hellflux, Hell's version of electromagnetic radiation," she told him. "It's like the entire spectrum of radio waves, microwaves, infrared and ultraviolet light, X-rays, and gamma rays here in the Living World, only in Hell it's all fucked up like everything else. All infernal energy travels through the Hellflux, even occult energy, and psychic energy."

"You said it's stronger now than during the last Merge?"

Nia was shivering at the strange static that was crawling over her body. "Yeah, I guess the extra power is coming from tonight's astrological signature, especially Venus being in the Sixth House." She looked around in more puzzlement. "Still, that wouldn't account for the Hellflux being *this* strong, I don't think…"

Westmore noticed that the static was crawling on him too, even under his clothes, and it was doing something else —

Holy fuck, I'm horny as hell all of a sudden, and when he looked down at the considerable bump in the front of his jeans, he thought, *Damn! Where'd THAT knockwurst come from?*

"Hey, Nia," he began his question very slowly, "Does, uh, does this Flux business also, uh, make you —"

"Horny as everliving fuck — yeah," she said, wincing at her own obvious sexual anguish. Now her nipples stood out beneath her top like football cleats. "And don't even *think* about getting any ideas with me!"

"I don't know what you're talking about," even though that was *exactly* the idea that had come to Westmore's brain.

"Oh, fuck! Look!" Nia pointed to an alley that hadn't been there a minute ago. "An Usher—"

"What's that? You mean like an usher at a church?"

Nia gagged. "No, you dickhead! An Usher is a specialized monster that's part of the Constabulary—the police! Only they don't protect and serve, they slaughter and mutilate!"

Westmore looked at the pallid gray thing in the distance, as it stomped down what used to be Brigantine Lane but was now Septicemis Avenue. *That's some fucked-up shit*, Westmore thought as he zoomed in on the thing. It must have been seven or eight feet tall, with sharpened horns curving outward from its anvil-shaped head. It had holes for ears and chisel-slits for eyes, and its skin could be likened to the skin of a slug, darkly spotted, exuding a mucus-like slime.

And it was coming right for where Westmore and Nia stood.

"We better run!" he yelled.

"It would catch us," and then she started walking *toward* it.

"Are you *crazy?* That's a fuckin' demon from Hell!"

"I got this," she said, surprisingly calm. "Just go hide, ya pansy."

I may be a pansy but I'm not insane! Westmore ducked behind fresh rubble. He watched through his zoom lens as the Usher increased the speed of its stride on stout corded legs. Nia stopped and raised the big revolver, waited a moment more, then—

BOOM!

The gun almost jolted out of her hand; Westmore could feel the shot's concussion even from where he was. And as for the Usher—

Its head no longer sat on its shoulders. Chunks of gray meat and brown skull fragments flew away in a starburst; its two horns shot off into the tinged darkness like bizarre boomerangs.

"What a great shot!" Westmore celebrated.

But Nia's eyes popped open wide, she shoved the pistol in Westmore's direction and—

BOOM!

Westmore ducked just as a Nether-Bat would've snatched him by the head and carried him off, no doubt to be its next meal, or perhaps worse.

Shaking, he picked himself off the ground (and yes, he'd peed his pants) and managed to stand upright.

"You're welcome!" Nia shouted.

"I-I—Holy shit, this place sucks..."

In the distance, in front of stray fires burning, more hellish figures began to emerge through stinking smoke. One of the things had to be twenty feet high, another was a massive tarantula with what seemed a grinning human face.

"The big thing's the latest incarnation of Golem," Nia said. "They're made of cursed riverbed clay and grave-dirt. The other thing's just a big-ass hybridized spider; it'll start spinning a web soon and loading people into it, then it pumps its eggs into the people, to incubate..." She aimed the Webley again; then came another BOOM! and that grinning human face on the tarantula disappeared and the thorax erupted something like green snot. Next, two more BOOMS and both of the Golem's eyes turned into holes that Westmore could see though.

"Can't kill the motherfuckers but if you blow out their eyes, they can't see you."

"Damn!" Westmore exclaimed. "You're a regular sharpshooter!"

"Yeah, lucky for you," she said and then winced when she looked at him. "Really? You pissed your pants?"

"N-no, I stepped in a puddle—"

She released the pistol's cylinder and looked grim. "Only two bullets left. Please tell me you have more."

"Uh, yes!" he replied. "There's a whole box in the car!" He ran back to his Prius, opened the door, but—

"Aw, no!"

In a sudden sound like pouring gravel, the car was sucked right down into the ground.

Nia was laughing. "Hope you got insurance."

Westmore could've howled. "I just made the last payment!"

"Step back," she advised next. "Something will probably come up in its place, something similar."

"Huh?"

The gravel-sound returned, and what raised out of the hole was a bizarre sort of canopied step van like a UPS van, only the front looked more like a miniature train engine, and there was a smokestack belching sulphur. Small port-holes surrounded the vehicle's back end, and in each port-hole was a fan.

Westmore and Nia both staggered backward at what was so far the absolute worst stench of the night. Westmore's belly sucked in and out, threatening to throw up again, but there was nothing left.

"Aw, shit!" Nia barked. "It's a Gestankvagen! The motherfuckers!"

"A *what?*" Westmore asked through a handkerchief over his mouth.

"A *stink* truck! They pack it full of corpses, poop, dead babies, and stuff like that and let it all rot. Then they drive around while those fans blow the stench all over the place. Satan wants his domain to stink."

Ridiculous! Westmore concluded. *Satan's an asshole…*

They staggered away from the abominable stench. When Westmore could breathe again he looked across to the downtown common area which, only minutes ago, had been a children's park with swing sets, seesaws, and jungle gyms but all that had been replaced with iron-maidens, racks, Catherine Wheels, strappados, and a Bed of Knives. The sign read POPE JOHN IX'S CHILDREN'S DAYCARE PARK. But past this Westmore noticed something even more disconcerting: six very obese nude women, holding hands and crossing the park. Silent bolts of black lightning shot from their heads up into the red sky, and with each bolt the sky's blood red actually brightened like neon.

"Shit, I knew it!" Nia yelled. "They're Arithmetri! *That's* why the flux is so powerful tonight!"

"They're *what?*"

"An Arithmetress is a female occult mathematician who can convert her massive amounts of body fat into quantified energy."

Westmore was looking at them closer with his zoom. Each one of the women must have weighed at least six hundred pounds, their breasts hung off them like pallid saddlebags, their faces so fat that their eyes resembled holes in dough, jowls swinging like wattles. But each one of the women had scribbles of tattoos all over their skin, markings like cryptic writing, sigils, and shapes. "What's all that shit written on them?"

"Secret infernal formulae that they're taught at the Cultes des Pythagorus," Nia informed him. "The formulae in combination with the non-Euclidean geometric symbols that are branded on them are what enable the energy conversion. Those women will burn off a hundred pounds of body fat per minute. They are to the Merge what a bellows is to a coal fire…"

Fuuuuuckin'-A, Westmore thought with his eye to his viewfinder. The hideous women were indeed getting smaller with each step forward and each launch of black lightning from their heads.

Down near the bus depot, there were no longer buses; instead there were rows of prison wagons being pulled by great horse-sized beasts that seemed to have the heads of dogs, and they were—

"They're Ghor-Hounds," Nia explained, looking straight at the fanged dripping animals. "Hell's beasts of burden. They're ideal because they never need food or water and they never get tired."

"How's that even possible?"

"Because they're dead, they're zombified. They're taking all those prisoners to the nearest pulping station."

What's a pulping... Westmore let the question die. He didn't want to know. He followed Nia and kept taking pictures this way and that...and this way and that he saw squads of armored soldiers with faces like lamprey eels marching in formation—

"Conscripts," Nia said. "Lucifer's infantry. They're mostly half-bred Demons who are surgically and chemically enhanced at the Institute of Teratology..."

—and a group of skeletal-looking women scuffling down what used to be Third Avenue and was now Penectomy Blvd. These women were unique in that not only were they emaciated, their bellies were completely evacuated.

"Zap addicts," Nia said. "They're called Gut-Jobs. They willingly sell their innards—and any other marketable body part—to Diviners, Alomancers, Extipitrists, any kind of fortune teller..."

—and several shrieking horrific things the size of basketballs rolled briskly across the lot—sort of like tumbleweeds, only they were roundish nodes of flesh-colored matter surrounded entirely by, by—

"Are those fuckin' *dicks?*" came Westmore's understandably alarmed question. "They look like tumbleweeds made of *dicks!*"

"Don't get in their way," Nia warned. "They're called Phalluphytes and, yeah, they're like Hell's version of tumbleweeds, only these things don't live in the prairie, they live in urban areas, rolling around endlessly looking for things to inseminate. Each one of those spikes are actually penises—or I should say things *like* penises—and they *never* go limp. The big lump in the middle is the testicle and semen reservoir. Those things will roll all over you and fuck any available hole. When a chick gets knocked up by a Phalluphyte...God knows what she'll give birth to."

Westmore winced. *Fuck this place!* "I've had enough! Let's get out of here! How do we get out of the Merge perimeter?"

"Behind where the 7-Eleven used to be—come on!"

Nia suddenly stopped and squealed when a rapid padding was heard, like a heavy person running barefoot, and out of more rank smoke there appeared a *thing* that looked like a giant human mouth full of teeth standing on two heavily muscled humanish legs. Several eyeballs of various sizes ringed its "forehead." Westmore emptied the rest of his bladder in his pants when the—whatever it was—lunged for him, jacking its immense mouth even wider in a clear effort to swallow Westmore whole but then—

BOOM!

—Nia squeezed off another shot, and the creature's head cracked, flinging a plume of indescribable slop all the way across the street. It sidled over, a tongue the size of a body pillow lolling. The stout, muscled legs kicked a few times, then went limp.

"What the FUCK?" Westmore bellowed.

"You're welcome again," Nia said and blew the gunsmoke away off the tip of the pistol. "It's a Dentataped. It's a hexegenically engineered species from the Office of Transfiguration. They make them specifically to clean up the

126

Mutilation Zones and eat all the corpses. Kind of like street-cleaners." She calmly snapped a picture with her cellphone. "I told you this shit was dangerous. Let's go."

Westmore's jaw dropped. "Yeah. Let's."

But just as she was leading him back through the lot where the 7-Eleven had been sucked down, the ever-familiar rumbling returned, the ground beneath their feet began to quake and then—

"Holy shit!" Nia yelled in something like exuberance.

What goes down, must come up…sort of. The previous crater was now pushing up, as if on a lift platform, another building in place of the 7-Eleven. It bore striking similarities, like huge plate-glass windows in front, aisles inside filled with what appeared to be products for sale, and a big neon-lit sign on top that buzzed and read 6-THIRTEEN.

"Oh, man, this is cool as shit!" Nia exclaimed.

"Whuh-what is it? A store of some kind?"

"Damn right it is! It's a 7-Eleven from Hell! Come on, we gotta check this out!"

"Bull-DICK!" Westmore shouted back. "We're getting out of the perimeter before we get our asses handed to us!"

"How can you not wanna see what's in here? Stop being such a pussy. This is a once-in-a-lifetime opportunity," and then she grabbed him by the back of his shirt and dragged him to the front door.

"You're the one who said it's too dangerous!" he objected.

"That was before this place popped up. Come on! We'll just be a minute!"

Typical ad posters hung in the front window: 2-4-1 SALE! MRS. ROTLEY'S PHLEGMON MERINGUE PIES! and SLAUGHTERY TICKETS SOLD HERE! and BILEWEIESER 12-PACKS, 13-PERCENT OFF! and DISCOUNT PHONE CARDS! CALL YOUR LOVED ONES IN THE LIVING WORLD AND

SCARE THE SHIT OUT OF THEM! and SNOT POCKETS! JUST
DROP 'EM IN THE TOASTER!

A bell rang as Nia dragged Westmore inside. "Take as many
pix as you can!" she ordered and then rushed away.

Westmore stood mute. There didn't appear to be anyone in
the store. At first glimpse, the place looked like any typical
convenience store...until he looked more definitively at the
inventory. A fountain-drink machine looked just like any other,
but there were no indications as to which spigots dispensed
what. Westmore grabbed a paper cup and started dispensing
from the first nozzle. He nearly fell backward from the smell
and the mere sight of the brown fluid.

"Nia!" he cried. "They're selling diarrhea where the
Slurpees should be!"

"And I'll bet that's not all. Check 'em."

So Westmore checked 'em. The second nozzle fizzed out
dark urine, the third produced what could only be gushes of
semen, and the fourth?

Westmore looked at the suspicious liquid. At first he
thought it must be tomato soup, on the thick side, but then the
truth cracked at him like a firecracker.

Aw, shit... A menstrual blood Slurpee, he realized.

Nia, in the potato chip aisle, called out to him in some
obvious zeal. She held out a bag of something. "Look at this! I
thought it was a bag of fried bacon rinds..."

"Think again?" Westmore queried. He squinted at the shiny
bag and saw its stylized letters: KRUNCHY McGEE'S DEEP-
FRIED FORESKINS! "Uh, let me know how they taste..."

"And look at this!"

Without too much enthusiasm, Westmore came around.
Nia stood in front of one counter on which sat one of those
familiar hot-dog rotisseries but there was nothing that looked
like Oscar Mayer on the wheel inside. There were several fat

kielbasa-looking things but they were grayish-brown and sweating beads of fat.

"Shit sausages," Nia said matter-of-factly. "They just tie 'em off in segments. From one of the Shit Farms, you know?"

"No, I don't know!" Westmore yelled. "You're telling me they farm *shit?*"

"Yeah, all kinds of different ways. For these sausages, they close off a fat person's anus with a Flesh Welder and force-feed him. When the intestines are good and bloated, they cut them out, tie them off, clip them, and them put 'em on the rotisserie where they roast and simmer in their own juices. They also force-feed people nailed to boards, and make Human Foie Gras. Their livers grow to the size of beach balls...but stuff like that only goes to the glitzy restaurants, not convenience stores."

Westmore had always liked sausage and foie gras...but not anymore.

Nia browsed the candy aisle while Westmore investigated the magazine rack. *Demonic Geographic, Popular Atrocity, Better Decapitations & Abortions, No Time Magazine, Bad Housekeeping,* and droves of others. Lower on the rack sat the obvious "adult" magazines whose glossy covers boasted untold examples of sexual congress between Hellspawn and damned Humans. One cover showed a gray, pointed-eared Imp in a doctor's lab coat and a stethoscope around his neck. Teeth like sharpened pyramids glittered through his impossibly wide grin; the Imp was feeding a fat, sore-pocked erection into a disconsolate nude Human woman on her hands and knees. It looked like the end of the Imp's penis was actually coming out her mouth.

The magazine's title? *The Doctor is IN!*

Still another mag, called *Severed Head Bukkake* sported, well, the severed head of a beautiful woman sitting lopsided on a stone slab. Around the slab stood several heavily muscled

Trolls all masturbating on the head. (The expression on the head's face was understandably morose.)

Wow, this porn really sucks, Westmore thought. Some torture mags lined the bottom row, which caused him to wonder, *Why is it always women who are the victims?* Here was another nude woman, chained to a chair; her face couldn't be seen because a strange stone bucket had been placed on her head. Scarlet-skinned demons (male, of course, and all sporting veiny erections, of course) took turns feeling up the woman's bodacious breasts, but at the same time an overhead chute emptied molten lead into the bucket. Gruelingly, on yet another cover, horned, leather-armored Constabularies jabbed pitchforks into the back of a nude woman on hands and knees. She was being forced to bob for apples in a tub of bowel movements floating in vomit.

Nia, now, was quite excitedly snapping pictures of infernal cereal boxes. (One was called *Roast Toasties*, which were apparently roasted fetuses covered with powdered sugar.) Westmore blanched when he looked at a reach-in freezer and saw mini-pizzas with scabs instead of pepperoni slices.

"Look at this!" Nia held up a jar that read DRAINED CARBUNCLE AND BLOODY PUS SPAGHETTI SAUCE.

"I can't even contemplate what they use for the spaghetti—"

"Farm-raised trichinosis worms, I think—Oh! And look at this! Hell's version of grated parmesan!" The green cylindrical container read GRATED DESICCATED SMEGMA.

Westmore choked back some near-puke. "Come on, let's go…"

"Just another minute," she said, oblivious, snapping more pix. She held up another can: HUMAN SPAM.

Fuck that, Westmore thought. "And how come there's no one working here?"

Nia looked back and forth. "Yeah, that is strange. There should be someone at the register." But then she pointed up at the ceiling. "At least they don't have to worry about shoplifters…"

Westmore looked up and saw shiny, weasel-sized things crawling slowly along the ceiling, upside down, but each one had a throbbing cluster of eyes for a head. Their bodies resembled garden slugs, only much bigger.

"They're Ocuslugs," Nia said. "They're like security cameras; they're trained to I.D. shoplifters and robbers."

Westmore frowned. "And then what? You're telling me a fuckin' *slug* knows how to call the fuckin' police?"

"No, genius. When it sees you stealing, it drops down on your head, shits down your throat, and then the shit dissolves all your insides."

"Oh…" On a rack he saw a bag of ears. CHIPOTLE-FLAVORED EAR JERKY, it read. The next bag read DICK JERKY - SPICY HOT! Westmore's shoulders drooped. "Come on, Nia. Let's just go. We've seen enough…"

"I said in a minute!" she yelled at him.

"But-but I gotta go to the bathroom…"

She grimaced at him. "Then fuckin' *go!* There's the bathroom right there! What, I gotta take you by your little hand 'cos you're just an old bearded little baby who pees his pants when he's afraid?"

I'm getting pretty sick of her, he thought and shuffled through the door that read BATHROOM.

Naturally, the bathroom stank but really no more than any convenience store bathroom in the Living World…which was interesting because this was a convenience store bathroom in *Hell.* Linoleum floor with a drain in it, a cracked white enamel sink hanging off the wall, a shitty metal-framed mirror with chips in it, even a rubber machine on the wall. But these commonplace similarities came to a terminus when he looked more attentively at things. A plaque read: EMPLOYEES MUST NOT WASH THEIR HANDS. A paper towel rack was mounted aside, but when he pulled a "towel" out, he had in his hands instead a severed face that had been pressed as if with an iron. The empty eyeholes blinked at him.

And the rubber machine?

It was not the usual type so common in rest rooms. CONDOMS! 25 HELLPENNIES EACH! FILLED, PERFORATED, OR PRE-INFECTED—YOUR CHOICE!

And of course, there was graffiti scrawled copiously on the walls: BAALZEPHON SUCKS DICK! SALOME LUVS TIBERIUS 4 EVR! Then—

"Hey, handsome," came a sultry female whisper. "Let's kiss, huh?"

Westmore looked down at the crusty drain in the floor. A tongue was sticking out of the grate, wagging.

"You're shitting me, right?" Westmore griped.

"Come on, sugar," urged the voice from the drain. "Put your dick down here. I'll lick it for ya..."

"Not today," he replied and turned quickly. Behind him stood a pale-green door as one would find in any commercial bathroom, with a gap under it and a partitioned compartment where the customer could defecate in privacy. And next to that stood a smaller, doorless compartment where the urinal hung.

This urinal, however, was not with the common run of urinals. It was merely a white metal box with a hole in the top.

What, I'm supposed to piss in the hole? he wondered, steadily more aggravated. *Fuck it, I gotta piss...*

So Westmore pissed, and it can be said that his marksmanship was laudable: the stream of his urine shot directly into the hole; only a few drops went astray as he was finishing up. He looked, then, for the flusher but discerned nothing that could be likened to that common implement.

Then…he heard a gargling sound.

Westmore stared down at the white box with the hole on top. *No*, he thought. *Please tell me there's not someone's HEAD in that box…*

He wanted to walk away but just…couldn't.

Oh, for pity's sake, he thought and surrendered to the impulse.

He detached the white box from the wall, to reveal nothing less than a living human head.

It stuck out face up, as if the body to which it belonged lay parallel to the floor on the other side of the wall, while the head itself stuck out through a hole.

"Hey, pal," the head said quite affably. "That's the best piss I've chugged in ages! Thanks!"

Westmore could not conceive of a way to respond to a man who'd just thanked him for pissing in his mouth. But the head seemed to strike some chord of very vague familiarity. Westmore squinted. *Is that… Is that…* It was the head of a Caucasian man, bald on top, with sprawls of dark kinky hair sticking out on the sides.

"Wait a minute!" exclaimed the head. "Are you from the Living World?"

"Uh, well, yes," Westmore admitted.

"No *wonder* your piss tastes so good!"

"Uh…"

"You got any more?"

"Any more…what?"

"Piss, man! Piss!"

"Uh, no. I'm done, uh, urinating."

"Shucks," said the head. "Look, bub, do me a favor, okay? Pull your pants down, turn around, and give me a Number

Two, right in the pie-hole, will ya? Compared to what I've been eating for the last fifty years, I'll bet it tastes like Swiss Miss chocolate fudge!"

"No!" Westmore yelled down. "I'm not shitting in your mouth!" and that was that. *I'm getting OUT of this fuckin' bathroom and then I'm getting OUT of this fuckin' fucked-up store, and I don't care WHAT fuckin' Nia says!* and then he jerked around toward the door.

But...

The possibility rattled him very severely—even to the point of outright despair—as he pushed out of the bathroom door.

Deep-seated childhood memories began to re-form and he thought he had a pretty good idea who the head was.

Larry from the Three Stooges.

His teeth ground, his face contorted in horror. *No! No! My favorite Stooge! It couldn't be him! Larry wouldn't have gone to Hell, would he?*

Westmore refused to believe it. "Nia!" he bellowed. "We're leaving! Now! I've had enough of this shit!"

Nia, still shooting pix, gave him her usual dirty look. "I told you! I'll be ready in a minute! Are you fuckin' deaf?"

"Well, *fuck you* then! Bossy bitch, you can kiss my ass! I'm leaving! You can stay here all night for all I care, but I'm *out of here!*" he declared, and then stalked toward the front door—

What the...

—but stopped in his tracks.

Some *thing* stood blocking the front door. One could say it was anthropomorphic in that it had a head, two arms, and stood on two legs. It wore, too, an orange-and-white-striped tunic, something quite similar to the garb worn by employees of convenience stores. Only here all similitude to the familiar vanished.

"Uh, Nia!" Westmore yelled. "I think I found the cashier..."

When she looked up at Westmore's meaning, her face turned sheet-white. "Holy shit. An Annelok…"

"What's a fuckin' *Annelok?*"

"It's your basic worm-demon, from the *Mephitus Annelia* phylum. Think of it, like, as a giant earthworm shaped like a man. The Department of Nefarious Commerce uses them for jobs like this 'cos nobody wants to work 'em."

The thing looked kind of dopey, like a Gumby doll, only its arms, legs, and head were made of tubes of flesh like an earthworm.

"At least it looks harmless," Westmore remarked.

"Oh, no! If you piss off an Annelok, it'll ram one of its worm arms right down your throat, grab your cock and balls *from the inside*, and then yank it out your mouth."

"Wonderful," Westmore said. "Excuse me, uh, Mr. Annelok? You're blocking the door and we'd like to leave. Could you please move?"

The ridged eyeless pink face traversed back and for in a definite *No.*

"Wait a minute!" Westmore exclaimed. "Shoot it! Don't you have one more bullet left?"

"Doesn't matter. It would be like shooting a hole in a side of beef. It's got no brain and no organs. It's just…worm meat."

But before Westmore could consider the predicament further, he felt some rumbling beneath his feet.

Nia looked at her watch, gulped, and yelled. "Holy fuck! I forgot that watches don't work in Hell!"

"So what?"

"So what? It means I lost track of time! Has it been eleven minutes since the Merge began?"

Westmore pondered. "I don't know but…yeah, almost, I guess…"

"We gotta get out of here before the Merge times out—"

Westmore's brow furrowed. "Well, what happens if we're still in this store when that happens?"

She looked bug-eyed at him. "The store gets dragged back to Hell and *we* go with it!"

"You never told me that!" Westmore shouted. "I thought the Hell stuff would just dematerialize and then our stuff would reappear—like, in a movie or something! What's it called? A lapse-dissolve?"

"Fuck! Fuck fuck fuck fuck!" Nia barked, then she addressed the Annelok. "Is there anything we can do to get you to let us out of here?"

The Annelok nodded, and it would've been looking right at Nia if it had had eyes.

"Okay, whatever it is, we'll do it. What is it?"

Westmore was not one who ever experienced anything that might even remotely be thought of as "psychic," but…

I think I know what it wants…

The Annelok pulled up its shirttail, revealing its decidedly *male* genitals.

"Oh, no," Nia mumbled.

Next, the thing pointed to its penis, which looked, as anyone might guess, like a stout length of earthworm: about ten inches long, two wide, with a big purple glans at the end. Then the Annelok pointed right at Nia's mouth.

Westmore could not refrain from laughing. "It wants you to suck its dick! I love it!" He stepped close to the creature, "Just for clarification, Mr. Annelok—do you mean if she sucks your dick, you'll let us out of here?"

The Annelok nodded, and then it began to…*play* with its penis, which sprang to a fully erect state. Now its eyeless face stared directly at Nia's bosom.

"Come on, Nia," Westmore egged on. "Get to it. You gotta suck this thing's dick and I mean fast. We might only have seconds left before the Merge is over."

"I-I don't think I can!"

"Why? What's the big deal? You suck dicks every night."

"Not *demon* dicks, you asshole!" In a rage, she grabbed Westmore by the neck and yanked him around. "If it's no big deal, then *you* suck it!"

"*You're* the hot chick in this duo, Nia. It doesn't want *me* to suck its dick, it wants *you*. So get your lip-lock going so we can get out of here."

Nia's face creased up in enmity, horror, and outrage. Her teeth chattered, and her lower lip trembled.

"Going to Hell in a hand basket is one thing," Westmore said, "but do you really want to go to Hell in a fuckin' 7-Eleven?"

Nia's defiance and rage collapsed; she let out a long sign of resignation. "Whatever," she whispered, and she got down on her knees, edged forward, grabbed the shiny pink worm penis, and commenced to performing fellatio on it.

"Atta girl!" Westmore said, and it looked to him that the woman's oral skills were formidable to say the least. He was about to suggest that she play with the thing's balls a bit, but then he noticed that the Annelok *had* no balls.

Nia's head bopped back and forth, and with each stroke back, the Annelok's limbs tensed up. Was it moaning in pleasure?

Nia certainly *wasn't* moaning in pleasure. The only muffled sounds from the back of her throat sounded like horrified *mewls*.

"And you probably know this, Nia, but he'll come faster if you stick your finger up his ass—"

She yanked her mouth off long enough to glower back at Westmore, yell, "SHUT UP OR I'LL FUCKIN' KILL YOU!" and then got back to the task.

Westmore peered listlessly out the front window. A glowing sulphur-pot street lamp with a sign that read RICHARD RAMIREZ BLVD suddenly tremored, then sunk completely into the ground only to be replaced by a regular street light labeled MADISON STREET. A brick booth that read MISINFORMATION CENTER boasted a sign: GET YOUR TICKETS HERE FOR THE GACY'S DAY PARADE! TEENAGE BOYS ADMITTED FREE! was sucked instantly into the ground, replaced a moment later by TICKETRON booth. All the while, a mild tremoring could be felt beneath him. Westmore squirmed in place, tapping his foot. *Come on, Nia, can't you blow a guy any faster than that?* Then, right out front, the big stink-gushing Gestankvagon disappeared into the ground, and a moment later, up came Westmore's Prius.

"Nia, I hate to tell you this, but shit outside is starting to change back. I don't think we have much more time, and I really don't want to spend the rest of eternity drinking diarrhea Slurpees, so if you could get the job done, like, *right now*, that would be super..."

Nia whined in her throat, that wet sucking-clicking noise getting louder as her head moved back and forth faster and faster. Suddenly—just as the giant medieval church outside disappeared, the Annelok went rigid, Nia mewled more urgently this time, and then the six-foot-tall worm-demon released a loud piercing celebratory sound much like an elephant in excitation.

Nia's cheeks ballooned, then she jerked back, gagging. "Aw, gross!" she hacked. What fell out of her mouth looked like a slew of ticks all slopped up in some kind of milky jelly sauce. Several more loops of the stuff shot out of the Annelok's cock, one hitting poor Nia right in the eye, another sailing directly into her agape mouth. "Oh, come on, buddy! Gimme a break!" At the prostitute's knees spread a great puddle of this demonic semen, the "ticks" jigging around in the sauce like Mexican jumping beans.

Just when Westmore feared the creature would go back on its word, the Annelok stepped aside and even held the door open for them...

"Thanks!" Westmore yanked the still-gagging Nia to her feet, then dragged her through the transom just as—

"Holy moly!"

—the convenience store was sucked completely into the ground, leaving nothing but a crater full of steaming rubble.

Overhead, the scarlet sky throbbed, the horrific thunderclaps returned, and in explosion-like bursts, the sky from Hell gave in to the familiar night sky from the Living World. Where Pope John IX's Children's Daycare Park had been, a band of very emaciated nude women trudged. "The Arithmetri," Nia said. "All their occult energy has been used up. Look, they're just skin-covered skeletons now..." *Wow,* Westmore thought. *That's losing weight the hard way...*

Beyond them, downtown Dannelton had ground back to the way it had been six hundred and sixty-six seconds ago...

Nia looked wiped out and wobbly where she stood, not a surprise, considering. "Thank God... Everything's back to normal—"

But Westmore squinted doubtfully. "Not exactly everything. Where's *our* 7-Eleven? It should be back now, shouldn't it?"

Nia was glancing down into the crater. "Step back! Here it comes!"

Before their eyes, their familiar 7-Eleven was upheaved and re-established on its former foundations. Even its bright lights were on inside.

"We better go in and make sure that Russian girl is okay," Westmore suggested.

"Fuck her! That mean, America-hating, foul-mouthed bitch can go fist herself—"

Westmore was inclined to share the sentiment, but mean, America-hating, and foul-mouthed or not, the right thing to do was check on her. After all, she'd just been to Hell and back, hadn't she?

Besides, he wouldn't mind seeing her boobs again, pressed up in that tight 7-Eleven top.

"Hey, miss?" he called out after he entered. "Are you all right?"

"Arrrrrgh!" came a gargly reply. "Aw, fark theese sheet!"

Westmore peeked over the counter, and his jaw dropped. His earlier wish to see her bare breast came true that instant, but...

"Holy martherfarkin' FARK!" she bellowed. She lay on the floor behind the counter, stripped naked. Her long shiny black hair was now long shiny *white* hair. And there was one more thing...

She had to be at least eight and a half months pregnant.

At first Westmore couldn't reckon how a woman could get this pregnant in just over eleven minutes but then—

He shrugged. *I guess everything's different in Hell, even getting knocked up.*

"Arrrrgh!" she yelled again. She curled up in a fetal position, her arms cradling the mammoth belly. "Those farkin' demons—they fark the sheet out of me! One of them had *three* farkin' cocks! They make me pregnant as FARK!"

Better her than me, Westmore reasoned. So distended were her breasts now that droplets of milk appeared to be squeezing out of her nipples. *Yeah, she's ready to drop...* He picked up the counter phone, dialed 911... "Yes, please send an ambulance to the West Street 7-Eleven—yeah, the one where the unfriendly Russian girl works," and then he hung up and walked out. *I don't wanna be anywhere near this place when she lets* THAT *bun out of the oven...*

"You did your good deed for the day," Nia griped, "now let's get the fuck out of here. See if your car starts."

Westmore didn't like the sound of that. "Why wouldn't it?"

"Oh, I don't know, maybe because it's been in another *plane of existence!*"

They both jumped in the car. Westmore put the key in, took a deep breath, and turned it.

The car started.

"How do you like that!" He reached behind his seat to get a beer but—"Oh, shit! Somebody in Hell stole my beer! Thieving bastards!"

"Consider yourself lucky. Now let's go."

As Westmore lead-footed it out of downtown Dannelton, they passed a caravan of emergency vehicles speeding in the opposite direction, their sirens blaring and lights throbbing.

"We-we made it!" he exclaimed after a few moments more.

Nia stared straight ahead, her mouth hung open. "Yeah. Shit. It's hard to believe we got out of there alive."

"And we got out alive because of *you!*" Westmore enthused, grinning over at her. "I owe you a *big* apology."

She smirked. "Yeah, I'd say so. You thought I was psycho, thought I was on drugs, thought I was an idiot. Didn't believe a word I said about any of it. Well, I'll bet you believe me now..."

"How can I not? And I'd be in Hell right this minute if you hadn't sucked that worm-demon's dick." He looked ahead dreamily. "I'll bet you're the only woman walking the Earth who can say she's given a blowjob to a worm-demon and even took the load in the mouth."

Nia winced. "Shut up, don't remind me…"

"And I'll bet that worm-demon's hard-on was bigger than any hard-on you've ever seen in your life. Was it?"

"What? Oh, shut up…"

"And tell me this—I'm curious. Does worm-demon semen taste like regular semen?"

"Shut the fuck up, you asshole!"

Westmore chuckled. "I'm just messin' with you. After all that, I figured a little levity might lighten things up."

"Levity's supposed to be funny, so shut up!"

Westmore pulled into a McDonald's drive-thru line. "I need a vanilla shake. What do you want?"

"I guess I'll take the same."

"Yeah, I'll bet *you* especially could use something to drink, you know, to get the horrible taste of *demon cum* out of your mouth," and then he started laughing.

"Fuck off and die, dick!"

"Okay, all jokes aside," he began. "Do you realize how rich we're gonna be?"

"How do you figure?" she asked, pretty despondently.

He was scrolling through the photo folder on his camera. "Look at all these pix I got, and you got a shitload too. Forget about the Dark Web—we'll put these up on YouTube, start our own channel! *Visions of the Real Hell*, we can call it, and we'll monetize the stuff! I'll bet we get a *billion* hits the first day!"

Nia mulled the prospect over, nodding to herself. "You know, you may be right. All these pictures are pretty convincing."

"Yeah, and there's something else too," Westmore said. His eyes were beaming at her. "When you were sucking that worm-demon's dick—"

"Stop saying that!"

"What? 'Worm-demon's dick'?"

"Shut up! Stop talking about it!"

He made an exaggerated expression. "Oh, Nia, don't worry. There's nothing to be ashamed of. You were saving our lives. You stepped up and did what needed to be done. You sucked the *bejesus* out of that worm-demon's dick—"

Her face turned pink when she yelled, "SHUT UP! SHUT UP! SHUT UP!"

"No, seriously, Nia. Here me out, okay?" He looked right at her and winked. "When you were sucking that worm-demon's dick, what do you think *I* was doing?"

"How the fuck do I know, you nut-job?"

Westmore held his camera up so she could see the LCD screen, then he pressed the little PLAY arrow.

Nia wilted as she watched. "No." Her eyes widened. "You *didn't*." Her eyes widened some more. Then: "You ass-motherfucking-HOLE! You filmed me while I was—"

"While you were sucking the worm-demon's dick," he finished for her, nodding. "But before you go apeshit, think about the possibilities."

"You fruitcake old fuck! What possibilities?"

"Forget about Kennedy and Marilyn Monroe. *This*"—he tapped the camera—"is the rarest, most unique, and most *valuable* porn clip ever to exist. Think about it..."

Nia's shell-shocked look slowly began to change to something a bit more positive. "Well...yeah. There's never been porn like this."

"You're damn right, there hasn't. This is a porn clip of a human woman—how do I say this?—engaging in oral sexual congress with a creature *from Hell.* Not even the best special effects in Hollywood could fake something this authentic. And in *today's* fucked-up society?"

Nia stared at the contemplation.

"People will *pay* to see a clip like this. *Lots* of people. Once we find the right platform to sell this on, it won't just be the talk of the town, it'll be the talk of the *world.*"

"I think you're-I think you're right!" Nia squealed. "We'll make millions!"

Westmore nodded confidently. "Yes, we will. Between this clip and all the pix from the Merge, we'll be world famous and richer than that bald guy who owns Amazon." He moved up in the drive-in line, to the speaker box, and said, "We'll take two vanilla shakes, please."

"Coming right up, sir. Drive around to the pay window."

Westmore drove the car around. "I'll bet they even make a Netflix series about us!"

"You're right!" Nia thrilled, and she actually put her arms around Westmore and kissed him. He appreciated her sudden affection and gratitude very much but—

Damn, I hope she doesn't still have worm-demon cum on her lips...

He looked up into the drive-in window.

"Two vanilla shakes!" the uniformed attendant called behind him.

And behind him, another attendant, was holding two cups out and—

"Raaaaalf!"

—threw up into the first cup, and—

"Raaaaaaaaaaaaaaalf!"

—threw up into the second. A straw was inserted into each cup, then the milkshakes were handed out to Westmore.

"Here are your shakes, sir. That'll be two Diocletian dollars—"

"Nia!" he yelled. "Something's fucked up here!"

"Oh, no no no no," came her response.

Westmore and his companion had been so caught up in their excitement that they hadn't noticed the oncoming incongruities. The attendant who'd just filled their cups with vomit was actually a reanimated corpse with one eyeball dangling from its socket and one cheek excised, showing a row of rotten teeth. Behind him several other employees busied themselves, but these persons were all either gray-faced Trolls, brown and smiling Imps, a Werewolf here and a Nekrotic there, and a two-headed, four-armed Hex Clone working the fries machine. Way in the back, a pair of busty Succubi were cutting hanks of flesh off of hanging human legs and dropping them into an automatic meat-grinder, for burger patties.

And overhead, without the notice of Westmore and Nia, the night sky was gradually changing over to a luminous dark scarlet, like the hue of deoxygenated blood. A black sickle moon emerged from behind a reef of coal-black clouds.

"The Merge is supposed to be over!" Westmore yelled.

"I know! But it must've shifted from Dannelton over to here."

"Why?"

"The occult cosmology, you know? Maybe the Merge got jinked up in the Hex-Flux, you know? An anomalous power-surge or something!"

Westmore yelled so loud his throat hurt: "But you're supposed to know about this shit! The trance-channelers and all that! They're supposed to be able to predict this!"

"Well, I'm sorry I can't know *everything!* Satan obviously decided to initiate another Merge! He's not exactly gonna consult us!"

What she said made sense, but the whys and wherefores hardly mattered at this point. Before Westmore could stomp the accelerator, he and Nia both were pulled out of the car by a crew of chuckling Broodren. The mischievous monsters made short work of stripping Nia nude and shorter work still of burying their erections into any possible orifice. Their penises, by the way, looked like warped pieces of radiator hose.

Westmore, on the other hand, hardly fared better. His Walmart jeans were ripped off his legs at the stitches, then his genitals were firmly grasped and twisted around and around and around until they popped off. The description of his vocal objections was not necessary to recount. Similarly, however, his head was grabbed and twisted around and around and around until it, too, popped off—

—yet even with his head no longer connected to his body, his sense of vision was able to register this final image:

The glowing golden arches at the entrance to the parking lot. The bright buzzing neon letters did not spell out McDONALD'S but instead McDAHMER'S.

THE BOUNCE HOUSE

Thirty-five-year-old Miles Bennell, whom one could say fit the mold of tall, dark, handsome, and a bit of a sexist pig, watched out the front kitchen window as the workmen from the party-equipment company rolled the deflated bounce house off the truck and centered it neatly in the front yard.

Miles' wife, Becky, fragrant from just having showered, came out, looked out the window, and immediately complained, "Oh, Miles, tell them to put it in the back yard! In the front it will look *ostentatious*."

"That's the idea, honey." He quickly eyed the curve of her buttocks. *God-DAMN, she's got an ass on her that won't quit, even after eight years of marriage...* "Ostentatious—what's that mean? Snobby, right?"

Becky tossed back her dark blonde jaw-length bob. "Yes, Miles. The neighbors will consider this a vulgar display of materialism and one-upsmanship. Just like with the Christmas lights last year, and our Halloween decorations. They'll think we're showing off." She shook her head, still looking out the window. "Don't we have more character than to Keep Up With The Joneses?"

"Fuck the Joneses. I'll *bury* the Joneses—they can eat my shorts. We're *better* than the fuckin' Joneses, for fuck's sake,"

Miles replied with some striking disdain. Then he glanced aside and cupped Becky's right butt-cheek until she jiggled away. "All these asshole neighbors? They need to know that when *my* kid has a birthday, he gets the best of everything—including the best and biggest bounce house available." He smiled out the window. "I mean, look at the size of that thing; it's twenty-five-by-twenty-five and fifteen feet high; they don't even *make* residential bounce houses bigger than that. You could fit twenty *adults* in there, much less twenty eight-year-olds."

"Yes, and it's twice as big as the one the Grangers rented for their twins—that's my point. It looks like we're doing it on purpose, just to show them up. 'Our bounce house is bigger than yours.'"

"Yeah," Miles said. "Perfect. The fuckin' Grangers *wish* they had our money."

Becky could only smirk, because she knew the futility of arguing with Miles. She looked closer out at the bounce house. "It must've cost a fortune," she muttered.

Miles couldn't resist. "No, what cost a fortune was your brand-new Cadillac V-Series Blackwing." *Ninety fuckin' grand, bitch, and don't you forget it.* Miles had bought the turbo-charged model for himself, and that cost another fifteen g's. He now had the two most expensive cars on the street, and that was *just* the way he wanted it. *How do you like me now, dipshits?*

"Don't get smart."

"And the bounce house only cost a hundred a day to rent. And no security deposit—"

Becky stared at him in disbelief. "Are you kidding me? When I was pricing them, the big ones all cost five hundred a day and a thousand security deposit! In *this* county? How'd you get it so cheap?"

Miles loved it when she didn't wear a bra. When he leaned forward next to her, pretending to watch the delivery men, he pulled half-wood just from peeking down the front of her Milano silk blouse. There were the goods: apple-sized, triangled by tan lines (she spent a lot of time in the backyard pool), and nipples poking out like amaranth-pink Hershey's Kisses. "I'll remind you, my dear, that not only did you marry a man who's wealthy and great in bed but one who is a masterful negotiator." In truth, there was no negotiating. The old guy at the store, Mr. Malpert of Malpert & Son's Party Equipment, gave it to him cheap, because a hundred dollars a day was better than no dollars a day, and Miles didn't see anyone standing in line.

"Oh, so that's it, huh?" She kept looking out the window. The workmen—they looked like day laborers—had quickly laid the base and were now unrolling the corner columns and inflating them with an air-compressor. She seemed astounded. "Really, I've never seen one that big."

"I know, right? Oh…you mean the bounce house."

"Yeah, Miles. The bounce house." She shook her head, smiling. "At your age, you're supposed to start *losing* interest in sex—"

He slipped over, stood right behind her, pulled out his now-three-quarters-hard penis, and pressed it raw against her rump.

"Does it feel like I'm losing interest?"

"Damn it, Miles! I'm not a scratching post!"

"You're not?" and that's when his left hand came around and started playing with her boob, and his right slipped right down the front of her jeans.

"Stop it!"

"Okay. I'm stopping it." He kept doing it. *God, I love this bald pie…* His middle finger angled right into her slit, which started to moisten at once. Then he slid it slowly up and down.

"Mmm," she said. "That's not bad."

"Good. Now pull your pants down so I can give peter some exercise from behind."

She paused, thinking about it. Miles knew how to read her. Then he started kissing the side of her neck, and that always amped up her mood. "Holy shit," he muttered into her neck. "I have the prettiest wife in the whole world. I'm *so* lucky…"

"Ok, you win," and then she started to unfasten her jeans. Meanwhile, Miles' cock had graduated to full hardness, and it was beating against the back of her Versace stone-washed jeans and leaving little dark dots on the denim. *Fuck, I can't wait to cum*, Miles thought. And just as Becky began to pull her pants down—

The doorbell rang.

"You gotta be fuckin—" Miles began.

Becky was chuckling. "No nookie today it looks like. I'll bet it's the bounce house guy. You better go get it."

Fuck! Miles swore in thought. *DOUBLE-fuck!* He stuffed his junk back in his pants, and half-walked, half-limped to the foyer, and opened the door.

And now might be an appropriate time for some elucidation as to the sequence of events taking place. The whole of the situation could be rendered as thus: Miles and Becky Bennell, a very well-off married couple living in an up, upscale neighborhood, were soon to commence with a birthday party for their tow-headed, fat, spoiled-brat son named Tommy. It's likely that Miles got that bun in Becky's oven a few months before they'd tied the knot; Tommy had been grunted out of his mother's loins a little less than eight months after she'd officially become Mrs. Bennell. But who gave a shit about stuff like that these days? After that he'd made damn sure Becky got an IUD because *one* bundle of joy was enough, and he didn't need any more Tommies sliding out of Becky's sausage closet. At first she'd suggested he use condoms but…*fuck that!* If a man devoted his love and life to a woman via the institution of wedlock, he sure as *fuck* had the right to dump raw nut into her cooter anytime he wanted — er, at least that's the way Miles saw it, and Becky didn't need much coaxing to go along with it. After all, being the wife of a young capable millionaire had its benefits...

It has likely been discerned by now that Miles wore his ego like he wore his Diamond/Gold Rolex: he needed *everyone* to see it. That people envied his material position in the world was a matter of great importance to him. In college over a decade ago, he'd been an insufferable fuck-horn, bragging to his friends at any opportunity about the abundance of attractive women he'd "scored" with, and it might be germane to mention that most of these female conquests were among the best looking in the entire school. Being, 1) handsome, and 2) overflowing with family money, helped Miles quite a bit in this department, but that was beside the point.

And, now, even deep into marriage, his inclination to brag about himself had followed him from college, and his son's birthday party was a perfect example. Seeing to it that little Tommy had a good time was only secondary; the imperative was to throw a birthday party that *blew away* every other neighborhood birthday in recent memory. That meant the best presents, the best caterers, the best clowns, and the best entertainment. Last year, Pete and Janice Cutler (Miles thought of them as the *Cunt*lers*)* had set up a go-cart track in their huge back yard for their Tastykake-filled sissy-britches son, Mark. That made a big splash, but then a couple months ago, the talk of the town had been the birthday party that Jake Grimaldi had thrown for *his* stuck up kid, Jimmy. The fucker had rented a twenty-by-twenty bounce house, and those were *real hard* to find. That wouldn't do for Miles, as we've seen — hence his twenty-*five* by twenty-*five* bounce house. He'd also hired a lifeguard for the backyard pool; multiple clowns *and* magicians, and he'd spent a fuckload on presents for *all* the kids, not just Tommy. In a neighborhood full of rich douche-canoes like this, one *had* to stay a step ahead.

Right now, Tommy was at the house of his best friend, Kevin Donovan; he'd spent the night, and Kevin's parents Jack and Teddi, would be bringing both kids over at one o'clock, the official start-time of the party. A bunch of other spoiled-rotten kids with their parents would show up around the same time.

And now that the stage has been fully set...

Miles answered the door to find, as expected, Mr. Malpert, the bounce house guy, standing opposite him. Malpert was old, grey-bearded, and kind of off-kilter-looking in his round spectacles, old dress slacks, and one of those old-style tweed sports jackets with elbow patches; the guy looked more like a college professor close to the skids.

"Mr. Bennell," he began, "the bounce house is set up and ready to go. It's maintenance free, but let me show you a few things just for your familiarization"

"Sounds good," Miles answered, still pissed that he'd come *this close* to banging Becky bent over the kitchen counter. What a rip-off.

They walked out to the front yard where the bounce house now stood fully inflated and quite grandiose. It had a red base, yellow corner columns, a blue roof, and was filled with multicolored balloons and beach balls. Heavy nylon screen formed the walls and allowed for the inside to be viewed at all times by vigilant adults. Off to the side sat a tanked air-compressor, which Mr. Malpert pointed to and explained, "You needn't worry about that; there's a pressure sensor so if the pressure gets too low, the compressor kicks on automatically."

"Great," said Miles. Now he was looking across the street where Mrs. London was washing her BMW in the driveway.

Ain't no way that tight-wad hubby of yours'll ever buy you a brand-new Caddy Blackwing like I bought Becky. Wouldn't mind blowing a big peckersnot in your hair, though... Mrs. London's killer-bod was ruined by the asinine curly mohawk hairdo. And the hair was the color of cotton candy. Only the 2020s would find such a hairstyle normal in high-end suburbia. However, her body from the neck down had provided Miles with some potent "beat-off fodder" on more than one occasion. Beatin' wasn't cheatin'.

Next, Malpert walked Miles to the front of the bounce house itself. "Here's the main pressure panel," he said, opening a lidded box on the side. "It regulates the firmness of the jumping pad." It was a simple apparatus, with buttons: low, medium, high. "You can play around with it; the kids like it when you alternate firmness while they're in there."

"Huh? Oh, yeah, sure," Miles muttered, "alternate the firmness," but now he was looking next door where Janet Brill, who looked kind of like Scarlett Johansson but with black hair and bigger tits, was getting her mail. She waved and smiled, then gave a conspiratorial wink. She and Miles had gone to high school together, where she'd been a primo nut-bucket (Janet Brill, not Scarlett Johansson). Miles had fucked the shit out of her on Senior Skip Day and a few more times that summer. *What a wonderful fuck-pig*, he mused now.

"Here are the light switches," Malpert said next, and opened another panel, this one mounted on the front column. "You can adjust the colors and the flasher speed with these knobs. It really looks great at night."

I'll tell ya what really looks great at night, Miles thought. *The smile on my wife's face after I make her cum, and that's what I SHOULD be doing now...* Several catering trucks pulled up just then, and the staff began wheeling their grills and food carts around to the back yard. Some of the staff were women, and

Miles eyeballed them without reservation, thinking, *I'd fuck her, I'd fuck her, I'd take head from her, no way I'd fuck Jobbessa the Hut, but…well, I'd let her jerk me off, I guess—*

Mr. Malpert cleared his throat to signal Miles' attention, "And one last thing, Mr. Bennell, this metal box down here." He pointed to a metal box mounted near the bottom wooden strut of the bounce house's base. The box had a Master padlock on it. "Inside here is the power coupler. Don't touch it for any reason. If you do, then it can off-calibrate everything and cause a big problem."

"Right," Miles half-heartedly replied. "Don't touch the power coupler—got it."

Just then, the trucks from the petting zoo pulled up, with the handlers leading the animals down the ramps and around to the back yard. A lamb, a baby pig, an alpaca, a pony, etc. Most of the handlers were female, and this just gave Miles more to eyeball. A couple of them were packing some outstanding cameltoe…

"So that's it, Mr. Bennell," Malpert said. "I hope your party is a smashing success. If you have any problems with the bounce house—don't worry, you won't—then call me. I can be here is ten minutes."

"Yeah, right. Thanks very much," Miles said, now watching the picture-perfect asses on the last three girls bringing the animals. *There's an all-you-can-look-at ass buffet if I've ever seen one…*

Becky came outside, and called to Miles, "It's time to go pick up the cake, honey."

"Okay, let's go," Miles began. The cake was six feet long, so this would require both of them to go pick it up.

But Becky was staring in almost awe at the bounce house. "Wow! It's even bigger up close."

"I know, right? Oh…you mean the bounce house."

Becky smirked just as her cellphone rang. "Hello?"

Miles was comparing Becky's cameltoe to the caterer's, and Becky, probably ten years older, was easily holding her own. Hopefully, he'd be drawing the end of his boner down that adorable groove before the day was out…

Becky just put away her phone; she looked exasperated. "Damn, that was the bakery. The cake won't be ready for another twenty minutes, they said."

"Well…" Miles got an instant idea. "Let's try out the bounce house for a few minutes before we go get the cake."

Becky's brow rose, then she kicked off her shoes. "What a great idea!"

Miles opened the framed entrance, then said "Ladies first," so he could get a bird's eye view of Becky's preeminent blue-jeaned ass. *The gift that keeps on giving…*

"I've never been in a bounce house before," Becky chuckled. "How does it work?"

"Simple. You get in and start jumping up and down."

Becky squealed delightedly when she stepped onto the bouncy, inflated floor and started vaulting around. The balloons and balls began to move en masse, and with them Becky bounced to every corner. Her hair flew up and down with each bounce, and so did her boobs beneath the silk blouse. "This is better than a trampoline!"

Miles somersaulted into the middle of the balloons and started bouncing around himself. Each time his feet hit the cushioned floor, the balloons shot upward. Next, several somersaults in a row, and it seemed like the whole world was upside down. A couple times he even bounced on his head.

The two of them were laughing out loud when they decided to stop to go get the cake.

"That was a blast!" Becky exclaimed, climbing out of the bounce house. Miles followed her. "Yeah, but we're not kids anymore. I'm a little dizzy."

"Me too, but—damn—that was fun!"

"Let's get Tommy's cake," Miles said, and they both walked to his Cadillac. *Damn, I'm feeling kind of weird*, he thought, getting in behind the wheel. He felt kind of prickly and hot but, of course, he'd just exerted himself. And, what? He felt kind of *icky* in a way he couldn't describe. As he drove down his road, he found himself smirking.

"What's wrong?" Becky asked. Just now her nipples stood out like golf cleats beneath the sheer Milano blouse, and the odd thing was, Miles didn't take note of that fact…

"Don't know. I just feel weird…"

"Want me to drive?"

"No, no, I'll be okay. I guess I overdid it, bouncing around in the bounce house like a little kid. I guess all the blood went out of my head for a minute, and it's just now coming back." This sounded reasonable and would explain the headache. But now he thought he felt hot flashes. "What about you?" he asked. "Do you feel okay?"

"I was dizzy for a minute but now I feel great," and then she did the strangest thing. She reached up and pinched her nipples for a second. "Kind of…horny, if you wanna know the truth. Why couldn't Mr. Malpert have come a little later?" and then she laughed.

But here was more strangeness. Miles had not reacted at all when his wife had admitted she was horny. This was clean contrary to his usual habit.

"Oh, shit," Miles said. "Jack's bringing Tommy and Kevin over at one, and that's about when the other kids will start showing up, but we won't be there yet."

"You're right," Becky agreed. "I better let him know." She whipped out her cell and called Jack's wife Teddi, who was also Becky's best friend. "Hi, Teddi, it's me. When you, Jack, and the boys get to our house, don't bother knocking, just go in; the door's unlocked and the maids and caterers are there. Yeah. Tommy's cake isn't ready yet, so we'll be a little late. Just start without us. The petting zoo animals are already there, and the bounce house is ready to go. Okay, see you in a bit," but after the call's termination...she pinched her nipples again and said, "Fuck..."

"What?"

She slid over next him on the big bench seat and whispered, "I *told* you. I'm horny all of a sudden." She slipped her hand between his legs, which made Miles flinch. "Get your cock out," she whispered hot into his ear. "Let me suck it..."

Miles' teeth ground. His mood felt skewed. "No, hon. I'm really not in the mood. Later."

Becky was fully taken aback by the response. She stared at him. "Did I hear you right? My husband, Miles Bennell, just said *no* to a blowjob offer?"

Miles saw her point. The idea of turning down a blowjob was beyond fathoming. He'd put his cock in a sack of greased-up salamanders if he could. But he just wasn't feeling it right now. "I got a headache, babe—"

Becky rolled her eyes. "That's supposed to be the woman's line..." Now she rubbed more intently between his legs. "Come on, pull over at the Hamburger Hamlet. I'll get this crotch-rocket interested," but then she squinted oddly, wedged her hand harder between his legs, then felt around down there. "What the... Did you stuff your cock and balls into your ass-crack?"

"Stop it!" Miles snapped. "I told you, I'm not in the mood! And did I stuff my...*what?*" and with that Miles put his hand between his own legs, feeling around. Immediately, he seemed alarmed. He slipped a quick hand down the front of his pants, croaked, "My God…" then yanked the wheel and pulled into the parking lot of the Hamburger Hamlet, tires squealing.

"Miles, what's wr—"

Frantic, Miles parked, pulled down his pants, and looked between his legs. Then he and Becky both yelled at the same time.

Miles' groin was utterly devoid of any evidence of cock and balls.

"Where's my junk?" he bellowed.

"And look!" Becky exclaimed, pointing down at the barren crotch. "You've got, you've got, you've got…a *vagina!*"

It was true, and there it was right before his wide-open eyes; the shock was just sinking in. His hands trembled with his realization, and he examined more closely the female sex organ that now occupied the area of space where his cock and balls were supposed to be. The closer he glared, the woozier he felt. *It's a fuckin' PUSSY!* the thought shrieked. *Shaved bald!* He could even feel some stubble. And then something occurred to him, something abstract issuing into his conscience: the pussy. That delectable groove, and the way that bubblegum pink minora was tucked back behind the lips, and the way the hood looked over the clitoris. "I've got a vagina, all right," he gasped, "and it looks a hell of a lot like—"

"*My* vagina," Becky finished, still staring. "I ought to know what my own vagina looks like, and that's sure as shit it!"

They were both staring down cockeyed at the vagina between Miles' legs. With all the times he'd licked, fingered, and fucked his wife's pussy, he knew it at a glance. Next, he jerked his gaze right at Becky. "Honey? Why is *your* pussy between *my* legs?"

"How the FUCK do I know?" she yelled back. It certainly wasn't *her* fault. "But wait a minute… If *my* pussy is between *your* legs…what's between *my* legs?"

Miles' lower lip tremored at the question.

"And come to think of it." Becky went on, "something feels a little *tight* down there right now…" Very slowly, then, she raised her hips off the seat a little, and pulled down her designer jeans—

Miles and Becky both yelled at the same time.

There, sprouting awesomely from Becky's bare crotch, was a sizable penis and pair of testicles floating in the crinkled scrotum. This, of course, was disconcerting enough, but more disconcerting was the obvious fact that it was *Miles'* sizable penis, balls, and scrotum.

Miles—ordinarily quite a macho man—instantly began crying outright, tears flowing down his cheeks.

"For fuck's sake, Miles!" Becky snapped. "This is no time to blubber like a baby! Some serious shit just happened to us, and we gotta find out what it was!"

Miles tried to get control of himself, but then he took another look down at his vagina and started blubbering again.

Becky sat there with her dick out, and she slammed her fists down on the Italian leather upholstery of the bench seat. "What the FUCK!" and then she paused, squeezed her eyes shut, looked down again. "What the FUCK!" She grabbed Miles by the collar and shook him to his senses, or at least tried to. "What caused this Miles? Something just switched our sex organs! What could it have been?"

Miles brought his hands to his temples, tears still squeezing from his eyes. "I don't know!" he exclaimed, voice quavering. "Global warming?"

"Oh for shit's sake, Miles! How could global warming switch my pussy with your dick?"

"Stop *yelling!*" Miles whined. "You've got me all out of sorts!"

"Oh, *I've* got you out of sorts? But my *pussy* between your legs doesn't? Quit whining like a three-year-old! It's not global warming, so what is it?"

Miles' face was pinkening in distress. "Maybe-maybe...something we ate?"

"That's *ridiculous!*"

"Well, wait a minute. There's that Air Force base on the other side of town—"

"Fuckin' *so what?*"

"I don't know. Maybe they're doing, like, secret government experiments on civilians."

This tamped down some of Becky's ire. Such things, certainly, had been heard of. CIA experiments in the '50s? MK Ultra? The Army supposedly putting reagents in the water supply of some town in Texas? "Hmm, yeah. Maybe you've got something there..."

"Or maybe *aliens,*" Miles blurted. "I just read the other day that the Air Force said there might be UFOs for real."

Becky's eyes thinned in contemplation. "I read the same thing. UFOs—yeah, that's a possibility..."

"Or...maybe we're having flashbacks. We did our fair share of acid back in the day. Maybe this is all a hallucination."

Becky grimaced at him, then grabbed his hand and made him grab her cock. "Does that feel like a fuckin' hallucination, ya moron?"

"Stop yelling!" Miles whined again, but when he tried to pull his hand way, she wouldn't let him.

"Keep doing that," she said. "Squeeze it some, play around with it..."

"No!"

Becky continued to manipulate his hand around her cock—er, actually, *his* cock—but between *her* legs. It got hard at once, and from Becky's standpoint, that was a *grand* feeling. "Fuck, that feels good. This is making me horny as a motherfucker," and then she began outright stroking the shaft with his hand and making him cup her balls. "Holy *fuck*. So *this* is what it feels like when a man gets horny. What a fuckin' treat!"

Miles gaped at her. "Becky, what's gotten into you? Since when do you cuss like that?"

She glared. "Since I pulled my fuckin' pants down and found your dick between my legs!"

"It's just not like you to be so profane."

"Can't you focus on the subject? Damn! What are we gonna do? Is it aliens, or government experiments, or what?"

"There's no way to tell," Miles sobbed. "Should we go to the hospital?"

"Oh, right, Miles. We'd be a big hit in the emergency room. What do you think they'd do when they were done laughing? Surgically switch us back?"

"I don't know!"

For the past moments, Becky had kept Miles' hand playing around with her hard-as-a-rock cock. And you know what? It felt a hell of a lot better than when he'd fingered her in the past. "Well, here's one thing I *do* know. I'm hornier than a fuckin' hyena in heat. Drive the goddamn car over there behind the dumpster."

Miles looked over with his lower lip sticking out. "Whuh-why?"

Becky grabbed a handful of his hair and twisted. "Because I fuckin' said so, goddamn it!" and then she kept twisting his hair till he started the car and parked it behind the dumpster.

"Since I've got a fuckin' dick, I'm damn well gonna use it!" Becky pulled her jeans all the way off. The erection bounced up and down like a diving board.

"What are you…" Miles began.

Then Becky pulled Miles' legs up on the seat, spread them, peeled off his pants, and grinned down at his vagina. "I've always wondered how a male orgasm compares to a female's— well, now, I'm gonna find out!"

"No!" Miles meekly rebelled. "I don't want to—"

"Twinkie, cry baby," Becky growled at him. "With all the times you've stuck this fuckin' thing in me, now *you're* gonna get some!" and with that Becky expertly spat right smack-dab on Miles' vagina, said, "I'm gonna fuck you till you can't see straight, bitch," and slammed that big log of an erection hard into that silly insignificant little vagina.

"Stop it!" Miles cried. "I don't like it! I don't feel good!"

"Shut up, you big steaming Nancy," Becky grunted into Miles' neck. She was pounding away at him, balls-deep with every stoke. It felt mind-bogglingly good, and there was something abstractly satisfying in hearing her balls slap against Miles' taint, and just *being inside* him, especially when he didn't want her to be. *Fucker*, she thought. *How's it feel?* Meanwhile, Miles lay spread-eagled like a bitch underneath his now-cock-wielding wife, and he was taking it hard. The outrage of this *intrusion*, this *physical violation*, left him in a ceaseless state of shock and helplessness. He continued sobbing, pleading, "It hurts, it's too big! Stop it!"

"Okay, I'm stopping it," she mocked. The sensations building up at her groin were intoxicating and unlike anything she'd known when she had a vagina.

"Fuck! Ugh!" she grunted, driving it home. "Oh, yeah! Shit on a stick, that feels good!" and then she lost all her breath as her orgasm broke. She lay paralyzed within the waves of ecstatic spasms and shimmied at the feel of those big spurts of semen she was now pumping without relent into her husband's "honey-bucket." One spurt after the next, each one as potent as a mainline of morphine. *I'm filling this bitch right the fuck UP*, she thought in primitive glee, *just like all the thousands of times he filled ME up, like I was his own personal fuck-dummy. His own personal cum-container...* Sweat darkened the full front of her blouse, and then her cheeks billowed at a long, relieving exhale. The bout of animalistic intercourse was over.

Miles lay still beneath her, still blubbering.

Becky lay there, greedily exhausted but then something clicked in her mind, her eyes popped open as if at an outrageous realization, and then she leaned up and—

smack! smack! snack!

—she unleashed a salvo of hard, vicious slaps back and forth across Miles' face, shouting, "You fuck! You piece of shit! You asshole!"

smack! smack! snack!

Miles lay back in total shock, terrified and shaking all over. "What? What did I do?"

smack! smack! snack!

"You motherFUCKer!" Becky wailed. "I had no idea that a male orgasm was TEN TIMES BETTER than a female's! It's not fucking fair! All these years I've been having piss-ant orgasms while you were having THAT?"

By now, Miles had all but been slapped senseless. He couldn't even cogitate what she was talking about. He hitched in his chest and stared up watery-eyed. "How could you *do* that, Becky? You-you-you...*raped* me!"

smack!

"We're married, dick-face! It'll be a sad day in American when a woman can't stick her cock into her husband's pussy any time she wants," but then her eyes narrowed as she considered, perhaps, the anomaly of what she'd just said. "Anyway, you've been banging me since the day we met. It pisses me off SO MUCH to know how much better your orgasms were than mine!"

smack!

Miles had to cover his face. "That's not *my* fault!"

"I know, but—"

smack!

"—it still pisses me off royal." She threw him his slacks. "Now put your fuckin' pants back on. We gotta figure out what to do."

Miles dared to cast her a defiant glance. "Well, the least you could do is go down on me…"

Her face turned into a repulsed rictus. "Fuck that shit, man! Yuck! I just filled that pussy up with *cum*—I'm sure as SHIT not gonna put my mouth there!"

"But-but, that's not fair!"

smack!

"Shut your pansy face before I *really* get mad…"

Miles continued crying while Becky hauled her jeans back on.

"Wait a minute," Miles said. "We forgot about the cake—"

"What?"

"Tommy's birthday cake—"

"Are you shitting me, Miles? Our genitals just traded places and you're worried about a fuckin' *cake?*"

Miles slumped. "It's his birthday, and—"

"That little piglet kid of ours can fuckin' *wait* for his goddamn cake. The fat munchkin'll probably eat the whole thing and not even say thank you. Spoiled little shit. I'll bet he sits to pee."

Miles looked horrified. "That's our *son* you're talking about!"

164

"Yeah, and he's a Hostess Ho-Ho on two legs who needs a good hard ass-kicking. He probably plays with dolls—"

"Becky!" Miles exclaimed. "What happened to you? You're a horrible person all of a sudden! Did you hear what you just said about our son? Your personality's completely changed!"

Becky gave her stuffed crotch a squeeze. "Yeah, and so has yours. You've turned into a whiny sissified little girl. Now what are we gonna do?"

"Well, well, I just thought of something," Miles said without much confidence. "Let's say it's a secret government experiment or some kind of alien ray—whatever. Did the same thing happen to other people, or are we the only ones?"

Becky nodded. "Good question. But how do we find out? It's not like we can ask the next guy walking down the street if he's got a pussy."

"Yeah, or stare at girls' crotches and see if there's a bulge—and, holy moly! I just thought of something else. What was the last thing we were doing before we left the house?"

Becky's jaw dropped. "We were jumping up and down in the bounce h—" but just then her phone rang. "Uh, yeah, hi, Teddi. Sorry we're late but we've, uh, we've got a little problem here—"

"YOU'VE got a problem?" Teddi wailed on the other end of the line. "You won't *believe* what happened! Get back here right away!"

"Why, Teddi? Tell me what happened."

"You have to see it for yourself. Otherwise you'd never believe me. Kevin and Tommy and a bunch of the other kids all got into the bounce house and, and—"

Becky's eyes bugged through a pause. "Don't tell me. Their genitals switched?"

Teddi shrieked. "Yes! How could you possibly know?"

165

"The same thing happened to me and Miles. We're on our way, and don't let anyone else into the bounce house," and when she hung up she yelled to Miles, "It's the bounce house!"

Miles chewed a nail. "What? You mean the bounce house was what made our genitals trade places?"

"Yes! And the same thing just happened to some of the kids! Now, drive—"

smack!

"—and DON'T drive like a woman!"

It was an exclusive manner of pandemonium that awaited them at the house, which was perfectly reasonable given the circumstances. Miles and Becky parked and ran past the empty bounce house, casting it an ominous glance, and then burst into the house. Miles ran with well, a little bit of a limp, like maybe he had a crushed beer can in each shoe.

A bunch of the kids were outside with the clowns and magicians, or petting the animals—oblivious to the chaos now taking place in the living room where Jack and Teddi had corralled the kids who'd used the bounce house.

"What the fuck, Miles?" came a very harried Jack.

Teddi, a statuesque brunette with killer implants, was just as disoriented as her husband. "They all went into the bounce house, then came out and were...changed! It's just not possible!"

"Tell me about it," Becky griped and pulled down her pants. The big cock hung there—kind of arrogantly, if such a thing was possible—like a mini elephant trunk.

"Wow, there's a bruiser!" Jack laughed.

"It's not funny!" Miles blared. "That's *my* dick! And look what I got—" Miles pulled his jeans down and showed off his shaved pubis and gorgeous vagina.

166

"Ooo," Jack remarked. "That there's some angel food cake!"

"Shut up, Jack!" Teddi yelled. Miles and Becky pulled their pants back up. "So how many kids were affected?" Becky asked.

"Every kid in the room," Teddi informed, "and it happened right after they all piled out of the bounce house. This is fucked up."

Becky's mind was racing, but she found herself fairly distracted by the presence of Teddi, who was looking quite foxy in her knee-high leather boots, denim miniskirt, and chiffon blouse. *Damn, I wouldn't mind putting the blocks to her,* Becky thought. *I'd joggle her fuckin' ovaries...* They'd fooled around in college a few times, drunk, but... *But that was before I had a dick.* The stray ruminations ended right then, though, when Tommy rushed up to her, teary eyed and lower lip sticking out. "Mommy! My peepee's gone! The bounce house made it go away, and now I have a girl-thing, you know, a cunny."

Cunny? Becky thought. *Is that what little kids call it?* "I know, honey. Do you know who got it?"

Chubby-cheeked Tommy pointed to a blonde girl with a ponytail. "Her, I think. Sherri McCoy."

Oh, that little troll. Her parents were perfect cunts. "Sherri, honey? Come here a minute, okay?"

Sniffling, eight-year-old Sherri shuffled over. "I-I-I-I—"

"I know, sweetheart. Lemme see. It's okay, you can show me, okay?"

Sherri pulled her skirt up and Cinderella panties down, and there it was: a bald little cock and scrotum with little balls in it. *Yep, that's Tommy's dick all right. Fuuuuuck me...*

"Why?" sobbed little Sherri. "Why did this happen?

"Because, honey," and then her mind went blank. *Because my fuckin' lame-brained husband HAD to get a fuckin' bounce house, and it turned out to be a FUCKED-UP bounce house...* "Don't you worry, honey. Just leave it to the grown-ups. We'll get everything back to normal—"

"Well you *better*," the little girl snapped, "'cos if you don't, my father'll sue!"

Why you little shit, Becky thought, wishing she could punch the little kid in the face and swing her around by her ponytail. Better yet, she wished she could kick her right in the dick. Now *that* would be fun. "Just...don't worry. Mr. Bennell will fix it. Now run along and go watch cartoons," *you smart-mouth little bitch!*

She walked over to where Miles and Jack were standing, listening to the rest of the whining kids whose genitals had been swapped. One kid, Cathy Wheeler, had her pants down and was twirling her limp little wiener around like a propeller. "Look! I'm a plane!" Jack frowned, "Cathy, put that away, and you there, Mike, is it? Put that candle down." But Miles was even more bewildered. It looked like a total of ten kids had been transfigured in the bounce house, five boys, five girls. Jack's kid, Kevin, sat on the floor crying, his pants down and his little bald vagina showing just plain as day. "Hey!" Miles shouted, pointing, "Diane, Lisa, stop that right now!"

Both eight-year-olds looked over with shit-eating grins; they'd been rubbing the ends of their penises together.

"This is madness, Miles," Becky marched over to say. "And it's *your* fault."

Miles was outraged. "How is it *my* fault?"

"You're the one who had to get the biggest bounce house just to show off to the neighbors—"

"I didn't know it was all fucked up!"

"Yeah, well, it's *still* your fault. Susie Jenkins was actually jerking off a few minutes ago. How do kids this age even know about that?"

"It's not my fault!"

"Settle down, guys," Jack said. Now the four of them stood in a circle. "I don't see that there's anything we can about this. We need some medical or scientific authority."

"How are you gonna get 'em here?" Becky ventured.

"Yeah," Teddi added, "and what could we tell them that wouldn't sound like a crank call?"

"Well, we better do *something* before the kids go home," Miles said. "Their parents are going to want answers."

Becky nodded with vehemence in her eyes. "Um-hmm. And that little twat Sherri McCoy already said that her father will sue. How do you like that little shit?"

A cast of dread came over Miles' face. "That's just what we need—"

"Not *we*, buster," Becky said. "*You.*"

"That's my loyal wife, all right. I can always count on her to have my back—"

"Shut up before I dick-spank ya—"

"Come on, you two," Teddi implored. "Quit fighting. We gotta think of something."

Jack was pinching his chin like someone with a goatee. "Did the bounce house come with instructions? Who brought it here?"

"Old guy named Malpert; it was from his company, down in Kenneth City. A couple of day laborers were with him, they set it up. This was the last bounce house Malpert had and…" Now Miles was pinching *his* chin. "Wait a minute! When he was showing me how to work it, he mentioned something about a— damn! What was it?"

"Come on, Miles!" Becky snapped. "Lay off the pot vape! This is important, so remember!"

"Well, I was—damn I hate it when you can't remember stuff." Miles squeezed his eyes shut. "Malpert was talking but I got kind of distracted looking at the butts on the girls from the petting zoo—"

"Terrific, Miles," Becky said, frowning. "What a great husband I wound up with, huh? I really picked a winner."

Miles glared. "Well if you don't like it then you can just—"

"What? Leave?" Now Becky stood, hands on hips. "You'd be sitting on the floor sucking your thumb without me. You don't even know how to do laundry."

"Yes, I do…I think…"

"Get it together!" Jack yelled. "Miles! What did this Malpert guy tell you?"

"Something—oh yeah! Something about the power coupler. Said it could mess up the bounce house if I tinkered with it."

"There's our only chance!" Jack said. "Do you know where the power coupler is?"

"Yeah, he showed me; it's on the bottom strut." But then his eyes thinned in some memory. "But it has a padlock on it."

"Do you have any bolt cutters?"

Suddenly Miles looked enthused. "Yeah! There's bolt cutters somewhere in the garage, I think."

"Teddi," Jack empowered himself, "you and Becky go find the bolt-cutters. Miles, you and me'll check out this power coupler."

Both parties split, Miles and Jack heading for the front door and Becky and Teddi heading for the hall, but not before Becky ordered the roomful of eight-year-olds, "Kids, don't leave this room till we say so. Then it'll be time for ice cream!"

The kids all cheered.

Becky led Teddi down the hall where the door to the garage was, but just short of it, she stopped, and pulled Teddi into one of the spare bedrooms.

"What the—" Teddi made objection. "This isn't the garage."

"Shh." Becky was grinning like a jack-o-lantern. "We'll get the bolt cutter-thing later. Let's do *this* now," and then she pulled off her jeans. Her cock was already standing up at full mast, throbbing.

Teddi started to make a face of disapproval, but then couldn't help but look closer at the big, beautiful boner sticking out from between her friend's legs. "Damn, girl…"

"Come on," Becky said. "Let's fuck!"

"N-noo."

"I'll betcha this cock is bigger than Jack's…"

Teddi hitched a chuckle. "Yeah. Like almost *twice* as big…"

Becky unbuttoned Teddi's blouse and let her hands frolic over the plenteous breasts, and next she was encircling a big nipple with the tip of her tongue. But when she reached to titillate the area between Teddi's legs, Teddi said, "Becky, no. It doesn't feel right. It would feel like I was cheating on Jack."

"Oh, fuck that hogwash!" Becky frowned. "Not if it's with a *girl*, for shit's sake. If it was with a guy, then that would be cheating, but I'm *not* a guy, I'm just a girl who happens to have a guy's equipment."

Teddi kept looking down at that throbbing, veined cock. Her stomach shimmied just *thinking* what it would feel like going in and out of her. "Well…"

Becky's eyes glittered.

"Okay—"

And that was that.

Becky threw Teddi down on the bed, pushed up her skirt and peeled off her panties, and then proceeded to fuck Teddi like a proverbial two-dollar whore. Teddi tensed up and hissed through her teeth when that big cock slid into her and started banging away.

"Fuck yeah," Becky grunted, then started sucking Teddi's neck. "I'm gonna tune you up, bitch…"

"Oh, oh, shit," Teddi whimpered. "That's so fuckin' good..." She wrapped her arms and legs around Becky's humping body and just let her keep pounding her. Each impact of Becky's groin to Teddi's sounded like somebody slapping raw meat over and over again. Teddi's tongue stuck out, her whole body tensing on and off beneath Becky's coital marauding. "Oh, fuck, yeah, you're hitting rock bottom, Becky! I'm gonna, I'm gonna—"

Teddi came bigtime beneath her hot, sweating friend, spasming hard like someone being electrocuted. But then the marvelous primitive sensations trebled when Becky grabbed Teddi's throat and squeezed hard. Teddi's face started turning pink. Finally, Becky let go, pulled her pulsing cock out, and just jerked it all off on Teddi's pussy, stomach, and bare tits. Becky's eyes rolled back in her head; each big pulse of semen only heightened the best orgasm she'd ever had in her life. "For shit's saaaaaake," she muttered, looking down at the huge spattering of cum all over Teddi. "That was some nut..."

Teddi would've been inclined to agree had she been able to talk; instead, she just lay there huffing and puffing. Tiny post-orgasmic twinges flared between her legs like after-notes of some devilish symphony. She was actually drooling.

"Told you I'd tune you up," Becky chuckled, then she grabbed Teddi's hand and used it to smear all that still-warm semen all over her front. "Does Jack hose you down like that?"

"Oh, fuck him. You just ruined me for life... But wait a minute. Wasn't there something we were supposed to do? Oh, yeah, get the bolt cutters from the garage."

———

Miles and Jack were both on their backs under the base-frame of the bounce house. The housing for the power coupler was easy enough to find but it seemed that Becky and Teddi were taking their sweet time getting the bolt cutters. Jack, frustrated, was trying and failing to pop the hinges with the screwdriver.

"This ain't doing it," Jack said, then he crawled back out and so did Miles.

Where are they? Miles fretted, kind of like a woman might.

"Why don't you go see what's taking them so long?" Jack said. But the problem was rendered moot a moment later when the two women appeared.

"What took you so long?" Miles asked with some irritation.

Becky roughly shoved the bolt cutters to him. "They were hidden under a pile of junk because *you* never clean the damn garage. Good job, Miles."

"Sorry," Miles peeped.

Jack took the bolt cutters and got back underneath the bounce house. "I'll open this thing or else…"

Miles stood between Becky and Teddi, then something subconscious caused him to sniff. It was a pungent and familiar scent that assailed Miles' nostril. *That's…cum…* It seemed to be coming from Teddi's direction and next he noticed some dark splotches in Teddi's blouse, like maybe sweat marks. He pulled Becky aside. "Hey, do you smell *cum?*"

Becky grinned back at him, then shot her eyes quickly to Teddi.

"You-you *didn't!*" he whispered. "You *didn't* fuck Teddi!"

Becky whispered back, "I fucked her and I came all over her—with *your* dick, fucker! And I'm gonna do the same to you if you don't fix this goddamn machine and get all these kids back to normal!"

Oh my God, Miles thought in a lightning bolt of despair. *She cheated on me, sort of*, and he actually brushed a tear out of his eye.

"Hey, Miles," Jack called out. "Get down here and check this out."

Miles slid back under the base. Jack had popped the padlock with no problem and had flipped up the lid to reveal a panel with two buttons on it, each the size of a half-dollar. The first button was red, the second green.

"Like a traffic light?" Miles ventured. He winced, finding it hard to concentrate because his pussy itched and those hot flashes were back.

"Red," Jack said. "Maybe that means, like, to *stop* the process, a way of reversing it. What do you think?"

Miles was gritting his teeth, scratching between his legs. And he felt ickier still down there, from all of Becky's cum dribbling and going tacky. *Damn! How do women stand being women?* And then the most dreadful thought of all struck him. *Am I about to have a period?*

"Jack! You listening? You're in LaLa Land. Come on, man, this is serious."

"Oh, yeah," Miles looked at the panel. Red, green. "I think you're right. The red must mean to stop the process. It's all we've got so we might as well try," then both men crawled back out. "Girls," Jack ordered. "We might have it here. Bring all the kids back out."

In less than a minute, Becky and Teddi were corralling ten whiny disoriented kids back out to the front yard. The bounce house door was flung open and Miles said, "Okay, kids! Everybody back in the bounce house! We think we've got a way to get you back to normal!"

The kids all piled back in, all too eager. But Tommy held back and looked up teary eyed at Becky. "Mommy, is this gonna make me back to the way I was before?"

"Yes, sweetheart," then Becky glared a Miles. "Your daddy says it'll work and you know Daddy. He's always right. Now up you go," and she helped Tommy back into the bounce house.

"What did you tell him *that* for?" Miles exclaimed. "I don't know if it'll work!"

"Well, it better work, because if it doesn't the poor kid will go through life thinking that his father's a putz and a loser and can't get anything right—"

"But that's not true!" Miles blubbered through a new round of tears.

"Sure it is, numbskull. Because it's *all your fault...*"

"Are we ready out there?" Jack called out.

"Yep," Becky replied. "Let 'er rip."

"Maybe they should jump around," Miles speculated, wiping more tears. "That's what we were doing when *we* changed."

"Finally!" Becky said, "Something *useful* comes out of your mouth. Okay, kids! Start jumping around in the bounce house! It's fun!"

"Here goes nothing," Jack said. There was a loud *click* sound. "I just pushed the red button."

Miles, Becky, and Teddi stood and watched the kids bouncing up and down through the screen. For a bunch of kids who'd just had their genitals switched, they looked to be having a good time. The balloons and beach balls bounced around them alternately. Each time the kids sprang up, the balloons and balls plummeted down.

Miles pulled on Becky's sleeve. He was still crying. "I can't *believe* you cheated on me," he whispered. "You broke my heart—"

smack!

Becky gave him a good one across the face. "Stop acting like a blubbering little candy-ass! Be a man, damn it!"

"What?" Teddi looked over and inquired.

"Oh, nothing..."

"How long do we do it for?" Jack asked.

Becky smacked Miles' arm. Hard. "You heard the man! How long?"

Miles voice quavered. "I-I don't know! Stop being mean!"

"Tits on a bull," Becky muttered. "I guess that's enough time." She opened the side door. "Okay, kids, everybody out!"

When all the kids were standing back in the front yard, Teddi said, "Holy shiiiiiiiiiiiiiit…"

At first the kids didn't realize something was wrong, but then they started looking around at each other…

Then they started squealing in mind-prolapsing terror.

This time, all their heads had been switched. Tommy's head was now on Sherri McCoy's body.

"Mommy!" Tommy wailed. "Why's my head on Sherri's body?"

"I don't know, honey. Looks like your father screwed up again."

Cathy Wheeler's head was now firmly attached to Mike Newberry's body, and vice-versa, and Jimmy Grimaldi's head sat atop Debbie Ross's body, and it went on from there.

"You gotta be shitting me!" Jack said when he stood back up and saw the damage.

"What do we do now?" fretted Teddi.

"But there's still the green button," Miles said. Did he scratch his pussy again? Yes!

"I guess that's the last resort," Jack moaned. "Okay, kids! One more time! Everybody back into the bounce house!"

Most of the kids did as they were told and were back in the bounce house jumping around. But not Tommy. He hugged Becky around her legs. "Mommy! I don't wanna go back in! Please don't make me!"

Little mamby-pamby fat fairy, Becky thought, then she hoisted Tommy up, heaved him into the bounce house, and slammed the door. *Can't believe I gave birth to that little tinklerbell…*

"They're all in, Jack!"

"Keep your fingers crossed," Jack suggested. Then he pushed the green button.

Becky, Teddi, and Miles stood anxiously aside, eyes fixed on the frenetic movement in the bounce house. The kids bounced up, the balloons fell down. The balloons bounced up, the kids fell down. If anything, it sounded like the kids were squealing in glee.

But in a few moments, those squeals of glee converted to ear-piercing, blood-curdling screams of horror.

"What the fuck?" Becky yelled.

"Something's happening!" Teddi observed. "Get 'em out of there!"

And Miles...well, he scratched his pussy.

It was a pandemonic melee; the kids didn't even wait, they banged the door open and began clamoring over one another to get out of the bounce house and back onto the yard. But when all of them had managed to escape, they all seemed to lay on the grass, kind of twitching and grunting, some still screaming. Becky noted with some disappointment that the highest-pitched scream came from Tommy, and there Tommy lay, arms and legs rowing in the air. "Mommy! Daddy! Help me!"

But no help was forthcoming, it seemed. Miles and Becky both stood frozen as statues, staring at the wriggling mass of eight-year-olds, while Jake and Teddi did the same. Then someone broke the dreadful silence and muttered, "This HAS to be the most FUCKED-UP thing to ever happen in all of human history..."

And that was probably an accurate assessment.

There was good news, and there was bad news. The good news was that each kid's head had been reattached to the right body...only *backwards*. In other words, the back of his head was now where his face should be. And that's the *good* news.

Here's the *bad* news: each kid's arms and legs had *transposed*. In other words, the arms were where the legs should be, and the legs were sprouting out of the shoulders.

"Oh, man," Teddi muttered, eyes bugging.

Jack added, "Looks like we're *really* in a pickle now…"

Some of the kids were trying to stand up on their feet, which sort of presented a view of someone standing on their head because their *head* was upside down between their legs. Other kids tried to stand up on their hands because this felt more natural, for their arms branched out of their hips and their heads were right-side up (but backward). But any serious ambulation failed after only a minute or so of effort, for whether they were walking on their feet or walking on their hands, the skewed positions were too much to reckon with, and balance was impossible to keep.

"The neighbors can't see this shit!" Becky snapped.

"Yeah," Jack agreed. "We gotta get 'em back in the house!"

"We're going in the house now, kids!" Teddi tried to sound enthused. "Who wants some snacks?"

But by now the kids didn't give a *fuck* about snacks. They all lay in an apoplectic twitching pile of disarranged arms and legs and backward heads, all sobbing and moaning and blubbering. Especially Tommy.

"Come on!" Jack yelled. "All we can do is grab 'em one at a time and get 'em inside!"

Jack and Miles managed two fucked-up kids apiece, one under each arm, and hobbled them into the house, while Becky grabbed Tommy and Teddi grabbed Kevin. The four kids who remained on the front yard conjured some resourcefulness and walked up to the house on their own on all fours, in a sort of "crab-walk." It was too bad no one thought to film it on their cellphone because it was one *very unusual sight* to behold, and would've made a splash on YouTube.

Back inside, the kids were all herded back into the living room, and the doors were closed. All four of the adults went *immediately* to the liquor cabinet and chugged some spirits. The kids were all curled up in weird positions on the floor, like armadillo bugs, still sobbing in their unfathomable trauma. Would they have to spend the rest of their lives like this? Or could some elaborate surgery offer a remedy?

And what was the exact *reason* for this outrage of physicality?

Tommy falteringly crab-walked over to his parents and looked up at Miles with his backward head. "Daddy? Mommy said you would make us all better but-but-but-but...you didn't. Why didn't you?"

Aw, fuck... Miles got down on one knee to personally address the really fucked-up thing that used to be his son. "I haven't given up yet, Tommy," he began but, really, what could he say at this point? "You can bet'cha I'll keep trying. And even...even if I can't get you back to normal, I want you to know that I'll always love you..."

Tommy contemplated the words, then his face screwed up, and he started bawling again and crab-walked away.

"Miles does it again," Becky sniped, arms crossed. "Could you maybe think of a more *hopeless* thing to tell a little kid, ya fuckin' empty-headed moron!"

Miles' face turned red and then he jerked toward Becky as if to pounce. "Get off my back! All you've done is give me grief since this whole thing started! It's not my fault!"

"It *is* your fault!" she cracked back at him. "You just *had* to get a bounce house, didn't you? You just *had* to get the biggest bounce house they make so you can show off to the fuckin' neighbors, huh? What a *dick!* If you hadn't insisted on getting that fuckin' bounce house, we wouldn't be in this mess! No wonder it was so cheap! God damn, I just *knew* I never should've married you—"

"Then why did you?" Miles bellowed back.

"Because you're rich and I didn't wanna work. But you can bet your ass I'll be filing for divorce now!"

With this comment, something in Miles' psyche snapped, kind of like a pencil might, one could suppose. His right hand tightened into a fist and he raised his arm. "What you need is a good old-fashioned knuckle sandwich!"

Becky leaned back and belly laughed. "Miles, if you even *tried* to hit me, I would beat your ass black and blue, and you know I could. Then I'd bang your pussy like you were a roofied bar tramp and make you suck your own dick! So go ahead! Hit me!"

Miles stood there with his fist raised and lower lip sticking out. Then...

His face fell into his hands and he started crying again.

"See what I get?" Becky mocked. "A regular macho man. But—wait! Here's something we can do!" She grabbed Miles' shoulders and jolted him to get his attention. "Hey, listen! Where did you first find the bounce house? Was there a rental lot or a place where that old guy did business?"

Miles looked up, sniffling. "Huh?"

smack!

"Where did you rent the fuckin' bounce house!"

"Oh, yeah." Miles gulped and wiped his eyes. "Place in Kenneth City, not far. Called Malpert & Son's."

Becky took command. "Teddi, Jack! You stay here and watch the kids! Me and Miles are going to Malpert & Son's!"

———

They approached Becky's Cadillac. Miles had a horrible stress headache, and what with everything else... "Honey, could you drive? I think I'm too upset—"

"What are you? Mr. Rogers all of a sudden?" Becky spat on the ground. "You're the *man*, so you drive! Get your fuckin' keys out, put 'em in the goddamn ignition, and fuckin' *drive!* If you don't, I'm gonna bend you over the hood and fuck you in front of everyone! All the neighbors will see your pussy!"

Miles whined, wiped his brow, started the car, and was off.

"How long does it take to get there?" Becky barked. She plucked her nipples subconsciously, then rubbed her fat crotch and smiled. "And step on it! You're driving like the little old lady from Pasadena!"

"Stop yelling at me!" Miles sobbed. "I-I can't concentrate! It's—I don't know—a ten-minute drive, I guess."

Becky nodded. "That's probably enough time," and then she hitched her jeans down and started playing with her big flaccid cock until it got hard. Then she started beating it.

Miles looked over, aghast. "You—You're *not!* You're not doing that *here!*"

"I sure as shit am," she replied, eyes closed, stroking away. "And you can bet your ass I'm not thinking about *you…*"

"Whuh—why not?" asked a now very agitated Miles.

"'Cos you're an obnoxious elitist pig—er, at least you were when you had a dick. Besides, that's just the way it is. Any woman who says she thinks about her husband while she's masturbating is a *liar.*"

Miles made a croaking sound deep in his throat. But he couldn't help side-glancing as his wife gluttonously pursued orgasm with *his* penis. Becky lifted up her blouse, hitched her pelvis up in the seat, then, "Aw, fuck, shit! Suck my sack, you bitch!" and then she tremored in grips of a raucous orgasm, semen looping onto her belly in thick ropes. When she was done, she just lay back, grinning. "Fuck, that was good. Ten times better than a girl's orgasm, you bastard."

"It's not my fault!" Miles whined.

"So what? It still makes me wanna kill *all men.*" With the edge of her hand she swiped up most of the semen off her stomach, then wiped her hand off on Miles' slacks.

"Hey! Don't do that!"

"Shut up," Becky said. She stuffed her dick back in her jeans and refastened them. "Are we there yet?"

Miles didn't think he could take much more. Finally, they'd arrived at the Malpert & Son's lot, so he pulled right in. Becky jumped right out of the car, but Miles stayed inside, trying to wipe the semen off with a Kleenex, but it wasn't working very well. *Will Woolite get this out?*

Becky yanked the door open and pulled Miles out. "Come on, shit-head! Don't *make* me break bad on you!"

At the end of the empty lot sat a little building and office. Becky hauled Miles along and banged through the door. A twerpy-looking guy in his thirties looked up from behind a desk with papers spread out. He looked stressed out. "Sorry, we're closed. All our bounce houses are rented out."

"Yeah, bub, and we rented one of 'em. We need to see Mr. Malpert, and I mean right now."

"I'm Pete Malpert," said the twerp. "The guy you talked to is my father; he got out—"

"Got out?" Miles said. "What do you mean?"

"Did he rent you the big one, the twenty-five-by-twenty-five job?"

"Yeah!" Becky yelled. "What do you mean he got out?"

"Oh, thank God I found it!" Pete said in a gust of relief. "My father didn't write down the address of the people he rented it to—"

But then a wan voice from some back room called out. "Help! Get me out of here! He's keeping me prisoner!"

Miles and Becky looked at each other, then they both looked at Pete Malpert. "All right, man," Becky said. "What gives?"

Pete's shoulders slumped in some obvious resignation. "If I told you, you wouldn't believe me…"

Becky wagged her finger at him. "Buddy, right now I've got my husband's dick in my pants, and he's got my pussy in his. And back at our house, we've got ten kids with their fuckin' heads on wrong and their legs growing out of their fuckin' *shoulders.* So don't worry about it. I'll believe you!"

"Okay," Pete announced. "You asked for it, so here it comes. My father is, for lack of a better term, a mad scientist. For thirty years, he was a researcher for this top-secret place in Virginia called the Air Force Aerial Intelligence Command. You ready for the kicker? They had aliens there, live ones—I'm serious. So naturally, like the good Americans we all are, we tortured the aliens for technological information. But one of the aliens made a deal with my father; it showed my father a blueprint for a machine that could transfigure matter, and the alien said it would give my father that blueprint if my father let it go. So…my father made the deal. He took the blueprint, then let the alien out of its cell, and, well, then he immediately called the MPs, told them about the escape, and the MPs shot and killed the alien."

"Wow," Becky remarked. "Your father's a grade-A prick."

"I know," said Pete. "Now, you would think he would immediately have given that blueprint to the Air Force—"

"But he didn't," Miles guessed. "He kept it for himself—"

Pete nodded.

Becky smirked, which was becoming second nature for her since she'd inherited some of Miles' hostile male hormones. "You're telling us that the old guy who rented us the fucked-up bounce house is a mad scientist?"

Pete looked her right in the eye. "Yes."

"And with alien blueprints, he made a machine that turned the bounce house into a contraption that switches cocks with cunts, and arms with legs, and heads?"

"Yes," Pete said. "See, I told you that you wouldn't believe it."

Becky looked at Miles, tapping her foot. They both thought about it for a moment, then:

"We believe it," they both said.

"It took him years," Pete went on, "to build the power couplers and transfiguration elements. But eventually he did, and they worked. However, the process won't work unless the subjects are engaged in rapid simultaneous motion when the element is turned on. So, a bounce house is the most ideal platform; the minute you get in it, you're moving rapidly."

Becky and Miles exchanged glances again. The whole idea sounded like pure bullshit, however: "Okay, we still believe you," Becky said. "But now, here's the million-dollar question. Can the effects of your father's machine be reversed?"

Pete held his hands up. "Of course. Just put anyone afflicted back into the bounce house and push the reset button. Then everything's back to normal."

Becky and Miles *yahoo'd* and hugged each other in a powerful jolt of celebration. But a question nagged at Miles. "Why on earth would he rent the bounce house out when he *knew* what would happen to anyone who got in it?"

Pete shrugged. "Because he's got dementia and went insane."

Becky nodded. "Well, that's a good reason, all right..."

Pete stood up. "Come on, I'll follow you to your house and change everyone back to normal."

All smiles now, Becky and Miles turned toward the office door, but then Miles stopped. "Wait," he said. "What about Mr.

Malpert? It kind of seems like he's being held captive against his will."

"Well, that's true to a point," Pete said. "This morning he escaped from his nursing home, then snuck here. When I was gone for lunch, he stepped in and rented you the bounce house."

"Don't believe him!" old Mr. Malpert voiced out to them. "Help! Let me out!"

Miles looked at Becky. "Wow, this sounds more serious than it first seemed. I think we should call the police, right?"

smack!

"You dog-shit-for-brains, dickless imbecile!" Becky yelled, then grabbed Miles by his collar and *shook* him. "You think I give a *fuck* about some nutty old man locked up in back? Dick-brain! Hammer-head! Back home, we got a living room full of kids with their legs growing out of their fuckin' shoulders! This guy says he can fix 'em, then *that's* the priority, not some nutty-ass old *fuck* locked up in a room. He can *rot* for all I care! *Fuck* him!"

Miles stood shocked at his wife's tirade. "Honey, that's a very hostile attitude. You'll be old some day too, you know. You should have more compassion for the elderly."

"*Fuck* the elderly and *fuck* him! We've got important shit to get done and here you are harping about some senile nut-job scientist with Alzheimer's! It's old motherfuckers like him who are bankrupting Medicare and Social Security—the government ought to put 'em all in a pile and bulldoze them into the into the fuckin' Grand Canyon!" and then she shoved Miles at the door. "I oughta kick your candy-ass up and down the street! You're a *disgrace* to manhood!" and with that Miles yet again burst into tears and stumbled toward the car.

Back at the house, all normalcy returned for the children. They were all put back in the bounce house, told to jump up and down, and Pete crawled under the base and showed Jack and Miles the hard-to-see little black button on the side of the panel housing. He pushed it once and, presto! Problem solved! Everybody had the right head, the right genitals, and their arms and legs were in the right place. The kids forgot about their previous quandary rather quickly, and soon were milling about with all the other kids, watching the clowns and magicians, playing Frisbee and Nerf darts, marveling over the animals, doing pony rides, and stuffing their mostly fat faces with the fantastic food the caterers provided.

And with the catastrophe behind them now, naturally, the adults retreated to the liquor bar to indulge in their favorite well-earned drinks. They decided at once not to tell anyone else what happened, and they would reinforce that suggestion to any of the kids who'd been affected. Who would believe such a tale? *They'd think we're all nuts*, Miles realized.

Ordinarily he was a beer drinker, but right now, loaded up with Becky's hormones, he was not at all hesitant to make himself a milksop, sissified Strawberry Lemonade Vodka Cocktail with a fucking little umbrella in it. *That's damn good!* he told himself. But then a sudden itch impelled him to scratch his pussy again and that's when it occurred to him: "Holy moly! We were so busy changing the kids back to normal, I completely forgot about me and Becky!"

"You're probably pretty anxious to get Becky's pussy out of your pants," Teddi laughed.

"You ain't kidding!" Miles guffawed. "And I need my pride and joy right back here where it belongs! Let's get out to the bounce house, Becky," but then he looked around and saw no trace of his wife. "Anybody seen where Becky went?"

"She probably went to the bathroom," Jack suggested. "Or maybe she's out back with the kids."

At just that moment, Becky was not in the bathroom, nor was she out back with the kids. Instead, she was speeding down the road toward the interstate, in her $90,000 Cadillac. The look in her eyes might be described as manically gleeful. By now Miles had left several messages on her cellphone, and on each one he sounded a little bit more disconcerted than the previous. "Honey," she could hear the message on speakerphone. "I'm getting a little worried. Where are you, baby? We need to jump back into the bounce house so I can get my dick back and you can have your vagina. Honey? Honey?"

"Fuck that shit, Miles," Becky whispered to herself and grinned. She turned off her phone, and then gave that big package between her legs a deliberate, satisfying squeeze. "If you think you're getting your cock back, don't hold your breath. Oh, and have fun spending the rest of your life with my pussy…"

THE JAR

*M*an, *this is some place to "sit,"* Alex immediately thought.
      He waited patiently, but still cruxed, in what the stone-faced doorman had called "the Sitting Room." It was probably a hundred feet long, fifty wide, and twenty high; expensive chairs and finely upholstered couches took up quite a bit of the floorspace.

The doorman, or whatever he was, got Alex seated at a table made of clear Lucite with matching chairs. "Mr. Sombrack will be with you shortly. His infirmities make it harder for him to get around these days, and he apologizes for the delay."

"Uh, no problem," Alex said, still a bit winded by the sumptuousness of the room, which only left him to wonder about all the other rooms in the house. A place like this, in the middle of a city? It was akin to one of those six-story Manhattan brownstones. And who exactly this Clifford Sombrack was, Alex had no idea, save for parsimonious references on Google about being a successful financier and entrepreneur.

Oh, well, he resigned. *I'm here, so let's see what this is all about...*

The walls of the immense room were covered by elaborately framed oil paintings. Alex was a digital artist himself, and his

view was this: *Digital is the future, oil is out. Oil is old hat.*
However, he had taken some prerequisite art history courses in
school and knew the real thing when he saw it. Most of the
adorning paintings *had* to be copies. He spotted one version of
de Kooning's *Two Women*, the original of which would be worth
millions; yet here it was, jammed amid other less recognizable
works, like an afterthought. Here, also, was a pastel version of
Munch's *The Scream*; Munch was known to have created
multiple prints and variants of his particular canvas, which
would enjoy a reputation of existing as one of the most valuable
paintings in history. Could this pastel here be one of those
variants—again, worth millions? Or, more likely, multiple
millions?

Alex rubbed his eyes. *Who the fuck is Clifford Sombrack?*

Another painting caught his eye, not from any potential
classical importance but due to a brazen and quite out-of-place
flavor of eroticism. It was a large oil of a nude, executed Pollock-
style by gobbets of paint seemingly dripped onto the canvas. It
depicted a blurred, curvaceous figure, nearly faceless save for
slits for eyes and a short blonde tumult for hair. But when Alex
narrowed his eyelids (much like the slit-eyes of the subject), the
painting shifted into an almost photographically sharp focus,
offering Alex a strained glimpse of a phenomenally attractive
woman with a radiant smile, a precise hairless gash between
her legs, and large buoyant breasts nearly three-dimensional.

"Shit," he muttered to himself, noticing a surge at his crotch.
"That's what I call effective painting…"

What had brought him here was an email query regarding
his digital artwork. A man named Martense was making an
inquiry for a man named Sombrack, the former being the
attorney for the latter.

"Mr. Sombrack would like to meet you, as he is an admirer
of your work and would like to discuss the possibility of

engaging you on retainer. Your airfare, accommodations, and all other expenses will be assumed by Mr. Sombrack. A ten-thousand-dollar consulting fee has already been sent to your PayPal. If you are previously detained or simply don't want to make the trip, you may keep the fee to defray any inconvenience."

Sure enough, when Alex logged onto his PayPal account, he found it mysteriously increased by $10,000.

The fidelity of the proposal was hard to question, so, as he was not "previously detained," Alex accepted the invitation (who wouldn't, under such conditions?), and several days later found himself here, sitting in a Lucite chair at a Lucite table in a giant room full of spectacular art.

So here I am...

The room seemed to exist within a void of awry proportions. One moment, it appeared larger than he'd first thought; the next, smaller. A number of alcoves and doors could be detected along the walls, whereas upon entrance, he'd not noticed them.

So this guy wants to buy digital art from me? He questioned the surmise. *It looks to me that digital isn't his thing...*

From somewhere deeper within the edifice, he heard two voices—just the tiniest drifts of sound: a man and a woman. The man's tone sounded cranky or displeased, though his words couldn't be deciphered. However, Alex was fairly certain he heard a female utter the words, "Fuck you, you old fuck..."

Interesting, Alex thought.

A mirrored door on the wall clicked open, and next, an old bald man in a wheelchair was being pushed toward the table.

"Thank you for coming, young man!" he declared. "I'm Clifford Sombrack and I'd like you to know that I'm thrilled to meet an artist of your caliber. As you can tell,"—he waved a crabbed hand errantly about to indicate the paintings decorating the room—"I'm very interested in art."

Alex stood up and nodded. "Thanks for the invitation, sir. And I have to admit, this room is totally intriguing."

"It is, isn't it?" The reduction of proximity now revealed Sombrack to be a man of indeterminate advanced age—eighties, nineties? It was impossible to tell. He sat in the chair in a navy-blue robe and black slippers, and he was very thin. A shiny bald head, narrow face, and sunken eyes were the man's most salient features, fairly generic.

The buxom blonde pushing Sombrack's wheelchair wore a tight sheer sundress, canary-yellow, which elucidated a centerfold's body. She was barefoot. She grinned sardonically and said, "Clifford's seventy-eight but he doesn't look a day over a hundred and ten."

Sombrack smiled. "Out of your starting blocks so soon, sweetheart?" He glanced back to Alex. "This is Lena. She's my... Let me think. Not exactly my employee, nor my advisor in any way. And certainly not my wife and not my daughter. Not my nurse, really. Lena? How would you describe yourself in relation to me?"

Lena's eyes lit up. "Well, I guess you could say I used to be your fuck-dummy, but you don't do too much fucking these days, do you?"

"I think I could better describe you as a human catcher's mitt for my sperm and rancor, no?"

These remarks struck Alex dumb.

"No so much *sperm* nowadays, darling," the blonde retorted, then she shot a grin toward Alex. "Oh, he can still get it up and cum sometimes, but his average load wouldn't fill half an eyedropper."

Alex's mouth fell open. *What the fuck IS this?*

Sombrack laughed. "Let's not bore Alex with our indulgent banter. He's come a long way at my request. I trust your flight was tolerable?"

"Yes, it was, sir," Alex said. "First time I've ever flown first class. Thank you."

"Excellent! And before we start, let's imbibe in a bit of refreshment, shall we?"

Sombrack pushed a button on a device like a TV remote, and moments later, the butler appeared, pushing a glittery cart. From the cart he removed a pilsner glass and a large dark bottle, and placed them before Alex.

"Would you prefer that I pour, sir?" he asked.

"No, thanks, I got it," Alex said, and began to fill his glass. After the long trip, a beer sounded pretty good now. The brand was one he'd never heard of: Baltika.

"To acknowledge your Russian heritage," Sombrack announced, "I've chosen one of your country's most popular beers."

It made sense, sort of. "Oh, sure. My last name being Petrov, you know I have Russian ancestry. But I'm really just a Russian by name. Never been to Russia, and don't speak the language."

"It's a beautiful country and quite unique to western eyes," Sombrack said, and nodded when the butler handed him a brandy snifter. "Thank you, Portafoy."

"Oh, Portafoy?" Lena rushed. "I'll have a glass of—"

Sombrack held up a staying hand. "She'll have a glass of exactly *nothing*, Portafoy. Because the last thing Lena needs is alcohol. Her utter intolerance for such beverages is the stuff of legend."

Lena grimaced. "Oh, kick off, Clifford."

"I will one day, darling." Sombrack grinned at her. "Just...not today."

Lena smiled again at Alex. "Guys like Clifford are like lawyers and telemarketers. Too many."

Sombrack nodded amiably. "You'll have to forgive us, Alex. My relationship with Lena—the love of my life, by the way—is diverse and unrepresentative. You could call it a hackneyed love-hate relationship, but it likely seems to you a *hate*-hate relationship."

Lena affectionately rubbed Sombrack's shoulders. "If Clifford's taught me anything of value, it's that hate can be a very empowering emotion…"

"Yes. How do I hate thee, darling? Let me count the ways."

Alex sat agog before his beer. He couldn't process what was going on here. "I-I…um…uh, your relationship is your business and none of mine. But, uh, you mentioned something about my digital artwork?"

"Of course," Sombrack replied, gently sipping his brandy. "There's something about lovely Lena's corrosive attitude that often veers me off track—"

"Th corrosiveness is all you, honey," Lena said. "As much as I'd like to take credit for it…you ridiculous old scarecrow."

Sombrack abruptly leaned forward to address Alex and effectively ignored Lena's comment. "Yes, I regard your artwork as unique and captivating, and your style is awesome."

"Thank you," Alex said, but even he had to admit that, in the landscape of digital arts, there was little "awesome" about his style.

Sombrack again indicated the countless paintings populating the vast room. "And as you can see, I'm a bit of an art-glutton, though many might refer to me as a 'patron,' of the arts."

"He spends a disgusting amount of money on artwork that he forgets about after owning it for a month," Lena added. She pointed high on the wall. "That sketch way up there? It's an original Hieronymus Bosch, just a doodle, really, from the late 1400s. Clifford paid millions for it—"

"I happen to like Bosch," Sombrack said.

"Yeah, but it's so high up you can't even *see* the motherfucker." She chuckled. "This arrogant putz actually tried to *buy* the *Garden of Earthly Delights*. That's like trying to buy the fuckin' *Mona Lisa*."

Sombrack, for a moment, looked disconsolate. "I admit, it's true. I offered half a billion, but those elitist curmudgeons at the Museum of Prado said they would never sell for any price. Oh, well. C'est la vie."

But Alex remained waylaid. *This has to be bullshit. Is Sombrack really worth that kind of money? Gates, Murdoch, sure. But I've never heard of this guy...*

"Ah, but on to business," Sombrack continued. "And, Lena? Do see fit to keep your mouth shut for at least the next few minutes, hmm?"

"Anything for you, prick," Lena replied.

"Here is my offer, Alex." Sombrack took some papers out of a pouch hooked onto his wheelchair. "I think you'll find my proposal generous."

"Proposal?"

"I'll be happy to pay you a retainer of fifty-thousand dollars per month for no less than one year—"

Alex nearly spat out his beer.

"I will expect one piece of artwork per month, whose subjects will be based on my desires. The subjects *I* would most like to see, in your style of course." Lena took the papers, walked them over, and placed them before Alex. "The contract is cut and dry, I should think," Sombrack went on. "But you needn't feel rushed. Feel free to have your lawyer look it over if you'd prefer."

Alex didn't have a lawyer and, as he was still trying to comprehend the details of this very bizarre offer. Too much was happening too fast for him to assume any kind of logical bearing. Breathing heavily, he looked at the contract.

"And here is your first month's fee," Sombrack added, upon which Lena placed five $10,000 bands of hundred-dollar bills on the table.

It was impossible for Alex to calculate how much time passed with him staring at the money with his mouth open. *Fuck it*, he thought and signed the contract. "I don't know what to say, Mr. Sombrack. Thank you very much. I won't let you down."

Sombrack smiled contentedly. "I'm sure you won't, and I'm happy to inform you that your first assignment will be a full-bodied nude portrait of Lena. There are many such portraits about the house." He pointed to the Pollockesque oil of the blurry nude blonde.

This caught Alex off guard; he looked at Lena. "Oh, wow, I didn't realize it was you." He squinted again, to enjoy the optical effect. "That's a tremendous technique."

"Yes," Sombrack agreed. "It's by a painter I hired from Mexico. I wanted something catchy, like the famous Dali work. Looking at it plainly, you see a woman on the balcony, but when you squint, you see Lincoln's face. But you needn't worry about such technical gimmickry; I just want you to paint her through the veil of your own creative vision."

"I'll get started as soon as you want me to."

"It's no rush. Let Lena model for you tonight. You can take some snapshots. Stay the night, at least, and then you can go back home and begin. Or stay here for as long as you like. Either way is fine."

Alex felt woozy in his seat. "Well, yes, thanks. Let me give that some thought."

"You'll find Lena a very inspiring model…"

I…guess so, Alex thought, side-eyeing the woman's curvatures. He was about to ask for more details, but a cellphone rang.

Sombrack looked at his phone and said, "It's Blickensderfer in Geneva. I'm afraid I have to take this. My apologies, Alex."

"No problem," Alex said.

"And while I'm busy, Lena can regale you with her razor-sharp intellect."

"Eat shit and die," Lena said.

"How lovely!" Sombrack began to wheel himself down a side-hall to take his phone call. "Oh, here's an excellent idea. Show Alex the Collections Room—"

This suggestion struck Lena oddly, and she showed a pointed concern. "Are you sure about that, Clifford? He might hightail it out of here if he sees some of that stuff."

"Oh, I'm certain he won't," Sombrack said, wheeling away. "I can tell he's a spirited young man. And call security; show him the vault as well…"

Lena sighed. "The boss has spoken. Get ready to see some fucked-up stuff."

Intrigued, Alex followed her down one side of the room and into a little doored alcove. "So I take it Mr. Sombrack's, like, a billionaire?"

"He sure is," Lena wistfully replied. "But he's not in *Forbes* magazine, and you'll never see him on any World's Richest Men lists. He might even be worth more than Musk and that psycho oil sheik."

Alex pondered this.

Was Lena deliberately walking with a seductive gait, hips cocking? She didn't seem like the kind of woman who needed to play herself up. "He spends a lot of money to make sure he's *not* on any of those lists," she said. "Did you look him up online?"

"Well, yeah," he answered, unable to take his eyes off those swaying hips. "But barely found anything."

"That's the way he wants it. He hates people meddling in his business."

"Sure, sorry. I don't mean to pry."

"Oh, you've come a long way on spec. You have every right to ask anything you want. He can be an asshole sometimes but he's very *unlike* most rich people. You seem like a nice guy so…"

"So…"

"If you want my advice, take everything you can from the old bat. You should've asked for more than fifty grand a month."

Man…

Lena produced some small electronic device like a fob, and then the door at the end of the alcove opened. "All the paintings and artwork in the big room? They're nothing compared to what's in here."

"More paintings?" Alex asked.

"A few, but mostly other things," she answered, unenthused. "In here you'll see the extent of Clifford's indulgence—or madness. Whichever you prefer."

When they entered the much smaller room, Alex was stopped in his tracks by an oil painting of multiple rectangles that seemed somehow three-dimensional. "Is that a real Rothko?"

"Yes, it is, unfortunately." She shook her head at the painting. "Fuck, *I* could do that. Sixteen million he paid for that piece of crap. Looks like the guy used a fuckin' paint roller. Big deal."

Alex was disinclined to agree with her assessment.

The room was no bigger than the average living room, but surrounded by bright, startlingly white walls. Situated around the room in various places were shelves, counters, and what appeared to be tall storage cabinets.

Lena opened one and withdrew, with a frown, a dull bronze rectangle of metal about the size of a closed laptop. "A genuine Gutenberg plate from the 1400s. A page of the very first printed book on Earth was printed on this plate. Wanna touch it?"

Alex's wide-open expression wobbled. How could he resist? He touched the plate with a fingertip…

"See? No big deal." she attested. "It's just a piece of metal. Clifford paid five million for it. Chump change."

Alex was awed. To him, at least, it was a bit more than no big deal. *I just touched a plate that made the first printed Bible. Before that they were all hand-written by monks…*

"Now, here's something that's a little more interesting—its effect, I mean." Lena led him to a long table lined with purple silk, upon which rested a cylindrical glass dome about the size of a wok lid. She lifted the dome and picked up between her fingers what appeared to be a piece of bone the size of a segment of a Tootsie Roll. "Open your hand."

"Looks like a finger bone. Whose is it?"

"Open your hand." Then she paused, her aquamarine eyes fixed on his face. "Alex, do you happen to believe in the supernatural?"

What a bizarre question… Alex answered as honestly as he could, with an immediate, "No."

Lena placed the bone fragment into his palm.

In less than a second, Alex nearly came off his heels, from a surge of current, almost like electricity, that snapped from his palm and branched out to his entire body. *What the fuck?* Suddenly he could hear his own heart beating, and Lena's. His vision sharpened as quickly as if he'd put on glasses as well; he looked back at the Rothko painting and was able to see it as if greatly magnified. He could see the particular brush strokes over the canvas as well as dimples in the oddly colored paint. He could see the depths between the various layers of oil paint.

"Impossible," he muttered.

"Think so?" Lena said, smiling. "Look at my dress. I'll bet you can— Well, just look at my dress."

Alex faced her and scanned his vision up and down her yellow sundress. *Holy shit...* He could see the individual threads of the fabric, and then he could see *through* that fabric, beholding her barely veiled physique. He could see her nipples, her belly button, her hairless pubis, all in a macro-focused dimensionality.

Lena explained, "This is a middle phalange of a man's index finger, which carbon dates back to about 100 A.D. It's said to be a finger bone of St. Ignatius of Antioch, a great evangelizer in what was back then Syria. He did just about everything Jesus did: healed the lame, made the blind see and the deaf hear. He raised the dead. The only thing he didn't do was turn water to wine. Anyway, the Roman Emperor Trajan had Ignatius imprisoned for heresy against the silly Roman gods. He was sentenced to be eaten alive by dogs, but Trajan gave him a choice. Ignatius could avoid being executed if he denounced Christ and accepted the Roman gods." Lena grinned. "Ignatius, in not so many words, told the emperor to fuck himself, and then willingly walked into the dog pit. How's that for faith?"

But Alex was still buzzing in this bizarre extrasensory euphoria.

"Of course," Lena went on, "even with the carbon-date, a naysayer would insist it was a finger bone from anyone who lived in that time. But what do *you* think? Being that you've been lit up like a pinball machine since I put the bone in your hand?"

Alex, hairs sticking up all over his body, looked at the simple piece of bone. There was no way it could be connected to some hidden power source, no way that any kind of battery could be secreted in it…

He gave the bone back to Lena, who replaced it beneath the glass lid.

"Well?" she prompted.

Alex's preternatural buzz vanished. "I-I think I'm leaning toward a belief in the supernatural now…"

"Everybody does, and after holding that? Only an idiot wouldn't."

Alex felt out of breath now, once his connection with the fragment had been terminated.

She proceeded to one of the cabinets. "One time, must be ten years ago, I had that fragment in my hand while Clifford was fucking me." She chuckled. "The orgasm I had was at least a hundred times better than I've ever known." She shrugged. "If I'd died right then and there…I wouldn't have given a shit." She stopped at another item mounted in a frame on the wall. "Here's something that Clifford was all gunned up about." Within the frame, there'd been mounted a big square-headed iron mace studded with metal points; it had a wooden handle.

"Looks nasty," Alex commented.

"It was definitely nasty back in the 1200s, especially to a guy named Eric Glipping. He was the king of Denmark, and he got his head bashed in with that mace by some dude named Marsk Stig. Now, you tell me. Who the *fuck* would want something like that hanging on their wall?"

Alex opened his mouth to respond but all he could do was shake his head.

"Here we go," Lena said next, pointing to a shadow-box containing a curl of hair secured by a ribbon. "This lock of hair was once, in 1692, on the head of a woman named Bridget

Bishop. She was the first of the so-called Salem Witches to be hanged. But she was *not* a witch. None of them were."

Next, she picked up a small translucent block which housed some odd, pink objects. The objects appeared organic.

"This is a scream. Jennifer Wilcox, or Nancy Wilcox — shit, I don't remember. Porn chick who started in the Seventies. She had mud-flaps, you know, so she got her sugar daddy to have 'em cut off by a plastic surgeon. But the sugar daddy wanted to keep them, so he had them preserved in this epoxy like stuff. Isn't that a howler? Labiaplasties are common these days, but see, this was the first pair to be preserved. When they went up at auction, Clifford just *had* to have them. Why? Because they were the first." She extended her hand. "Pussy lips, I'm not kidding. Clifford paid a couple hundred grand for some tramp's pussy lips."

Alex, in spite of the morbidity of the item, had to chuckle. "Next, you'll be telling me that Mr. Sombrack's got John Holmes' penis in a jar."

She shot him the strangest look. "No such luck; Holmes was cremated. But it's funny you should mention such a thing..."

Back came Portafoy, sided by two giant meat-racks in suits. Each had a bulge under his right armpit. The men were each six-five at least and the arms in their suit sleeves were about the width of Alex's thighs.

Portafoy nodded blank-faced to Lena, pulled back a curtain, and exposed a stainless-steel vault door with a round wheel in the center, like a vault in a bank. Into a keyhole, he inserted a key on a chain around his neck, then Lena stepped over and did the same. They turned the keys and a loud CHUNK! was heard.

Are they opening a door or launching an ICBM? Alex thought.

Then the three men departed.

"Were those two guys bodyguards?" Alex asked. "They look like football players."

Disinterested, Lena answered, "One used to be in Seal Team Six. The other was an Army Ranger or some shit. Clifford's paranoid about all this junk he owns. And if anyone breaks into *this* house?" She shook her head. "They're leaving feet-first."

Next she pulled open the vault door. Lights came on automatically.

She looked at Alex with a bemused smile. "Very few people have ever been allowed to set foot in this room. You're not gonna believe the shit that's here. There are people starving in the world, and Clifford spends his money on outrageous crap like this."

Alex followed her into the vault.

Three carmine curtains stood at the small room's rear wall. Lena pulled the cord on the curtain at the left, which revealed a glass or clear Lexan box about three feet high and two wide, on a pedestal that stood knee high. Sitting in the box was nothing more than an ordinary metal bucket.

"A bucket," Alex intoned.

"Yeah, but a special one if you're all fucked up in the head like Clifford." Lena seemed dour. "On November twenty-third, 1963, President Kennedy's autopsy, after much to-do, had been performed at Walter Reed Army Medical Center. During that autopsy, Kennedy's brain had been removed from his skull at the request of a ballistic examiner. After the autopsy, Kennedy's body was put in a coffin and taken out of the building by Secret Service men and several military officers. However, the brain had not been put back into the skull. Several hours later, Kennedy's physician, Rear Admiral George Burkley, arrived at the hospital and demanded custody of Kennedy's brain, with orders from Bobby Kennedy, the president's brother, who also happened to be the attorney general of the United States. No one argued with Burkley. He left the hospital with this bucket, containing Kennedy's brain. But no one knows where the brain is now. Burkley claimed he put it in Kennedy's coffin at Jackie Kennedy's request; other sources claim that the brain, or at least some of it, was kept at the National Archives. Where it is now — who knows? But what's relevant here is that this bucket is undoubtedly the bucket that transported Kennedy's brain out of the medical center, and at the bottom of this bucket are still traces of what is called 'cranial debris' and some of that debris is composed of a small amounts of Kennedy's gray matter. It's hard to see, but…look close."

Alex peered downward and saw, at the bottom of the bucket, some rust, some tiny flecks of things that could've been skull splinters, and some splotches of a dark desiccated material that was otherwise difficult to describe with any clarity.

"So that little bit of stuff at the bottom is a tiny bit of JFK's brain," he said more than asked.

Lena nodded, almost as if embarrassed. "Brain is brain, if you ask me. I don't care if that brain belonged to the country's most beloved president, or just another guy who schlonged Marilyn Monroe. It's just *brain*. But to Clifford?" She shook her head.

For whatever reason, Alex wasn't terribly impressed, and was not inclined to ask or even wonder how much Sombrack had paid for the bucket, nor how he'd managed to procure it.

He looked at the second curtain.

Now Lena was grinning rather sardonically. "Okay. This one's a doozy. Who's the greatest singer in American history?"

Alex thought for a moment, was about to answer, but then was hit by a jolt of alarm. "No. No. Please say you don't have Elvis Presley's head behind that curtain."

"Not Elvis's head," she said and opened the curtain. "Try Elvis's *shit*."

Alex gave a thousand-yard stare at this next Lexan box.

No, was all he could think. How such a thing as this could be preserved, he couldn't fathom. Sealed in a vacuum? Suspended in epoxy? Alex didn't know and didn't want to know.

All he knew was what his eyes verified: he was looking at a *huge* pile of feces. It had to be enough feces to fill Admiral Burkley's bucket twice; that's how much shit sat plopped inside the display case. Alex was incapable of speech.

"Everyone knows the story," Lena began. "Elvis died while trying to take a shit. He hadn't had a bowel movement in a long time, because he was a chronic Demerol addict. Opioids, when not used as per prescription, cause *serious* constipation. He was trying to huff out a grunter on the toilet, managed to drop a two-foot-long turd, felt a twinge in his chest, stood up, then had a massive heart attack and collapsed to the floor. That's where he died. His girlfriend and some other people did CPR, but it was a no-go. He'd previously been hospitalized for several serious health problems, including an enlarged heart, malignant hypertension, diabetes, irregular heartbeat. Add obesity to all that, and it's time-bomb city. But here's the kicker. When Elvis died, he weighed three hundred and fifty pounds." Lena paused dramatically, then grinned. "Thirty-nine of those pounds, according to the autopsy report, were excrement ballooning his bowels." Then she extended her hand to the display case.

Alex could only keep staring. "And Mr. Sombrack *bought* Elvis's shit…"

"That's right. It was removed from his intestines at his autopsy. DNA tests verified that it's Elvis' poop. Cool, huh?" she said sarcastically, then made a gag gesture. "And if you think that's something, *I'll* show you something…"

The third curtain opened.

"Gimme a break," Alex uttered.

What looked back at him from another pedestal was a dick in a jar.

Granted, it was a *big* dick, an elephantine penis still attached to a wrinkled scrotum that seemed still to house the testicles. The entire works floated eerily (corona pointed down) in what Alex could only presume was formaldehyde. He leaned forward, squinting at the foot-long piece of tubular meat, hoping for a dead giveaway that it was fake.

It didn't look fake. "Fuck," he said.

Lena seemed a little antsy as she stood in place. Was the sight of this gargantuan sex organ stimulating her a bit? It seemed so.

"Who's the lucky guy?" Alex ventured.

"Do you know who Grigori Rasputin was?"

Alex peered at her. "The whack job Russian mystic? Sure, I took history classes. The guy was an orthodox minister or something, sweet-talked his way into Czar's inner circle, evidently was able to stop the Czar's hemophiliac son from bleeding whenever he cut himself."

"Exactly. He was a devoutly religious man—in his own way, I mean—and led church services several times a day. But he was also a raging sex maniac. No hypocrisy there, huh? This guy fucked just about every woman in the Czar's palace. Once word got around how big his dick was? Are you kidding me?" She pointed to the monstrosity in the jar. "The women followed him around like puppies; he couldn't get rid of them. He must've fucked at least five women a day. Most notably, he was regularly boffing Czar Nicholas's wife, Alexandra. She couldn't get enough of that wang."

Alex wearily rubbed his face with his hands. "So...somebody killed him, right?"

"Damn straight. Remember, this was right before the Russian Revolution in 1917. The government, the military establishment, and the Czar's power men were all in chaos. There was one guy named Prince Felix Yusupov who thought Rasputin was using his influence over the Czar to undermine the war against Germany. Add to that, Yusupov, even though he was married to the Czar's niece and had a kid, was gayer than fuckin' Liberace. He had the hots for Rasputin, but Rasputin wanted none of that shit. So Yusupov, one of the richest and most powerful men in the country, didn't take to being rebuffed. He got his buddies together, got Rasputin drunk and fed him with cake laced with enough cyanide to kill a gorilla. But Rasputin didn't die. So then they shot Rasputin in the chest, but the fucker *still* didn't die. Then they beat him with clubs, but Rasputin crawled out of the palace, so then they shot him again and drove over him with a Rolls-Royce Silver Shadow (Clifford bought the car from a collector in Ukraine). And, wouldn't you know it? Rasputin *still* didn't die. But they had to get rid of the body, so they said fuck it, and stuffed Rasputin in a canvas sack and dropped the bag into a nearby river. It's interesting to note that when Rasputin's body was pulled out of the river the following spring, the coroner found the cause of death to be drowning. Creepy, huh?"

"Yeah, creepy," Alex said. "But what about—"

"Oh, yeah, but before they dropped Rasputin into the drink, Yusupov cut off his works and put it in a jar of formaldehyde. See, the prince absolutely *envied* Rasputin's giant whopper of a cock. And that's what you're lucky enough to be looking at now." Lena stooped over and grinned more intently at the hideously large genitals floating in the jar.

My God, Alex thought. *Who ARE these people?* But, all the while, something had been ticking in the back of his mind. *Rasputin's dick. Cut off. Put in a big jar …*

Then it struck him. "Wait a minute! I've read about this! That's not Rasputin's dick. Mr. Sombrack got ripped off hard.

Look it up on Google. Rasputin's severed cock and balls are on public display in a museum in St. Petersburg, in a jar of formaldehyde. There are tons of pictures of it!"

Lena now stood with her arms crossed, nodding and grinning all the more. "Oh, there's a dick in a jar in St. Petersburg, all right... but it's not Rasputin's, it's a substitute. Some other poor bastard's giant dick has been standing in for the real McCoy for over a hundred years. Clifford's research department got wind of the switch, so Clifford bought the cock and profiled its DNA from a tooth from Rasputin's son, Dmitri. The DNA from the tooth was a match. Ain't no doubt about it. The cock in that jar once swung between the legs of the Mad Monk Grigori Rasputin."

Alex was left to stare, head tilted, at the absurd and grotesque thing in the jar. "How-how much did Mr. Sombrack pay for—"

"Don't ask," Lena said. "The number would make you sick to your stomach."

"I suspect it would. It would likely sicken the *nation*," Sombrack's voice surprised them from behind. He wheeled his chair into the room, smiling contentedly. "But what a man does with his money is his business. Do you agree, Alex?"

That dick must've cost millions... Alex didn't know what to say but he was not about to criticize a man who just put fifty thousand dollars in his pocket. "If you want some guy's severed cock and you can afford it...why not?"

"Excellent! I so admire honesty, Alex. Most people are just so disingenuous, it's beyond belief. Lena, for instance, constantly lambastes me for not giving money to the so-called *poor*. But then, when you take into account how much money I've given *her* over the years, and I assure you, it's enough to collapse the Parthenon, she's given *not one thin dime* of it to anyone."

Lena fumed. "Why don't you roll that chair into heavy traffic, Clifford?"

"Oh, but sweetheart, you wouldn't want me to do that, would you? Then you'd go back to being a homeless drunk, grifter, and prostitute, yes?"

Lena smiled, unfazed. "If you don't shut up, Clifford, I'll tell Alex all about how you need Trimix injections just to get your dick hard."

Oh, boy, Alex thought

"I don't see anything to be embarrassed about in that, darling." Sombrack countered. "A man my age?"

Lena veered her near-perpetual heinous grin at Alex. "Listen to this shit; I'm serious. I stick a fuckin' *hypodermic needle* in the base of Clifford's cock anytime he wants to get it up, and it makes for the happiest moment of my day. Oh, yeah, he says it doesn't hurt, but gimme a break. It's a fuckin' *needle*. In his *dick*. And any time he winces from the pain...my pussy soaks."

Sombrack rubbed his hands together. "Yes, and then I fuck her like a two-dollar whore. It provides for an exemplary satisfaction, believe me. But now, away with Lena's juvenile animosity. I'm glad you've had the opportunity to behold the most esteemed item in my collection."

"I gotta admit," Alex said, more in a daze. "I thought Elvis's shit was the kicker, but—"

Sombrack nodded. "But Rasputin's cock in a jar? You don't see that every day, hmm?"

"No, sir, I don't."

"Something to tell your grandkids someday!" A sudden shift in the old man's demeanor, from the garrulous to the laconic, changed his disposition. "But here's something you should know, Alex. Mr. Rasputin's genitals serve as the chief reason I called you here."

Alex blinked at the inexplicable words. "I...don't understand."

Sombrack raised an invigorated finger. "Ah, but you will, when I explain at dinner, which is served, by the way, in a few hours. I'll see the two of you then." As he began to wheel away, he said, "And, Lena, dear. Do show Alex the Garden of Gethsemane. Oh, and—"

"Need help changing your Depends?" Lena called out.

"Oh, no thank you. I need to fill them up some more before I order Portafoy to smother you in them. Ta-ta, my darling!"

This is so fucked up, Alex thought. "What the hell did he mean by that?"

"That the dick is the main reason you're here?" Her magnificent breasts rose and fell as she shrugged. "Got no idea. But we'll find out."

"And what else did he say? The Garden of Gethsemane? Isn't that where—"

"Jesus was betrayed by Judas," she refreshed his memory. "The actual garden is still intact in Jerusalem, by the way." Now her gaze on him darkened with something like veiled prurience. "Let's go down here. You like art."

Alex felt a jolt when she took his hand and led him down the hall.

"Look, this is bugging me," he said. "What does Rasputin's dick have to do with me being here?"

"I don't know, but you're really curious, aren't you?" They walked hand in hand down the main gallery, millions of dollars of art looking down on them. "Clifford is nuts. Don't worry about it."

Alex couldn't have felt more awkward. "He wants me to do an NFT of Rasputin's *dick?*"

"I don't know. Wouldn't surprise me, though. Like I said earlier, take as much as you can from that withered old fuss-budget. Whenever he offers you money, hold out for more."

Several yards down the gallery, she turned into yet another concealed doorway, and led Alex into a spacious, high-ceilinged room whose front wall was almost completely occupied by a huge framed oil painting of Jesus. Along the three remaining walls stood tables displaying old books.

"Check out *this* library," Lena said with a smirk.

Alex made a cursory examination of some of the books, many covered by tooled leather and with gilded bindings. They all seemed to be in Latin, Greek, and other foreign languages. Religious iconography and full-page illustrations were found in all, in the form of skilled engravings: representations of Jesus, Moses, King David, the Apostles, all powerfully rendered.

"Evidently, Mr. Sombrack has a serious interest in divinity," Alex observed.

"In a sense, that's very true."

"But in another sense?"

Lena paused. "Let's just say he's a fan of both sides of the fence."

This, Alex contemplated, as he moved to the next table, and picked up a tome entitled *Fuga Satanae* by someone named Stampas, printed in 1619. *Song of Satan?* he guessed at the translation. "So I take it Mr. Sombrack is a satanist?"

"Oh, no." She cocked her hip again, which for some reason compelled an excruciatingly erotic image. "He believes in God and he believes in the Devil. He believes in Heaven and Hell, in good and evil."

Alex didn't see what this had to do with anything pertinent, but he had to ask, "Do *you?*"

Her current pose in the sheer summer dress suggested that her breasts existed without flaw. "I believe I don't give a fuck.

And why should I? It doesn't matter one way or the other. Here's what I believe: I believe that old fossil in the wheelchair should buy me a fuckin' Lamborghini. But he won't, just to bust my chops. Fuck, he bought Portafoy one, and he bought the goddamn housekeeping manager a new Corvette."

Alex just kept looking at her, in spite of her hypocrisy. That body. Those curves and breasts. The thought barged into his mind: *I wish I could fuck her…*

"But the painting's what it's all about," she said, and then opened a fold-down chair and placed it several yards back from the painting of Jesus. "Sit here. Give it a good look." Lena remained behind him as he took his seat.

The details of the painting were thus: kneeling before Jesus was a man in leather armor whose left cheek was swathed in blood. Jesus, meanwhile, held His hand against the bleeding man's left temple. In the background stood several Roman soldiers and astonished men in tunics, and surrounding them all were olive trees and flowers. The painting had something of a classical flare, but not much was noteworthy.

Big deal, Alex thought. He was waiting for something to happen, perhaps something like what happened when he held the finger bone of St. Ignatius. But after a minute, no untoward experience was observed, nor did anything amid the painting's composition take his notice.

"It's by some no-name painter from the 1500s," Lena said, "depicting Christ's arrest in the Garden of Gethsemane. But, according to Clifford, it's the best rendering of the scene."

"The scene?"

"This happened the night before Jesus was crucified. Judas squealed to the Romans where Jesus would be that evening, and it's where the infamous Judas Kiss took place. That's how Judas let the Romans know which guy was Jesus, by kissing his cheek. Several messengers from the high priest Caiaphas stormed into the garden to help arrest Jesus, and one of them is that dude there with blood on his cheek. His name was Malchus. When Malchus reached to grab Jesus, John the Apostle stepped forward, drew his sword, and cut off Malchus' ear. Really fucked him up." Lena smiled cunningly. "This pissed Jesus off bigtime, and that's when He said, 'Those who live by the sword die by the sword.'"

Alex was reflecting back. "I think I remember this from Sunday school."

"Yeah. Jesus picked up the severed ear, pressed it against Malchus' head, and healed him. The fuckin' ear *grew back.* I'm pretty sure it was Jesus' last miracle."

"Okay." Alex sat duped. Overall, in point of technique and dimension, the painting was mediocre. "And *why* did Mr. Sombrack want me to see this?"

"Who the fuck cares?" Lena said, just as she came around from behind. She'd skimmed off the sundress and stood blaringly nude right in front of him.

Alex could've melted like butter into warm bread.

"Let's do this," Lena said, stepping over his thighs and sitting down. "You've got nothing better to do now, right?"

Alex couldn't answer. The sight of her nude, perfect body, her weight on his thighs, and the brazen proximity of her breasts left him in a dense, euphoric trance.

She was looking down, with an expression of intent concentration. One hand felt up his crotch, hardening his cock in his pants and making it leak.

"You can fuck me here, and fuck me again tonight when I pose for you." She sighed. "It's been so fuckin' long since I've had a cock in me that's not ancient."

Alex squirmed, pinned down in the chair. So much pre-ejaculatory fluid pumped out of his squashed cock that it began to leave a wet spot. She squeezed more intently, harder and with more precision.

Don't cum in your pants! he ordered himself. Now she was unbuckling his belt, his cock pulsing.

But that's when something snapped in his mind like someone breaking a pencil.

He grabbed her wrists, made her desist. "Fuck! I can't do this!"

She made a face at him. "Why the hell not? You can't be gay. If you were gay, your cock wouldn't be harder than a nightstick right now."

He started to push her off his spread thighs. "I can't..."

"Feels to me like you can. I'm not hot enough? I'm pretty sure I'm better looking than most woodpile snakes."

He was staring right into her body. Perfect, perfect. Even the pores in her skin were perfect, erotic somehow. Those mind-boggling breasts, those big delineated nipples not a foot from his face. He began to lean forward, sex-drive manipulating his consciousness, to suck one of the nipples.

"Go on," she whispered. "Suck it if you want..."

He was halfway to actually squeezing her breasts, when the pencil snapped again. "I'm not gonna fuck the girlfriend of a guy who just gave me a shitload of cash!"

She began to scowl. Veins were beating perceptibly in her breasts. "Don't be an idiot. He *wants* you to fuck me." She pointed to a high corner in the room where a video camera was mounted. "He's a voyeur. You fucking me is part of what he's paying you for."

Overload. His thought processes were skewing, and finally he pushed her off and stood up.

"I don't believe you," she said, visibly perturbed.

"This is too fucked up. I don't even know what all this is about!"

Lena shook her head, smirking. "Right now, it's all about me trying to get laid."

"This scene is too much for me. I'm not fucking in front of a camera, for shit's sake! And the guy just made my year by the money he gave me! I'd feel like I was pissing on him!"

Her magnificent body seemed to droop. "Wow, you're a weird one." She looked up at the camera in the corner. "You hear that, Clifford? How's that for loyalty? He won't fuck me because he's loyal to you."

Alex was trying not to look frantic as he rearranged himself. "I gotta get out of here. Where am I supposed to go till dinner?"

Silence dropped.

Alex looked up at the massive panting and suddenly felt asinine. *I've got a hard-on in front of Jesus.*

Lena put her sundress back on. "Come on," she said. "I'll show you your room. And don't worry, there are no cameras there, so no one will see you beating off…"

———

Dinner was served. The dining room was in a more distant wing of the house, densely appointed in a Colonial motif, and they all sat at a twenty-foot-long stained-oak table. Murky paintings adorned the wall. Servants, overseen by Portafoy, laid out the food with antique silverware. Alex looked at one of the forks and saw evidence of its maker imprinted on the back: Paul Revere Silversmiths.

"I thought it would be fun to indulge the cuisine of your homeland," Sombrack informed him. "These are all very authentic dishes; in fact—" He pointed to a plate of dumpling-like things—"unless I'm misconstrued, Pelmeni is Russia's national dish."

But Alex was still out of sorts. The Pelmenis looked like dim sum. He was unable to appear impressed, and he didn't give a shit about Russian cuisine. *Where's a fuckin' McDonald's?* All he could think to say was, "It looks great."

He sipped his Baltika beer, not really tasting it. The weird business with Lena was pushing his tolerance to its limits. He didn't know which end was up. And he knew this: Sombrack seemed to have no real interest in digital artwork.

Other dishes were identified and explained to him: Blinis — caviar-filled "pancakes"; the ubiquitous Beef Stroganoff; Shashlik — akin to ka-bobs of meat-chunks and onions; marinated beef strips in aspic; and, of course, Borscht. Alex could take or leave any of it.

Sombrack sipped Russian Gold Standard vodka, while Lena frowned at her lemonade.

Amusedly, she said, "Alex asked me if you believed in God."

"And I trust you told him that I most assuredly do," the old man replied, "just as I very much believe in His counterpart. One without the other makes no sense. Do you mind discussing your own religious beliefs, Alex?"

It was an annoying query. Alex merely said, "This is probably a very dull answer, but I don't really believe in anything."

"Ah, but perhaps you will before long." Sombrack looked at Lena, and she glanced back at him, as if sharing some mysterious comprehension. "The large painting of Jesus healing Malchus, for instance." Sombrack took a bite out of his Volga caviar-crammed blini. "It says so much more than what it shows — the goal, I should think, of any conscientious artist. It suggests all the questions of the universe and challenges the viewer to genuinely confront his or her believes."

Alex didn't get it. "How so, sir?"

"Well, traditionally people tend to say that they don't believe in anything they can't see, correct? But that's fallacy. I can't see a hydrogen molecule, but I still believe it's the most abundant element in the universe. I didn't see the Battle of Leipzig, but I believe it put an end to Napoleon's military capabilities. Do I believe that Jesus brought Lazarus back from the dead? Yes, because the number and quality of the witnesses strike me as credible. Mary Baker Eddy, founder of the Church of Christian Science, one day saw a row of handicapped children on the beach, all paraplegic and in wheelchairs. While walking along the shoreline, after she'd passed them, all of the children stood up and began to walk, and walk they did for the rest of their lives. There were scores of witnesses to this event. I believe it, and I believe that Moses parted the Red Sea and God created the Universe. It's said in the Bible that St. Peter, after Christ's death, approached a crippled beggar who'd never walked in his life. The beggar's legs were just bones covered with skin. Peter told him to stand up and he did, and instantly the beggar was standing on healthy muscular legs. But I'll have you know that none of this is fantasy, nor can it be explained by mysticism or magic. It's simple science. Granted, a science that's too complex to be fully understood or objectified, but science nonetheless. It's *celestial* science. But there must be a counterpart, yes? The reverse pole? We can call it whatever you like, but I choose to think of it as *occult* science."

"Are we having fun yet?" Lena asked, smirking. She'd replaced her yellow sundress with a low-cut evening gown of glittery sapphirine material, which turned her into a cleavage-fissured pedestal for awesome breasts, sparkling in place. "Be a little *more* boring, why don't you, Clifford?"

Sombrack steepled his fingers in front of him. "One day, dear, I'll build for you a solid gold gibbet and hang you from it."

"In a wheelchair? Don't make me laugh. I'd kick your ancient, wrinkled ass up and down the street. You're older than coal, Clifford."

Sombrack shrugged. "I'll get the guards to do it. Then get baseball bats and have a piñata party. But there's no candy in *you*, I don't suspect. Just searing, steaming hatred. It's not my fault you never made *anything* of your life. And back to the topic of Rasputin… Oh, if he were alive today! I'd pay millions to watch him fuck the living shit out of you with that obscenity between his legs. Indeed, I'd pay him to fuck you to death."

Lena smiled at Alex. "Sweet, isn't he? I'm so lucky to have a boyfriend as nice as Clifford!"

Sombrack sighed. "There are other elements that highlight my, shall we say, incised *proclivities*. We'll have to show you the chapel."

"Chapel?"

"Yes. The room in which abodes my faith. The White House has a chapel, and so does the Hall of Versailles, the Kremlin, and the Great Mosque. Well, there's one here too. Why shouldn't I have my own? A specific place, a sanctorum, in which I give praise and thanks to my Creator?"

Alex dully shivered as Lena surprised him by running her foot up his leg under the table. He looked at her just as she silently mouthed to him, *I wanna fuck you…* After this, she said aloud, "I think you'll like the Chapel."

"But getting back to our primary discourse," Sombrack intruded, devouring a duck tongue. "The painting of Jesus healing Malchus, reconnecting the latter's ear to his body, in a fully functional state. I've explained this miracle as an example of celestial science. And if we accept that, then there's no logical choice but to accept evidence of the opposite. Do you agree?"

Alex was feeling headachy and tired. "Oh, yeah, why not? God's science, versus the Devil's? Is that what you mean?"

Sombrack's brow rose and he veered another glance to Lena. "Yes. All science is, when you get down to the nitty-gritty, is math. For instance, the scientists at Los Alamos knew the atom bomb would work long before they tested it. Because they did the math. In their heads, they all *knew* it would work. They weren't even surprised when the first test proved a colossal success. So, yes. Math. Following me yet? Malchus's ear?"

Alex squinted now, groggily confused. "Not...really..."

"Two plus two doesn't *always* equal four," Sombrack replied with the tightest of smiles.

"In this case, it equals twelve," Lena added, "as in twelve *inches*." She got up, walked around, and stood behind Alex's seat.

Sombrack chuckled. "I'm afraid the young man's a bit distracted by your horn-dog tits and bowery-tramp air. But I can hardly blame him for that!"

By now, Alex's head was spinning like a centrifuge. Lena leaned over and began to overtly rub his crotch, prodding the limp, confused parcel of flesh satcheled between his legs. "Can I give him a last one for fun?"

Sombrack waved the suggestion off. "Don't bother. I'm too excited to get on with this..."

Two and two equals twelve, Alex's thoughts echoed.

His vision was dimming as Lena's hand played over his crotch, either erotically or mockingly.

Alex had only time to think, *Stupid! I just fell for the oldest trick in the book...* and then his consciousness turned black, and in the most hackneyed fashion, he went face-first into his Stroganoff.

Echoic darkness. A cloudy sensation like floating in murk. And a steady distant beeping sound...

What the fuck?

Gradually the rim of his vision admitted more light and then slowly expanded, and the clarity of the beeping sharpened, until he realized that each beep coincided with a beat of his heart.

His mouth felt desert-dry. At the peripheries of his sense of sight he detected the movement of what could only be people. Then he stared.

Several middle-aged men were removing blue masks and garments like surgical gowns. Then they each donned suit jackets, all displaying poker faces.

"Thank you, gentlemen," Sombrack's enlivened voice leapt out of view. "Your expertise is greatly appreciated. I'm sure I'll have more assignments for you in the future."

The men said nothing in response; instead, they seemed glum, sullen. Portafoy passed to each of them a briefcase as they left, and then the door was closed, sealing in more beeping silence.

The grogginess was lifting; Alex was able to let his eyes wander.

He was in something like an intensive-care suit, surrounded by various pieces of hospital equipment. An I.V. stand was at his left, like an attendant, with a line of tubing extending down to his arm. Every minute, a blood-pressure cuff inflated automatically on his upper arm.

"You're back, Alex!" Sombrack's voice enthused. "How delightful! Any dreams? Any somnambulant images that you recall? I'd be very interested in hearing them."

Alex disregarded the intrusive chatter; instead, he was looking around the room's walls now, noticing how this chamber sorely differed from anything close to a surgery suite.

On the walls hung dozens of framed art-objects depicting an obvious leitmotif of diablerie or artistic praise for Lucifer.

Diagrams, sigils, picturesque representations, spells and incantations on ancient parchments, etc.

"The very blueprints of occult science," Sombrack said, "and the very essence of what we've been discussing. Quite a bit of it is all about faith, Alex. To you, these framed displays on the wall are no more than flamboyant artwork and arcane ancient script. However, when amassed in proper the domain of *faith*—" Here, Sombrack raised a withered finger. "—they are all power totems. They are all aligned *devices*. Think of an accumulation of batteries, if you will. When one conglomerates a number of single batteries, what is the result? More power, more *energy*. And when that surplus of energy is wielded by devoted practitioners, the energy can be utilized for many wondrous things. This room is more than a chapel, it's a nethersphere. It facilitates a certain kind of science, similar to the celestial science that Jesus harnessed in order to heal Malchus' ear. Unfortunately, Jesus wasn't available today." Sombrack's eyes widened and he smiled, sniffing the air. "There, you can smell it, can't you? These totems have positioned us very closely to the veil…"

At that moment, then, Alex did indeed begin to smell something like the subtle redolence of smoke intervened by wafts of ozone.

"Sure, you think it's all bullshit," Lena said. She'd come around to look down at him, her macabre, sexually-charged beauty refined in the stark-white luminance. "The ravings of a madman billionaire with too much time on his hands. But you'll see." She put her hand on his chest and began to rub. "It was really hard for Clifford to find you, you know."

Alex knew by now that he'd been set up. The art patronage, Sombrack's admiration of his digital work, even the cash… *All a crock of shit…*

Sombrack wheeled himself into view. "Indeed, yours is a privileged and very singular heritage, Alex, and it's a pity you've never been aware of it."

"What are you talking about?" Alex's voice grated. All the while, that rising redolence began to make his eyes and nostrils sting.

Sombrack contentedly folded his hands in his lap. "Grigori Rasputin was quite the lady's man, as we've discussed. But he also sired seven children through the loins of his wife. Four died very early on. His surviving son, Dmitri Rasputin, died from dysentery in 1937. It's not known if Dmitri had any legitimate children, but it's better known that the gentleman did court a few women in his time…"

Alex simply continued to stare, not so much at Sombrack's face but at his words. He was just on the fringe of knowing where this discourse was going.

"Dmitri got around, in other words." Lena's fingers dawdled over Alex's hospital gown. "He sowed his fair share of oats. Of course, nobody knows if his dick was as big as his dad's, but it's an uncontested fact that he knocked up a Russian farm girl in 1936, and she pumped out a boy. The farm girl never married, but her last name was—and I'm sure you've guessed by now—Petrov."

Anesthetic still buzzed in Alex's head. "Buh-bullshit," he sputtered, and determined not even to listen to the rest.

"From there the line perpetuated," Sombrack went on. "Dmitri was cremated, but as is often the case, his teeth survived the process, and my purveyors were able to obtain one. The DNA from Dmitri's tooth and *your* DNA were a perfect match. It was my very good fortune that you enlisted in the Navy out of high school."

Lena grinned, then she looked inquiringly back to Sombrack. "So what is it, Clifford? Is Rasputin Alex's great-grandfather or his great-*great*-grandfather?"

"Great-great-great, I believe, darling." Sombrack continued to gaze at Alex's lengthening face. "It was crucial to 'keep it in the family,' so to speak, and so I have. The process works much better with that genuine admixture. Beyond all doubt, Alex, in your veins runs the blood of Grigori Rasputin."

"If you'd never joined the Navy, we'd never have known," Lena said.

Alex tried to propel his thinking beyond the veil of his mental fog. "You got my DNA info from my naval records?"

"Sure. The U.S. Privacy Act doesn't apply to billionaires. Throw a bunch of money in the right place, at the right people, and you can find out anything. Neato, huh?" Lena asked, still grinning brightly. "But I guess the rest is a bit of a bummer, right? You inherited Rasputin's DNA, but you sure didn't inherit his giant dick."

With this, she bent over something out of view, then raised her hand high. Tweezed between her thumb and index finger was a limp and rather insignificant lump of flesh. Via the manner by which Lena held the thing aloft, it swayed slowly back and forth like a pendulum.

Alex's appalled eyes thinned to take closer note of the mass's details. There wasn't much of a shaft in this bloodless state but eventually he was able to detect the shriveled glans and testicles depending in the scrotal sack. It looked sad, and, sadly, all too familiar.

Sombrack turned up some lights, which illuminated more effectively all the occult arcana hanging on the walls. Planetary symbols, large gold letters similar to Hebrew and others in Old Latin. A complicated mosaic of teeth fashioned to represent the demon Apollyon.

Lena indicated the freshly severed genitals. "Garbage can, Clifford?"

"Oh, no, dear. Put it in the jar. In a way, it'll still make for an interesting collector's item."

Something like insanity was blaring in Alex's head. He tried to reach forward, to feel his crotch but suddenly realized his wrists were strapped down.

"Let him see, darling," Sombrack said.

Lena raised a hand mirror and angled it obligingly.

There were no bandages, as one might expect. Instead, Alex's splayed groin was now occupied by a preposterously large penis and scrotum.

The heart monitor's beeping increased to a distracting degree. Lena turned it off.

Petrified, Alex lay back, breathing fast. Thoughts in the form of outraged words tried to form in his head, but they crumbled just before reaching coherence.

"I guess it's too early to play with it, huh?" Lena asked Sombrack.

The old man gave the question some contemplation. "Why, I don't know exactly, but I shouldn't think there'd be much recovery time needed. In 1696, Etienne Roulet, the infamous occultist of the Rhode Island Colony, cut a snake in half and then healed it as a demonstration of Lucifer's powers. There was no recovery time; the snake was reconnected instantaneously. Just as Jesus' healing of Malchus' ear was instantaneous. Likewise, when Jonas Trenair, the Wizard of Mareuth, reconnected the severed hand of a hanged witch onto the wrist of member of his following, the recovery time was equally instantaneous." Sombrack's eyes suddenly beamed. "Go ahead and touch it, sweetheart. We *know* what will happen, don't we?"

In something like hushed awe, Lena's hand reached down.

On his back, Alex couldn't see what she was doing but he could feel it with great sensitivity.

He felt Lena's deft fingers trace slowly up and down a very long nerve-charged tube of flaccid muscle. In an eye's-wink, that flaccid tube engorged before a gust of pleasure more potent than the first time Alex had ever had a woman's hand on his cock. At once, his loins were buzzing, despite his hips cringing in place.

"Damn, Clifford!" Lena squealed delightedly. "It's harder than a fuckin' barbell, and it only took a second!"

"Such is the power of our king, dear." Sombrack wheeled around for a direct view. "My goodness! Only a true fool would doubt such radiant power!"

Lena was leaning over, inspecting this new addition to Alex's unwitting body, marveling at it. "There's not even a seam!"

"Of course not, dear. It's science. It's perfection…"

Alex's consciousness continued to gyrate in his head. Lena was stroking the massive thing now, whipping up sensations in Alex's brain like none he'd ever felt.

"A masterpiece!" Sombrack celebrated. "This cock hasn't been hard since 1916!"

Lena moaned. "I can't wait anymore! I've gotta sit on this big motherfucker *now!*" With this erudite declaration, she skimmed off her clothes and, like a dog in heat, climbed up onto the table, her tongue actually wagging…

The supernatural erection spired upward, such that Alex could see it without craning his neck. *My God*, was all he could think.

"More than a reasonable trade-off, don't you think, Alex?" Sombrack inquired, "Let's face it, your artwork is mediocre and hardly the means to a successful career. But now? You get to spend every day for the rest of your life stuffing Lena like a turkey with that hideously large cock, and carrying on the great tradition of Rasputin, eh?"

Lena's eyes rolled back when she lowered her crotch onto the throbbing erection; she even grunted in the process. She gazed up at the sigils in breathless ecstasy.

Inch by inch, Alex felt himself burrow up into the hot, wet confines. The sensations were as euphoric as a mainline or high-grade heroin. He was dead-ended in her pussy before she could even take it all, and he knew he would cumming in her momentarily.

Sombrack nodded. "Imagine your cock as a plunger, Alex, and Lena's pussy is a gas station toilet—let 'er rip! Fuck her so hard her eyeballs switch sockets!"

The pleasure was incogitable.

"I want this money-grubbing hosebag knocked right the fuck up," Sombrack went on. "I want her treacherous pussy *filled* with Rasputin's sperm, so she'll be pumping out his children like a goddamn vending machine! Finally, the tramp has a purpose in life!"

Just as Alex was beginning to ejaculate, Lena squealed, "Oh, Clifford, I love you so much! You say the sweetest things!"

ABOUT THE AUTHOR

Edward Lee is the author of over 50 horror, fantasy, and sci-fi novels, and dozens of short stories. He has also had comic scripts published by DC Comics, Verotik Inc., and Cemetery Dance. Many of his novels have been reprinted in Germany, Poland, Japan, Italy, Russia, Spain and other countries. He is a Bram Stoker Award Nominee; his Lovecraftian novel INNSWICH HORROR won the 2010 Vincent Price Award for Best Foreign Book (Austria), his novel WHITE TRASH GOTHIC won the 2018 Splatterpunk Award for Best Extreme Horror Novel, and his collaborative novella HEADER 3 (with Ryan Harding) won for Best Extreme Novella. In 2020 Lee won the J.F. Gonzales Lifetime Achievement Award. In 2009, the movie version of his novella HEADER was released by Synapse Films and is available now on Tubi; several of his novels are currently under option. Lee has also sold a collaborative film script (with David Hayes) to Sub Rosa Studios; the film is tentatively entitled OUIJA SLUMBER PARTY, and has a release date in mid-2025. Lee is a U.S. Army veteran and lives in Seminole, Florida.

Curious about other Crossroad Press books? Stop by our
website: http://crossroadpress.com
We offer quality writing
in digital, audio, and print formats.

Subscribe to our newsletter on the website homepage and
receive a free eBook.